OUT
OF
REACH

BALLANTINE BOOKS \ NEW YORK

OUT
OF
REACH

PATRICIA LEWIN

A Ballantine Book
Published by The Random House Publishing Group

ISBN 0-345-44320-9

Book design by Julie Schroeder

Manufactured in the United States of America

For Ed

ACKNOWLEDGMENTS

Thanks to all those who shared their knowledge and professional insight. Sharon Reishus, for the CIA details and her endless patience in supplying them. Jonathan M. Sullivan, M.D., Ph.D., who once again answered my dozens of e-mails on all things medical. Patricia McLinn, friend and fellow writer, for helping me navigate the Washington, D.C./Virginia area. Peter Van Wie for the German phrases. Jennifer Stern and Agent Mick Fennerty for responding to my FBI questions. Lesley Matthews, shodan, and Sensei Peter C. Litchfield, sandan, for choreographing my martial arts scenes and showing me how a woman can take down a man.

All mistakes (or literary license) are mine.

Thanks also to Gin, Sandra, Ann, Pam, Donna, Anne, Pat, and Deb for the brainstorming and general moral support. You keep me sane.

As always, thanks to my husband, Jeff, for believing I can do anything. And to my daughter, Andrea, for cheering me on.

Thanks to Meg Ruley, the best of agents, and Charlotte Herscher, who deserves a medal for her patience and for maintaining a calm demeanor while navigating rough waters.

OUT
OF
REACH

PROLOGUE

THE NEW KID was finally crying.

Softly. Into his pillow while the rest of the mansion slept. But Ryan, standing outside the door, heard, and a touch of sadness squeezed his throat. This one had held out longer than most. He'd been here two days, with no sign of breaking. Ryan had to admire that.

Shifting the tray to one hand, he unlocked the door and slipped into the room.

The crying stopped.

Some of the kids broke right away, the soft ones, sobbing nonstop for their parents. Others took longer. The street kids, the fighters. They got angry, hiding their fear with hateful words. The really strong ones, the leaders, said very little, telling Ryan and the rest to go fuck themselves without uttering a word. This boy, pretending to sleep as Ryan crossed the room, was one of those, refusing even to eat.

But his defiance had finally begun to crumble.

The tears were Ryan's cue to offer comfort. One child to

another in a scary adult world. Though Ryan wasn't much of a kid anymore. Sixteen on his last birthday, he'd long outgrown any usefulness other than tending the new arrivals.

"I thought you'd be hungry," he said, and set the tray on the nightstand.

At first there was no response from the bed. Then the kid's survival instincts kicked in as the smell of fresh bread and hot chicken soup teased his empty stomach. He swiped a fist across his eyes, then rolled over.

"I'm not supposed to bring up food after hours." Ryan sat on the edge of the bed. "But it won't hurt this once."

The boy pushed up against the headboard. "Who are you?"

Ryan felt the squeeze of sadness again. "My name's Ryan." He hesitated, then broke one of his own rules. "What's yours?"

"You don't know?"

Usually it was better that way, easier, not knowing anything about the kids he cared for. Not even their names. "They don't tell me much around here." The truth, but something more, a common bond between them.

The kid looked doubtful, or maybe he was just figuring out the downside to sharing his name. Finally he said, "Cody Sanders," then, "Where am I? And what is this place?"

Ryan glanced around at the large bedroom and sitting area. Like all the others in this wing of the house, it was designed for a time when the wealthy owners entertained overnight guests. But that was all in the past. Now it was little more than a gilded prison. "Just a house, or I guess you'd call it a mansion." The rest, that he didn't know the exact location of the estate, he'd keep to himself.

Cody hesitated, then asked, "Where is he?"

"Trader?" The word came out as a question, though Ryan knew exactly whom Cody meant.

"Is that his name?"

"I doubt it, but it's what the staff calls him." When they

dared speak of him at all. "Don't worry, he's not here right now."

"Why did he bring me here? What does he want from me?" As usual, once the questions started, they tumbled out one after the other and begged for answers Ryan didn't have. Or was willing to share.

"Look." Ryan shoved off the bed. "I better get going." It was easier than staying. "I just brought you the tray."

Cody looked at the food, obviously hungry, but made no move toward it. "Help me get out of here." Not, *I want my mom or dad*. Just, *let me go*.

"I can't." Ryan started for the door. He could no more leave than Cody. Nor did he want to. He was safe here, safer than anywhere else he'd ever lived.

"Are you afraid of him?"

Ryan couldn't deny it. Trader was the scariest man he knew, and Ryan hadn't survived this long by defying men like him. "Eat your soup, it's good."

"You could help me if you wanted."

"It's just not possible, okay?" Ryan hadn't planned to explain himself to this kid, but the words came anyway. "There's no place to go. We're in the middle of nowhere." There were guards. And the dogs.

"So you're a prisoner, too."

That touched off a spark of anger. "This is my home." In a few days this kid would be gone, but Ryan would still be here. "I live here."

Cody studied him for a minute, as if evaluating Ryan's claim, then said, "I *will* get out of here."

Ryan didn't answer. What was the point? The kid wasn't going anywhere until Trader came for him. Sooner or later he'd figure that out for himself.

"I'll check on you later," Ryan said.

As he closed and locked the door behind him, something

slammed against the other side, then slid to the floor. Ryan pictured the tray, the shattered dishes and food in a puddle on the expensive rugs.

"Damn." It would be his job to clean up the mess.

The kid was going to make this difficult. Too bad. Because he *would* break. They all did. Eventually.

I

He was big.

Two hundred, two hundred and twenty pounds at least. Visibly strong. And young. No question his body had made the journey to manhood, but the stupid grin on his face said his mind was stuck in adolescence.

He'd taken an aggressive stance, feet planted wide, arms flexed. "You're going down, bitch."

Erin backed up. "Whatever you're trying to prove, this isn't the way."

"I'm not the one with something to prove." He edged toward her.

She put more distance between them, reaching for the calm that would get her through this. Instead she found something else, something darker.

"Where do you think you're going?" he asked, a smirk in his voice and on his face.

He was right. She had little maneuvering room. Though she doubted more space would make a difference. If she ran, he'd be on her in seconds, and it would be over. Her best bet was to stand her ground.

"Look—" she started.

He made a sudden and unexpected grab for her, his big hands clamping brutally around her forearms. But the move was based on brute strength not skill, and she twisted and brought one elbow up to slam into the underside of his chin. He grunted and released her.

She backed up again.

The next time, she saw him coming and ducked and rolled out of reach. Back on her feet, she pivoted to face him again.

"You're quicker than you look," he said.

"And you're clumsier." The reply escaped before she could check herself, and he obviously didn't like it.

"Enough of this shit." He came at her again, fast and straight this time.

Erin blocked him, her foot outside his, ankle to ankle. The heel of her right hand slamming against the underside of his chin. Her left striking his biceps, then delivering a stunning blow to the side of his neck and forcing his head sideways into his shoulder.

At another time, the shock on his face might have been comical, but today, she wasn't laughing.

She seized his elbow, twisted, and he landed on his back. Hard. But she kept him rolling onto his stomach and jammed her knee against his kidney. His arm wrenched behind him, bent at the wrist. Her free hand shoving his head to the floor. And he frantically slapped the mat in surrender.

The class applauded.

Erin held him a few seconds longer, then let go, releasing his arm and backing away.

"Good job, Erin." Bill Jensen, head martial-arts instructor at the CIA's Farm, stepped away from his trainees and extended a hand to the man on the floor. "Sorry, Cassidy. It's the price you pay for being the biggest SOB in the class."

The younger man ignored the offered assistance and sprang to his feet. "No problem." He rotated and massaged his shoulder. "I like getting roughed up by a woman half my size."

"Life sucks sometimes," Erin said as she retrieved her towel from a corner of the mat. "Especially in the Company."

She was still edgy. More than she should be, more than would be healthy if this had been real. Maybe that was the problem. This had all been a game, and she didn't like games.

"Go ahead," Cassidy said, "rub salt in my already shredded ego."

She looked him over. He was probably ex-military, and the CIA wasn't known for recruiting people with low self-esteem. The combination meant it would take a lot more than one fell to do serious damage to his ego. "You'll survive it."

"Okay," Bill said to the others. "Do I have to interpret these results for the rest of you?"

"I want some of what she's got," said a short, compactly built young woman in front.

"They don't hand out balls to wimps, Sheila," goaded a man behind her. He was nondescript in the way of many nice-looking American men: medium height and build, muddy eyes, and dark blond hair. Perfect raw material for the CIA.

Sheila turned a brief, cold stare on him, then dismissed him with a sneer. "You should know, Chad."

The class whooped, congratulating her while offering condolences to her target.

"Okay, joke if you want," Bill said. "Just don't miss the point. Which is . . ." He looked from one career trainee to another.

"Size don't mean shit," said Sheila. "The big ones just make more noise when they fall. And the small ones . . ." She threw another quick glance at the man behind her. "They squeak."

Another burst of approving laughter, and again Bill cut it short. "That's right. You can be strong as an ox, and this little lady"—he gestured toward Erin—"will use that strength against you. Any questions?"

"I've got one," said another of the women. "That was very impressive, Officer . . ." She hesitated, evidently unsure what name to use, though it was Farm policy not to use an officer's last name—even if you knew it. "Erin."

"But?" Erin knew what was coming, the question asked after every demonstration. And it was always one of the women who did the asking.

"Well, you're obviously well trained. What are you, a black belt in tae kwon do?"

"Erin holds several black belts," answered Bill. "What's your point?"

"Well, what happens when she comes up against someone who's just as good, *and* he outweighs her by a hundred pounds?"

Before Bill could answer, Erin said, "No matter how good you are, there is always someone better." She glanced at him, saw him nod, and went on. They both knew it was the women who wanted an answer, and they wanted it from her. The men needed to hear it as well, but would never admit it. "And in this business you're bound to run into that person sooner or later. Whether it's someone your own size, or"—she glanced at the hulk she'd just put on the mat—"or not."

"So what do you do? Hope for the best?"

"You train and acquire as much skill as possible. You get good." Erin paused, letting her eyes drift from one face to the other, wondering how many of them understood what she was saying. They were young and brash, the best of the best in their respective fields. Or else they wouldn't be here. The CIA recruitment criteria were very tough. Every one of them was used to winning. "Then it comes down to heart, and the will to survive." Not win. Survive.

"It becomes a chess match," Bill offered. "You fight with your head as well as your—"

"More than that," Erin interrupted, frustrated with him. They needed to know this wasn't a game. "It's a question of which of you is willing to pull out all the stops." She looked pointedly at the guy she'd taken down. "And who gets meaner, quicker."

For a moment, no one spoke.

Then, "Okay, thanks, Erin," Bill said, indicating the end of the session. "Now pair off.

"Chad, I want you and Sheila together. I'm pretty sick of the two of you, so work it out." Then, almost as an afterthought, he added, "Just don't kill him, Sheila. The paperwork for dead CTs is a bitch."

Dismissed, Erin started toward the locker rooms. As always, she left wondering if anything she'd said or done would have an impact. Would they take their training more seriously and understand the inherent dangers of the job? Had she listened when she was a trainee? Probably not. It wasn't until you got out in the field that reality set in.

Bill fell in beside her.

"Sooner or later, one of your gorillas is going to wipe the floor with me," she said.

"Sounds familiar."

She grinned and threw him a sideways glance. It wasn't the first time they'd had this conversation. "That was an accident."

"So you've always claimed."

Four years ago, as a CT—career trainee—in Bill's class, she'd put him down in a demo similar to the one she'd just given for his current class. It never would have happened if he'd taken time to read her student file, which revealed her years of martial-arts training. Instead, she'd caught him by surprise, embarrassing him in front of a class of newbies, and he'd never let her forget it.

She suspected, however, that he'd also never repeated the mistake of ignoring student files. "So this is your way of getting even. You're *hoping* one of your recruits can take me."

He laughed abruptly. "I'm not holding my breath, but it wouldn't exactly break my heart."

"Easy for you to say. You'd be watching from the sidelines."

"As you said, life in the Company sucks."

She laughed and shook her head. "You have a wicked streak, Officer Jensen."

He grinned. "Yeah."

They'd reached the women's locker room, but as she went to open the door, he said, "Wait up a minute, Erin. We need to talk."

She stopped, aware of the sudden shift in his voice. "Okay."

He hesitated, briefly. "You were a little rough on him. Cassidy, I mean." He backstepped and planted his hands on his hips. "You put him down pretty hard."

"Please." She rolled her eyes and held out her arms, splotches of red showing where Cassidy had grabbed her. By tomorrow, they'd be black and blue. "The guy was looking to hurt me."

"He was playing a part."

"And I wasn't?" She folded her arms, not believing he was serious about this.

"I'm not sure." He looked away for a moment, then met her gaze again, head-on. "Sometimes you play the part a little too well."

She frowned, surprised. He meant it. He was actually worried that she'd hurt one of his handpicked testosterone junkies. "This isn't a game, Bill, those recruits—"

"This isn't about them, it's about you."

"What are you talking about? The only reason I do this is to give them a taste of what they're up against. If—"

"Look," he interrupted. "I know you're not crazy about working in the States."

He wasn't making any sense. "What does that have to do with anything?"

"You're angry, and it shows. Hell, Cassidy really pissed you off out there."

"Give me a break. You know better than that." In a fight, anger could get you killed. Bill knew that as well as she did. It was one of the realities drilled into all serious martial arts students.

Still, she had to admit, Cassidy had irritated her with his Neanderthal tactics. But she hadn't been angry. Not really. Or maybe . . .

"I'm worried about you," he said. "You don't belong at Georgetown babysitting a bunch of foreign students."

It was a guess, but he wasn't that far off. Knowledge of a covert officer's assignment was on a need-to-know basis, but it wasn't much of a leap for someone who'd been in the Company as long as Bill. Erin had been trained for the clandestine side of the Company and reported to the Directorate of Operations, as Bill well knew. Then responsibility had dragged her home.

"What do you want from me, Bill? You want me to play nice with your CTs?"

"Either go back overseas, or—"

"You know that's not an option."

"Then get your anger under control. Talk to someone, see a counselor or a . . ."

"Or a what? A shrink?"

He rubbed a hand down his face, looking distinctly uncomfortable. "All I'm saying, Erin, is—"

"I know exactly what you're saying." She stepped forward, into his space. He was the one making her angry. "And you're out of line. My career, my life, is none of your business. I come here for one reason only, to show those recruits just how nasty the real world can get. So, if you want someone to coddle them—"

"That not what I—"

"—get yourself another demo queen. Because I've been

out there, and it's no game. And the sooner they"—she gestured toward the group across the gym—"learn that, the more likely they are to survive."

She spun around, grabbed the locker-room door, and slammed it open. A few strides later and she was alone inside, collapsed against the lockers, the adrenaline pumping through her system. Balling her fists, she barely kept herself from pounding the cold metal behind her.

Damn it. Damn him.

Except for her supervisor, Bill was the only one of her colleagues who knew about Janie and Claire. Thanks to a few too many drinks when she'd first returned to Langley, they'd ended up in bed one night. Which was hard enough to live with, but the things she'd told him . . .

She shook her head at the memory. Embarrassed.

Her family situation was private, and she'd been afraid word would get around. However, fifteen years in the Company had taught Bill the art of secrecy. He'd kept her revelations to himself, never mentioning it again to anyone. Not even her.

Until now.

He wanted her to see a shrink, for God's sake. There was no way. That was her sister Claire's territory, and Erin wasn't about to trespass.

Since age twelve, when Erin had watched the adults in her life flounder in the wake of Claire's disappearance, she'd sworn she would never be a victim. No one would ever have that power over her. She'd kept that promise. She'd made herself smart, topping her class in every subject, and she'd made herself strong, her martial-arts training bordering on obsession. And she'd managed to keep herself together when everyone around her had fallen apart.

With a groan, she remembered saying those exact words to Bill. Boastfully. As if she'd accomplished something remarkable. When in truth, all she'd done was survive.

Suddenly, she realized what he'd done. As quickly as it had surfaced, her anger vanished, and she bit her lip to keep from laughing aloud. Leave it to Bill, always the teacher, to demonstrate his point by showing her how close to the edge of anger she treaded. He'd pushed until she'd flashed, lashing out at him for daring to see too much.

Of course, he was right. She was miserable at Georgetown.

She'd joined the CIA because it fit her. Working undercover suited her temperament and her training. And because no one would expect that of Claire Baker's big sister.

Then, a year ago, fate had twisted her life.

Her mother's illness had been sudden and unexpected. Cancer. During a routine cleaning, Elizabeth Baker's dentist had found a spot in her mouth and suggested she have it checked out. Six months later, after two rounds of radiation and another of chemotherapy, she was dead.

Erin blamed the doctors and their radical treatment of a woman who'd felt fine until they'd started treating her. She also blamed her mother for her three-pack-a-day habit and the vodka that had gotten her through the nights. And Erin had blamed herself. While her mother had been dying, she'd been overseas running agents for the U.S. government, but more to the point, if not for her, Elizabeth would never have smoked and drunk to begin with.

Erin sighed, the mistakes of her past a burden she couldn't ignore. Any more than she could walk away from the responsibilities of her present.

Standing, she headed for the showers, stripping off the Farm-issued sweats as she went.

She'd returned to the States for the funeral and never left again. With her mother gone, there was Janie to care for. And Claire. Always Claire.

Now Erin was stuck.

The CIA didn't know what to do with her. She wasn't

an analyst or a techie, so they'd placed her at Georgetown while they tried to figure it out. Armed with a Ph.D. in International Studies, which she'd earned before joining the Agency, she taught Ethics and International Relations to twenty-year-olds, while keeping her eyes open for potentially violent anti-American sentiments among the foreign student population. And she worked the embassy circuit, attending parties two or three times a week.

Not that she minded teaching. She enjoyed it and found hope in the bright young minds, but it wasn't what she'd spent her entire adult life training for. As for her unofficial assignments—watching foreign students and embassies—on the surface they seemed similar to what she'd done overseas. But it was different on American soil, where she had strict orders to take no action and only report what she saw.

Meanwhile, her bosses seemed to have forgotten her.

So, yeah, she was angry. But, as she'd told Cassidy, sometimes life sucked.

A few minutes later, she left the locker room wearing army fatigues, the standard dress code for CTs and their trainers, with her one-day temporary ID clipped to the breast pocket.

Bill was waiting for her. "Still mad?" he asked.

She started toward the exit. "Should I be?"

"Look, Erin, I'm sorry if I upset you."

"Who do you think you're kidding? You meant to piss me off."

He threw her a glance, obviously gauging her mood, then smiled. "Well, yeah, but . . . Okay, hell, I'm not the least bit sorry. But hey, what are friends for, if not to meddle in each other's lives?"

They stepped outside, the bright fall sunlight cool and crisp. She turned toward him. "Is that what we are?"

"I thought so."

They fell silent, the memory of that one night awkward and

strained between them. Erin retreated to a safe subject. "So, do I come back for your new class next month?"

He laughed shortly and nodded, obviously deciding he'd said enough on the subject of her anger. "Yeah, I want you." It was the wrong thing to say. "I mean—"

She held up a hand. "It's okay. I know what you meant." She gestured toward the visitors' lot—a half mile on the other side of the complex. "I better be going."

"I'll be done here in about half an hour. Join me for a drink?"

She shook her head. "I can't . . ."

"Just a drink, Erin."

"It's Friday, Marta's night out, and Janie and I do the pizza thing. Plus, I have a long drive home."

"Invite me along."

That surprised her, and she was half tempted. Despite the family that occupied her every free thought, she'd been lonely this last year. Still . . . "I don't think that's a good idea."

Janie had suffered too much loss already. Erin wouldn't parade men through her life as well.

"Okay, then what about tomorrow? I'll drive up and we'll make it dinner. I'll treat you both."

"I can't."

He hesitated, then said, "You know, you don't have to handle this all alone, Erin."

She knew what he meant. "Yes, I do. They're my family, my responsibility."

"Erin . . ." He started to say something more, then obviously thought better of it and backed off. "Okay, but if you ever need anyone."

She reached out and touched his hand. "You're a good friend, Bill."

"I'd like to be more."

"There's no more of me to give."

He looked about to argue further, but dropped her hand and stepped back instead. "Okay, go on and get out of here. You got a kid waiting for you."

Smiling tightly, she turned away and started across the grounds to the parking lot. She suspected she was throwing away her chance at a good man, a man who understood her, maybe better than she understood herself. But besides her job, there was no room for anything or any "one" besides Janie and Claire. That was a reality she'd just have to live with.

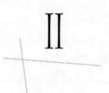

II

Two hours later, Erin pulled into her driveway. It was a small, two-story redbrick house in Arlington, one of the quiet suburban neighborhoods servicing the metropolitan D.C. area. She'd bought it ten months earlier, before moving Janie and Marta north from Miami.

She'd never pictured herself as a home owner, and certainly not a resident of the suburbs. But with her mother's death, everything in her life had changed. Even this. Janie needed a place to be a child, a family area where she could grow up. Even if the only family she had was an unconventional aunt, an aging family friend, and a mother who'd spent most of the last seven years in and out of various mental institutions.

As Erin pushed through the back door, Janie looked up from the kitchen table and grinned. "Come see what I made, Aunt Erin."

Erin's mood lifted. No matter how frustrated she'd become with her job, she loved having this little girl in her life. The real-ization had come to her gradually these last few months and had surprised her. She'd never thought of herself as the maternal type, but her niece had crept into her heart and taken hold.

Closing the door, she went to see Janie's latest creation.

"You like it?" Janie asked, eyes wide. "It's for Mommy. I want her to know what my new school looks like."

"It's great."

Janie's talent was unmistakable. Even Erin, who had no experience with children, could see the child had a special gift. She'd used colored pencils to draw her school, an older, three-story brick monstrosity, flag in front, children's drawings in the windows. On the sidewalk in front of the building walked a little girl with curly blond hair, two women at her side.

Erin recognized herself on Janie's right: an angular woman of medium height, thick dark hair—her one good feature—cut short because she didn't have the patience to mess with it, and a little wild looking because even short it took too much time to style. Marta walked on Janie's left: smaller, older, and rounder, with a noticeably maternal air.

Erin had taught Janie to pay attention, to notice her surroundings, the small details in everyday things. And people. But her talent for putting what she saw onto paper was all her own.

"It's the first day of school," Janie explained. "Remember? When you went with us?"

"I do." Janie's eye for detail translated into a realism Erin found difficult to believe came from seven-year-old hands. "And I knew exactly what day it was." She ruffled Janie's hair.

Just then, Marta entered the kitchen, a basket of laundry in her arms. "You're home early."

"I got lucky. No students pounding on my door today. Here"—Erin started toward the older woman—"let me help."

"Don't be silly." Marta sidestepped her and crossed to the basement door. "I may not be as young as some people, but I'm still capable of carrying a basket of dirty clothes."

"Erin likes my drawing, Marta." Janie had returned to her

colored pencils, adding a few straggly flowers along the edge of the building.

"Of course she does, dear," Marta said, and disappeared down the stairs.

"Your flowers look sad," Erin said, referring again to Janie's drawing.

"That's because they know summer is over, and soon it will be cold outside."

"Do you miss Florida, sweetie?" Erin asked, trying to keep the concern from her voice. "Because remember, you and Marta are going down for a visit next week when your school closes."

"I know." Janie went back to her picture. "I miss Grandma. But it's nice here, too. I can't wait to see the trees change colors."

"Aren't you excited about the trip?" None of them had been back to Miami since moving north, but with two teacher work days coming up, Marta had thought it would be a good opportunity to take Janie home for a visit.

Janie shrugged.

Erin stroked her fingers through Janie's bright curls, wondering if she should say more. Ask questions. Her niece had experienced more than her share of upheaval. She'd never met her father, and Claire . . . Well, Claire had never been well enough to be a real mother to Janie. That role had been left to others, to her grandmother and Marta. Then, after Erin's mother's death, Erin had moved Janie away from the only home she'd ever known.

Although Janie showed no outward signs, Erin knew all about burying one's pain. So she worried. Was she doing enough? Could she fill the void the other two women had left in this child's life?

"Are we having pizza tonight?" Janie asked, obviously unaware of her aunt's concerns.

Erin smiled. "I promised, didn't I?"

"Yes." Janie pumped her arm in the air, a new gesture straight from her peers. "I love pizza."

"Give your aunt a few minutes to catch her breath," Marta said, reentering the kitchen. "She just walked through the door."

Erin smiled at Janie, rolling her eyes a bit, making Janie giggle.

Marta ignored their antics. "Are you done with your drawing, sweetie?"

"Almost," Janie said, picking up a pencil and adding touches of yellow to the trees. "See, even the trees know winter is coming."

Erin laughed at the first creative license Janie had taken with the drawing. The leaves would turn, but not for a few weeks, not until mid to late October.

"Well then," Marta said, "put it away. You need to get cleaned up before going out."

Janie pursed her lips, looking ready to argue, but stopped as Erin shook her head and took Marta's side. "Go on, honey. It's pizza night. You'll have time later, or maybe tomorrow, to finish your drawing."

"O . . . kay." The word came out in two long syllables as Janie carefully put away her pencils and slid her drawing into her pad. "Can I at least leave it down here so I can draw when we get home?"

"Sure," Erin said, bending the rules a bit and leaning down to give her niece a quick kiss on top of her head. "Now go on, I'm hungry."

Janie scurried out of the room, bouncing her way up the stairs to her bedroom.

"Slow down," Marta called, to no avail.

Stairs, Erin remembered, were another thing the seven-year-old loved about living here. And climbing them, up or down, at various paces—none of which resembled a walk.

"Such energy," Erin said, once Janie was out of earshot. "Sometimes I wonder how I'll ever keep up with her."

"You'll manage." Marta busied herself with putting away the remains of Janie's after-school snack. "You always have."

"Yeah, well"—Erin dropped onto one of the counter stools— "that was before a certain seven-year-old came into my life."

In truth, Erin didn't know what she'd do without Marta. The older woman supplied a sense of stability and normalcy in Janie's life that Erin couldn't manage alone. Although her current assignment with the CIA kept her in the D.C. area, she worked odd and unpredictable hours. And making the rounds on the embassy circuit required that she attend parties and receptions as often as three times a week. Then there were the occasional last-minute calls from Langley, when she'd have to drop everything and go in. Plus the possibility that the Company would send her somewhere without notice always existed and wasn't particularly conducive to raising a child. So, Erin was eternally grateful for Marta.

Besides, Marta had been part of Janie's life from the day Claire had brought the new infant home. Erin had been away at school, having just started her doctoral program, and her mother had been too preoccupied with Claire to pay much attention to the baby. So Marta had stepped in, taking care and loving Janie as if she were her own.

Marta had been Elizabeth's closest friend since she'd moved to Miami's Little Havana with Erin's father. A blond, blue-eyed Lauderdale girl, Elizabeth had been an outsider in the largely Cuban community. Marta had taken the younger woman under her wing, helping her navigate a culture more distant than the thirty miles that separated their two communities.

Together, they'd weathered Elizabeth's two pregnancies and

births, her divorce from Erin's father and short-lived second marriage to Claire's. Then Claire had disappeared, and Elizabeth leaned even more heavily on Marta, who'd always managed to bear the weight.

Marta had been there for Elizabeth and her children. Now she was here for Janie as well.

Erin smiled at the other woman. "You're so good for her."

"And you're not?"

Erin shrugged. "Not like you."

Marta walked over and flipped open the drawing pad Janie had left on the table. "Do you see the look on that child's face?" She pointed to Janie on her first day of school. "She adores you."

In the picture, Janie had eyes only for her aunt, for Erin. She'd completely missed it before, skimmed right past it when looking at the drawing with Janie. Maybe she'd wanted to miss it, because she hadn't wanted to see how much Janie had come to depend on her. Claire had depended on Erin once, and it had cost her dearly.

"Children are smarter than you think," Marta added. "She knows you will always be there for her."

"She knows I'm all she's got." Just the thought frightened her. She'd failed Claire. What if she failed Claire's child as well?

Marta folded her arms. "And that's such a bad thing? You are her mother's sister. Her blood. You give her time, and you give her love. It is all she needs."

"You make it sound so easy." When Erin knew from experience it was anything but.

"Easy? No. Simple? Yes."

Erin didn't know how to answer that, what to say. For ten months she'd been worried that she wasn't enough for Janie, that the little girl needed someone else. A real mother. And here Marta was telling Erin that none of that mattered, that what Erin gave Janie was enough.

She pushed off the stool, deciding it was best to leave this conversation while she could. She didn't want to delve too deeply into her role as surrogate mother to Janie, not even with Marta. Because despite the older woman's kind words, Erin was afraid she'd come up short. "I better go change or Janie will be down here . . ."

Then she spotted the newspaper on the counter.

48 HOURS AND COUNTING
CODY SANDERS STILL MISSING
POLICE AND FBI NOT GIVING UP

A wave of nausea rolled through her. She'd heard those exact words herself, standing next to her mother, nineteen years ago. "We're not giving up, Mrs. Baker."

But of course, they'd had to. Eventually.

As for this little boy, this Cody Sanders . . . Forty-eight hours. Too long. By now there was a good chance the boy was dead. And if not . . . Well, that wasn't something she wanted to think about.

"Why do you torture yourself?" Marta asked.

Erin looked up, saw the concern on the older woman's face, and struggled to control her own features. "Should I avoid the news because it's unpleasant?"

Marta snorted. "You are not kidding anyone, Erin. It is time to stop blaming yourself for what happened to Claire."

"Who should I blame, then?"

"The madman who took her."

"I was supposed to be watching her." Erin wrapped her arms around her waist. "She was my responsibility."

"You were twelve years old. A child."

"Old enough—"

"No." Marta moved from behind the counter, planting two round fists on her hips. "Now you listen to me, Erin Elizabeth. I loved your mother. She was more of a sister to me than my own. But I never, *never,* agreed with how she left you to watch Claire while she worked."

"She didn't have a choice."

"There are always choices." Marta tossed her hands into the air. "Your mother just refused to consider hers. And watching the two of you afterward, the way you blamed yourself and each other . . ." She shook her head. "Well, it hurt my heart."

"It hurt all of us." Erin went cold inside, rigid. "Claire most of all."

For a moment, Marta seemed at a loss for words, searching Erin's face. When she finally spoke, she kept her voice low. "Let it go. It is over. Done. The monster who took your sister is in jail."

"And what about Claire?"

"Claire is exactly where she needs to be. You have seen to that. And someday, she will be well. But even if she never gets well, you're doing everything you can."

Erin didn't answer. She knew she couldn't win this argument. Marta only saw the good in those she loved, never the failures. So Erin lied. "You're right." She gave the other woman a quick kiss on the cheek. "I'm sorry. And I'll try to remember that."

Marta eyed her, possibly detecting the truth, but didn't challenge her. "Okay, then. Now go get ready before Janie goes crazy waiting for her pizza."

Erin headed upstairs.

Despite what Marta said, Erin knew she'd been at fault. She'd lost Claire that summer day nineteen years ago. And they'd all been paying for that mistake ever since.

III

FBI SPECIAL AGENT Alec Donovan shuffled through the glossy eight-by-tens on the table. Cody Sanders. His mother, Ellen Sanders. Roy Vasce, Ellen's current live-in boyfriend. And their seedy, rented row house, off the rail yards in South Baltimore's Locust Point.

Alec had gone through the entire file. He'd studied the pictures, read and reread the reports, gone through the interviews, all meticulously gathered by his small team of agents and police officers, without coming up with anything new.

Something was missing.

He could feel it, but just couldn't put his finger on what.

Pushing away from the table, he moved to stand in front of the storyboard on a large display panel attached to the wall. A picture of Cody was front and center, and beneath it, the time line tracking his movements the day of his disappearance. On one side was a list of friends and family whom the investigation team was interviewing. On the other, a list of questions that needed answers. In essence, the storyboard was a compilation and summary of all the details, the scores of interviews and reports, contained in the files.

Something.

Alec would just have to go over it again. And again, if necessary.

"Have you been here all night?"

Startled, he turned toward the woman in the doorway, then glanced at the windows where the first flush of gray shaded the sky. Across the room, on the far side of the temporary command post, a new set of faces manned the twenty-four-hour tip line. Alec hadn't even noticed the shift change. "I don't suppose you'd believe me if I said no."

Cathy Hart, one of the team of agents working for Alec on the Sanders case, pulled off her jacket and tossed it over a chair. "You look racked."

"Thanks." He turned his attention back to the storyboard. "Would it be politically incorrect to ask you to make fresh coffee?"

"Yeah, it would, but I'll do it anyway. *If* you agree to go back to your room, take a shower, and get some sleep."

Even though he and Cathy worked out of Quantico, an easy ninety-minute drive south of Baltimore, they'd taken hotel rooms. When every passing hour decreased the chance of finding a missing child alive, they couldn't afford to waste any time on driving. Or sleeping.

"After we find Cody," he said.

"He needs you sharp, Alec. You're not going to do him any good if you're exhausted."

"It won't do him any good if we find him after he's dead, either."

His bluntness shocked her. He could feel it in the sudden stillness behind him, and in the way, after a few seconds, she left the room without comment. To make coffee, he hoped.

Cathy was a good investigator, sharp, dedicated, and in an

odd sort of way, still innocent. Even after two years as an FBI CAC (Crimes Against Children) coordinator, working at his side on some horrific child abduction cases, she'd maintained her spark of optimism. Something Alec had lost years ago.

When she returned, she brought two steaming mugs.

"Thanks," he said, accepting the offered salvation. "I'm on coffee duty tomorrow."

"I'll hold you to it."

He breathed in the aroma, praying the caffeine would shake something loose in his brain. Because Cathy was right about one thing. He needed to remain sharp.

"Anything new?" she asked.

"Just more questions." He rubbed a hand over his face. "And the nagging suspicion that I'm missing something obvious."

"If it was obvious, Cody would be back home by now."

She was right. Maybe he *was* too tired.

He couldn't remember how many hours he'd been awake. Too many. Since he'd gotten the call about Cody Sanders . . . when? Two days ago? He'd been assigned the case because the CAC coordinators in the Baltimore office were involved in Operation Innocent Images, a case involving child pornography on the Internet. So he and Cathy, fresh off a case in Chicago, had driven up from Quantico.

"Go through this with me, will you?" he said. "Maybe a new pair of eyes will see what I'm missing."

Cathy grabbed a notepad and scooted up onto the table facing the wall. "Let's go."

Over the past two years, they'd learned to bounce ideas off each other. They had different strengths, different weaknesses, and together they often saw things neither one could see alone. It was a great partnership, and he'd come to depend on her common sense and insight into human, and particularly child, behavior.

Alec started. "Cody Sanders, age nine. Fourth grade, Francis

Scott Key Elementary." He pushed up onto the table next to Cathy and sipped his coffee. They'd been over all this before, but they were going to do it again, and again. Until they found the missing pieces.

"According to his mother, Ellen," he continued, "Cody left for school around seven-thirty. She claims there was nothing unusual in their morning routine. Roy Vasce—"

"The boyfriend."

"Verified her story."

"But the agent who interviewed Roy," Cathy added, "doesn't buy it. According to the neighbors, Roy and Cody don't get along. Lots of noisy fights."

"Any signs of physical abuse?"

Cathy shrugged. "No one's saying."

"Check the local hospitals. See if they have records of Cody being admitted to the emergency room under questionable circumstances. And try the school nurse. She might have noticed something, a broken bone or two, anything that might tell us if Roy was heavy-handed."

"The locals are already checking the hospitals, and I'll visit the nurse today."

"Good. So, the question is, did Roy and Cody argue that morning?" The scenario—more common than most people would believe—that Alec hated the most. "And did Roy . . . or Mom and Roy . . . decide the boy was a pain in the ass and get rid of him?"

"Nothing in the mother's demeanor suggests she had anything to do with it." Compassion was one of Cathy's strengths, and her weakness. Accusing a family member was always her last choice. Where she assumed innocence, he saw guilt. Both could be a problem.

In this case, however, "I happen to agree," he said.

Certain behavioral patterns and clues inevitably surfaced when a family member murdered a child. A mother might use the word *kidnapping* before most bereft parents could psychologically admit to the possibility. Or a father would overthink a cover-up, making false assumptions about kidnappers and their behavior. He might send a note to himself, or something of the child's to the police, as evidence of the child's abduction—which only a kidnapper interested in collecting ransom would do.

Ransom was certainly not a question in this case.

Ellen was a single mom, hustling drinks in a dive off Light Street in South Baltimore. She was consistently behind in her rent on her deteriorating, formstone rowhouse, and Alec suspected the parade of men through her bedroom were more often paying customers than boyfriends.

Nor had Ellen or Roy exhibited any other behavior that would have Alec hunting for a body instead of a terrorized boy. Yes, there was the friction between Roy and Cody, but that alone didn't make Roy capable of murder. Or more specifically, of successfully covering it up.

"They don't strike me as smart enough," Alec said. "But let's not rule it out." He didn't want to blind Cathy with his opinions. He wanted her eyes open and looking at all possible scenarios. "I want you to push a little harder on them. If nothing else, they might know more than they're saying. Get a polygraph."

"They've already refused."

"Find out why. If they're telling the truth, they should have no objection."

"You're the boss."

"What about the biological father?" Alec asked. "Have you found him yet?" He'd skipped out when Cody was four, and according to Ellen, they hadn't seen or heard from his since.

"Not yet, but we're working on it."

"I doubt he's involved." Men who'd deserted their families didn't usually show up years later to kidnap the children they'd abandoned. "But we need to make sure."

"We'll find him."

Alec waited while she made notes on the storyboard, joining Ellen and Roy's names with a bracket and drawing an arrow to the word *polygraph*, question mark, in capital letters. When she was done, he brought up another common scenario. "Cody could have run. If he had a problem with Roy, the boy might have decided he'd had enough, picked up, and taken off."

"That's what the locals think," Cathy said, recapping the marker she'd used on the storyboard and dropping it on a nearby table. "And it wouldn't be the first time."

Cody had run three times in the last year, which accounted for the limited manpower working the case. The locals just didn't believe this was a kidnapping, but the case was getting a lot of media attention and so they'd called in the FBI and the CACU.

"What do *you* think?" Alec asked, trusting Cathy's instincts on child behavior more than those of an overworked police force.

She hesitated, considering, taking her time before answering. "If he ran, it was spur of the moment. According to his mother, nothing is missing." Cathy crossed her arms, again weighing what she knew. "And I went through his room as well. I don't think she's lying. He left behind his clothes, his Walkman, a stash of money under his mattress—two hundred dollars that I don't want to even guess about how he got. Everything a nine-year-old boy takes when he runs."

Again, Alec agreed. It was a matter of looking for patterns, behavior that fit the specific outcome. Given certain stimuli, most people reacted in predictable ways. Cause and effect. It was what made profiling work.

"Okay," he said. "We'll assume an abduction, but keep our options open."

She nodded, going to retrieve her coffee.

"Let's move on." Alec pushed off the table and pointed

toward the second point on the time line. "Cody arrived at school before the eight-fifteen bell. He was in his homeroom and the rest of his classes at the designated times throughout the day."

"And no one remembers him acting differently or doing anything else unusual." Cathy took a careful sip of her coffee and put it down. "Although, I wasn't too impressed with the interviews, especially those done at the school."

Alec wouldn't have put it quite so nicely. He was seriously undermanned, with only a half-dozen agents from the Baltimore office working the case and another half-dozen locals—all rookies—doing the legwork. There just weren't enough experienced agents or officers to go around.

"I want a second set of interviews. Call Quantico and see if Matheson can spare a day, just to interview the kids at the school." Matheson, a specialist in child interviews, was in high demand. No one was going to be eager to let him head up to Baltimore for a day on a case the locals believed was a runaway. "He owes me. So tell him I'm collecting."

Cathy grinned and made a note. "And if he's still unavailable?"

"Get over there yourself. You're the closest thing to a trained specialist we have, and probably just as good." Like most CAC coordinators, Cathy had a background in child-related work. She held a Ph.D. in child psychology and had practiced for five years before joining the FBI. "If Cody even ate something different for lunch, I want to know about it."

"I'll make the call."

"Okay, let's get back to the time line," Alec said. "Cody left school around two thirty with Melinda Farmer, age ten, and a class ahead of him in school. They walked partway home together, split at the corner of Hull and Marriott, a ten-minute walk. Tops. Less than three blocks from Cody's house. And, as far as we know, she's the last person who saw him."

"You want Matheson to interview her as well?"

"No, you take her. She's more likely to talk to a woman. She walked with Cody almost every day. If anyone knows anything, it's Melinda. If he ran, she'll know. She may even know where. And if Roy used his fists, she'll know that, too."

"I'll make it a priority. And what do you want me to do with the locals?"

"Get them walking the streets again. Expand the search. Get them over to the docks and Cross Street Market. I bet the kid spent some time there. Someone saw something, and I want to know who and what."

"You got it."

Alec tossed down the last of his now lukewarm coffee. Hot or not, he needed the caffeine. "So, assuming Cody got home, say anywhere between three and three-thirty, he was supposed to call his mother, who was working an afternoon shift. He didn't, but she claims he often forgets. So when she didn't hear from him by four, she called home. No answer. She assumed he went out, and though irritated with him, she wasn't concerned. Again, she claims he's been getting harder and harder to control lately."

"Which is backed up by the fact he's run away three times in the last year."

"Yeah." Alec sighed and dragged a hand through his hair. He didn't like where this was headed. "Okay, Ellen arrives home at five thirty, and Cody's still not home. Now she's angry. She starts calling friends, neighbors, but no one's seen him. Finally she calls the police at four minutes past ten, seven hours after Cody's been missing."

She might already have been too late.

Seventy-four percent of the children murdered during a kidnapping are dead within three hours of the abduction.

But Alec didn't believe Cody was dead. He had no good reason, except an odd feeling that there was something different about this case. Moving away from the storyboard, he dropped into his chair at the large conference-room table. Leaning back, he closed his eyes and this time dragged both hands through his hair.

"So, what's your gut telling you?" Cathy asked.

He didn't want to say it, but the facts were staring him in the face. "Stranger abduction." The hardest type of case to break.

"Yeah." She sounded deflated. "Me, too."

"And it was high risk." Alec leaned forward. "Cody's a street-smart kid. He's not getting into a stranger's car. Hell, he'd probably be more likely to pop a tire with a switchblade."

Since his father had left, his mother had paraded one man after the another through their lives. Cody had spent a lot of time on the streets. He knew the score.

"And look at him." Alec picked up Cody's picture and slid it across the table to her. "He's beautiful."

"They're all beautiful."

"Not like this kid." He had an angel's face, though he tried to hide it with a scowl, dark blue eyes ringed with sooty lashes, and hair that, even shaggy and dirty, looked touched by gold. "I bet he's been fighting since he was five, just because of that face." Alec tapped a finger on the glossy photo. "This boy was targeted."

"Okay." She shrugged. "So he was targeted."

"High risk *and* targeted." The worst possible combination. "Whoever took this boy was a pro, someone who's done it before, a lot, and knew what he was doing."

"And?"

Reality was a bitch, but Alec had never been one to shy away from her. "The only way we're going to find Cody is if we get very lucky."

"Or the kidnapper gets stupid."

Alec arched an eyebrow, then shook his head slowly. They both knew the chances of that one. "Not likely."

IV

THE FIRST MILE was always the hardest, before Erin hit her stride, before her mind and body slipped into a place of pure physical effort. Then her thoughts shut down, the constant mind chatter finally quieting. She forgot about Claire and the CIA, her classes and students at Georgetown, this month's constant stream of bills, her mother's death, and even her concerns for Janie.

Instead, Erin concentrated on her breathing, the steady beat of her heart, and her feet pounding the hard-packed dirt. She slipped into a world of silence that she found only while running.

She'd started jogging in her early teens, in the months following Claire's disappearance. The first time had been after an argument with her mother. She couldn't remember what they'd been fighting about—though she didn't doubt it had been fueled by their grief over Claire. Angry, Erin had raced out of the house, with no particular destination in mind. She'd just run, away from her mother, away from the ghost of Claire, away from her own fear and guilt over both.

Two hours later, she'd returned home physically spent but rested, too, in an odd sort of way. She'd then been able to face her mother, who'd been so relieved when Erin returned that she hadn't punished her for taking off. At the time, Erin hadn't understood. She did now. After losing one daughter, Elizabeth Baker would never have survived losing a second.

From then on, Erin had run regularly, anytime her sister's disappearance closed in around her or the life of a teenager became too high pressure. She'd found it helped with her martial-arts classes as well, making her stronger and faster while increasing her ability to focus.

Even now, after all these years, running was part of her discipline, part of the regimen she followed to stay in top form. During the week, she got up before the rest of the household and walked the few blocks to Jamestown Park, the starting point of a jogging/biking trail that followed one of the dozen streams flowing into the Potomac. Round-trip it was an eight-mile trek, with mile markers all along the way. Monday through Friday she did six, but on the weekends she slept in, waiting until nearly seven before heading out and doing the whole eight miles.

Today she was even later than usual. Thanks to her conversation with Bill, sleep had eluded her for most of the night. His observation about her anger had gnawed at her. She knew he was right, but after hours of restless tossing and turning, she'd realized he'd been wrong about the source. True, she missed the excitement of working as a covert officer overseas and the knowledge that she was making a difference, serving her country in a way that suited her. Here, her position within the CIA was in a holding pattern while her superiors decided what to do with her. However, there was one major compensation for her stagnated career. Janie. It had taken only a few months for Erin to realize what she'd almost missed, and now she wouldn't have exchanged this chance to watch her niece grow up for anything.

Still, her anger hovered close to the surface. Bill hadn't been wrong about that. The question was why, and the answer went back to Claire's kidnapping, to the single act that had forever altered the lives of everyone Erin loved. The monster who'd stolen Claire's innocence and shattered their family was still pulling invisible strings, shaping the people they had all become and how they lived their lives.

Erin hated it, despised that she had no control, that she was still no less a victim than she'd been at twelve years old. That was the true source of her anger, the underpinnings of what kept her ready to lash out at any moment. And she didn't know what to do about it.

Finally, just as the eastern horizon had hinted at the approaching day, she'd drifted off, sleeping fitfully until Janie bounded in at eight thirty. The seven-year-old brought morning sunshine and pure energy as she bounced on Erin's bed to wake her sleepyhead of an aunt. A half hour later, Erin had headed for the park.

Now, as she came to the end of her run and the path leading back to the entrance, she considered going an extra mile or two. She was still edgy and in need of physical exertion.

Then she remembered Janie and their plans for the day. By the time Erin got back to the house, her niece would be at the breakfast table, too excited to eat. Like Friday night pizza, spending Saturday together had become a routine as they explored the sites around the D.C. area.

They'd done the normal tourist stuff: walking the mall, visiting monuments, and touring museums. Janie particularly loved the National Gallery of Art and had begged Erin to take her back three times already. The child's artist eye took in everything and later transferred it to her own drawing pad. But they'd found things of particular interest for kids as well, and today they were headed for the National Zoo. Janie had been talking about it all week. She wanted to see the pandas.

So instead of going an extra mile or two, Erin slowed to a fast walk and headed for a nearby bench. Spending time with Janie would be worth forgoing the extra running.

As she stretched out her heated muscles, she looked around.

A playground dominated this area of the park. In the center sat a brightly colored labyrinth of slides and tunnels, ladders, and climbing or hanging bars. Flanking it were a pair of swing sets, a slow saddle type for babies and toddlers on one side and a flat-seated highflier for the bigger kids on the other. Plastic animals on heavy-duty springs, seesaws, run and push merry-go-rounds, and a wooden sandbox filled in the spaces.

The park was quickly filling with people, mothers pushing carriages or children on swings. Fathers, too. Families. Erin wished Janie could experience a normal family, but that wasn't likely. Her father's identity was lost somewhere in Claire's damaged mind, if she'd ever known it to begin with, and Claire . . . well, she'd hardly qualify as your standard PTA mom.

Erin dropped down onto the bench, resting her head against the back and closing her eyes. The sun felt good on her skin, warm and nourishing. It was a beautiful day, perfect for an outdoor excursion, and she wasn't going to waste it worrying about things she couldn't change.

Fall had temporarily retreated, giving summer her way with the sunshine and temperature. Overhead, the cloudless blue sky was so sharp it almost hurt her eyes. The trees still shimmered in their greenery, and the last of the summer flowers reached toward the sun: lilies, impatiens, and cyclamen.

Erin, who'd never cared much for growing things, mentally checked off the names she'd once learned as part of an under-cover operation, where she'd posed as a florist. She didn't understand the mystique of tending plants, but she did gain an appreciation for their beauty and a satisfaction in knowing their names.

A high-tinkling bell sparkled the air.

Erin sat up. An ice-cream vendor pushed a cart along the walk toward the playground. Excitement rippled through the surrounding children, who pleaded with parents for money, then raced toward the man and his cart, small fists tight around dollar bills.

Too bad Janie wasn't here. It was a little early in the day for ice cream, but that would make it even more fun. Erin stood and started toward the small crowd of children, thinking she could buy Janie a treat for later.

When she got closer, however, she saw that the vendor wasn't dishing out ice cream. Not yet, anyway. Instead, he was performing simple sleight-of-hand tricks for his captive audience. A squeal of delight escaped one little girl as he pulled a coin from her ear, then made it disappear again with a sweep of his other hand.

He wasn't bad for a playground magician. In fact, the longer she watched, the more she realized he was very good. And there was something familiar about him. At first she couldn't say exactly what, but then realized it was his hands. The way they moved, with an economy of motion, plucking a coin from the air or stroking a child's cheek, without quite touching . . .

Erin shivered.

Where?

She studied those hands, and him, certain she'd seen him before. It nagged at her, tugging at a memory and making her uneasy. Nothing else about him helped place him. He was between forty and fifty. Five-ten or -eleven. Pale blue eyes. Balding. Soft around the middle. And nondescript. Which in itself bothered her.

When he finished his act, he started handing out ice cream

to his eager audience. The children, however, weren't done with him and begged for more tricks. He accommodated them, giving out another ice-cream bar and making the dollar of the boy who'd bought it disappear in midair.

Erin had to know where she'd seen him before.

She started across the grass to ask, then stopped, natural wariness or her CIA training taking over. Besides the sense that she should know him, there was something else disturbing about him, something that seemed not quite right. She told herself she was being foolish. He was, after all, only an ice-cream man, and none of the kids seemed the least bit shy around him. Still, Erin hung back, standing among the watching parents, taking note of the name on the cart—KAUFFMAN FARMS FINE ICE CREAM—and memorizing his features.

When the children finally released him, Erin fell back with the others. Though she kept an eye on him, with a quick glance or two as he closed down and readied his cart to move on. She gave one of the children a quick push on a swing, smiling at the mother who was busy with a toddler on a nearby plastic duck. Another quick look over her shoulder, another push, and Erin stepped away from the swing set.

He walked down the path, heading for the picnic grounds, his little bell announcing his approach.

Erin followed, weaving through the children as they raced from one piece of equipment to the next. She'd reached the edge of the playground, where she'd have to head across the grass toward the path . . .

"Miss Baker!"

Startled, she turned toward the child's voice.

"Look, Mama, it's Janie's aunt." A little girl, familiar, ran toward her, a woman about Erin's age trailing behind. "It's me, Alice. Don't you remember?"

The child slid into place. Last week, when Erin had picked

up Janie from a birthday party, she'd given this little girl a ride home.

"Of course I remember you," Erin said, glancing at the retreating ice-cream cart.

"This is my mom," Alice said, tugging on the woman who'd just caught up to her daughter.

Erin wanted to hurry after the man as he disappeared around a bend in the path, but what could she say? *Excuse me, but I think I've seen the ice-cream vendor before, and I want to follow him to see if I can remember where.* Put like that, it sounded ridiculous.

So she forced a smile and tried to focus on Alice and her mother. "Hi, Alice's mom, I'm Janie's aunt Erin."

The other woman laughed. "Please, call me Rose. Thanks for bringing Alice home last week. My car picked the wrong day to get a flat tire."

"Is there ever a good day for that type of thing?" Erin resisted the urge to again look after the man selling ice cream.

"You have a point."

"Where's Janie?" Alice asked, tugging on Erin's hand.

"At home. I was out running."

Alice looked crestfallen. "Can you go get her?"

"Alice," her mother reprimanded. "I'm sure Erin has better things to do."

Erin grinned, loving that Janie had made friends here. "It's okay, Rose." She had an idea. "Actually, Alice, I'm taking Janie to the zoo today. Would you like to come along?"

Alice brightened and turned to her mother. "Can I, Mama?"

"I don't know, honey . . ."

"Oh, please."

Erin interceded. "It wouldn't be any trouble, Rose. Janie will have a better time with one of her friends along. And then, so will I."

The woman laughed shortly. "Well, you're right about that. So, sure, why not? But you've got to promise to let me return the favor and take the girls someday."

"It's a deal," Erin answered.

"Yippee." Alice jumped up and down and clapped her hands.

"We're leaving around eleven, so how about if we swing by and pick up Alice then?"

"Sounds good." Rose took her daughter's hand and squeezed. "Okay, Alice, we better get home and get you ready."

"One thing before you go," Erin said, stopping them. "Did you happen to see the man selling ice cream?"

"Yeah, he was a little early today."

"So, he comes here all the time?"

"Well, this is the first time I've seen this particular man." Rose hesitated. "The usual one shows up later in the afternoon. But the coin tricks are a nice touch. I figured the regular guy couldn't make it. Why?"

"Oh . . ." Erin suppressed the ring of alarm in her head. "I just thought Janie would enjoy the show, that's all."

"Well, maybe he'll be back tomorrow."

Somehow, Erin didn't think so. "Maybe."

"I guess we need to go get you cleaned up," Rose said to her daughter. "We'll see you in a bit, Erin. And thanks again."

Erin watched the two head across the park, then she turned and started down the path where the man with the ice-cream cart had gone. At the edge of the park, she stopped, looking up and down the quiet suburban street.

He was nowhere around.

It was probably nothing, she told herself. But as she headed toward home, she didn't believe it.

By late afternoon, Erin had gained a new appreciation for teachers, camp counselors, and anyone else who had to deal with seven-year-olds on a daily basis. So much energy, bottled up into such small packages. If she could bottle it, the country would no longer be dependent on foreign oil.

The zoo was packed. Evidently, a lot of people had had the same idea for how to spend this last glorious Saturday before chilly weather set in.

The girls didn't seem to mind the crowds, however.

They went from display to display, hand in hand, their friendship cemented by the shared adventure. The elephants and rhinoceroses awed them, the big cats frightened them, and the scores of brightly colored birds enchanted them. They giggled over the antics of the bears, fell in love with the pandas, and spent an hour at the hands-on "How Do You Zoo" exhibit, where the children could experience what it was like to be a veterinarian or caretaker at the zoo.

They ate hot dogs and ice cream, snow cones and giant pretzels. Erin had initially said no to the cotton candy, believing both girls had had enough sugar for a month, much less a single afternoon. Then she'd given in to that as well. After all, how often did any of them get to spend a day where their biggest concern was whether cotton candy was one treat too many?

By the time she loaded the two of them into her car, Erin was exhausted. Although the girls seemed ready to go for another hour or two. That thought lasted for less than five minutes, when one glance at the backseat before exiting the parking lot told her how little she knew about children. Both girls were sound asleep, bent in awkward, uncomfortable positions that would have an adult racing for the ibuprofen once they awoke.

The drive home was blissfully quiet.

Alice's mother must have been watching for them because as soon as they pulled into her driveway, she came out. She took one look at the girls in the backseat and gave Erin a knowing smile. "Wore you out, did they?"

Erin laughed softly, and Rose maneuvered Alice out of the car. "Thanks," she said, "next time it's my turn," and carried her sleeping daughter inside.

At home, Janie barely stirred when Erin lifted her from the car and carried her inside. Marta clucked like a mother hen, following them up the stairs, then shooing Erin out of the way after she laid Janie on her bed. Erin stepped back, gratefully relinquishing control as Marta tended her chick.

"I don't suppose she's had dinner." Marta pulled off the grimy shorts and T-shirt. "And she needs a bath." She tsked and slid a clean nightgown over Janie's head. "Well, it will have to wait until morning."

Erin slipped out of the room, leaving Janie in Marta's competent hands.

Time with Janie had been exactly what Erin needed. It had a way of putting things into perspective and making her see them more clearly. Earlier in the day she'd worried that her niece needed a typical family, but that fear was groundless. She and Marta were Janie's family. And Claire, whom the child loved despite her shortcomings as a mother. It would have to be enough.

In the kitchen, she found a pot of chili simmering on the stove, but Erin needed to unwind before eating. A glass of wine and a shower were highest on her priority list. She took a chilled bottle of Chardonnay from the refrigerator and poured herself a glass, then headed for the family room.

She turned on the television, sipping her wine and flipping channels for something mindless. Instead, the local news station caught her. She'd actually passed over it before what she'd heard registered. Then she quickly backtracked, sinking onto the couch as she listened to the anchor.

Words jumped out at her.

Five-year-old girl. Chelsea. Missing. Last seen, early afternoon. Jamestown Park.

And the memory snapped into place.

The ice-cream man. Nineteen years ago. Miami. A neighborhood park in the heart of Little Havana. The day her sister, Claire, disappeared.

V

THE SCENE WAS A NIGHTMARE. One Alec had visited too often.

Police cruisers, their blue lights stroking the night, surrounded the park, blocking off entrances. A combination of wooden barricades and bright yellow crime-scene tape held back the walking traffic, while uniforms paced, keeping the curious and the grief-stricken at bay.

Off to one side, a man and woman huddled. The parents. She was trying to be brave, gripping her husband's arm in an iron fist, tears streaming unchecked down her checks. Every few minutes, she gave in to the sobs, and the man at her side held her close—to comfort or for comfort—Alec couldn't guess. Beside them, a young police officer stood watch, helpless to offer any kind of support or assistance.

Their little girl was missing.

Alec ducked beneath the crime tape and headed for his car.

He had no jurisdiction here. In that regard, each kidnapping was unique. The locals could call in the FBI or not, and so far they'd made no official request. Plus, there was nothing to indicate any connection between this girl's disappearance and Cody Sanders. Alec had come as a courtesy. He knew the detective in charge and had offered to take a look, hoping he'd find some commonality between the two cases, something that would help them find both children.

The two disappearances were a mixed bag that pointed at once to the same perpetrator and to two different ones. Depending on what aspects of the cases you focused on.

On the one hand, the similarities between the two couldn't be ignored. Even if you discounted the closeness in timing—approximately forty-eight hours apart—and the proximity—one disappearance in South Baltimore, the other in Arlington, a distance of roughly fifty miles—even then, two other points jumped out.

First, both abductions were high risk, a rare and dangerous undertaking for most kidnappers, who usually found easier targets. Cody had vanished on his way home from school. A high-risk abduction, made even riskier by the boy himself, who knew the streets. While the girl had been snatched from a park, where she'd been sleeping in a stroller, a dozen or more kids and parents within sight, and her own mother no more than a couple of yards away.

Second, the lack of evidence in both cases was telling. Contrary to what the media would have you believe, most kidnappers were caught quickly. Usually they knew their victims or were just plain sloppy in their attempt to secure a child. To have two predators, operating at the same time in such close proximity to each other, stretched the bounds of what Alec could dismiss as coincidence.

However, there was one other major factor that said the cases were unrelated: the children themselves.

Sexual predators had preferred victims. Age. Coloring. Sex. It all mattered. And except in unusual circumstances, they didn't stray. Cody Sanders, age nine, blond and blue-eyed, from the South Baltimore streets, was the opposite of Chelsea Madden, age five, female and dark, from suburban Arlington. And on this point alone, the experts at Quantico would be quick to claim there was no relation between the cases.

Still, something else, a gut feeling whispered to Alec that they were connected. If only they could find something, just one small clue to prove it.

More times than he'd like to admit, it had been just such a hunch that had led him down an unexpected path to a missing child. For years, he'd been the butt of Bureau jokes. "Hey, Donovan," someone would say, "got your crystal ball with you?" They'd call him Mulder and make snide, *X-Files* comments. Once, a pack of tarot cards, wrapped in black paper with bright silver moons, had shown up on his desk. Alec had laughed, realizing he was an oddity in an agency known for its protocol and by-the-book methods of solving crime. But as he closed more and more difficult cases, the teasing had turned to respect, and he'd learned to accept and rely on these instinctive nudges.

Tonight, however, it seemed they'd led him astray.

The police were combing the park with dogs, but so far, nothing. The darkness made it harder, but by morning it might be too late for Chelsea Madden.

Of the more than 58,000 children abducted by non–family members every year, approximately 115 are victims of more serious, long-term abductions. Of those, 56 percent are recovered alive, while 44 percent are killed. And of those murdered, 74 percent are dead within three hours of their abduction.

Alec wanted a cigarette. Badly. Instead, he took a roll of Tums from his pocket and popped one in his mouth. It had been nearly two years since he'd quit smoking. Usually he didn't miss it. Except on nights like this, when his stomach burned and his head ached.

He glanced again toward the parents. They were no longer alone. A priest was with them now, mumbling words of comfort Alec couldn't hear, words he no longer had within him to offer.

It was nights like this when he considering leaving the Bureau, or at least the CACU. Nights when he didn't think he could face one more heartbroken mother or angry father. Nights when he thought it was time to let someone else search for the lost innocents.

Then they would find a child. Alive. Frightened. Maybe even damaged in some visible or nonvisible ways. But alive. And on those nights, he knew he couldn't walk away. If it killed him—which it probably would someday—he'd have to keep going.

Just to save one more life if he could.

He prayed with everything in him, to whatever powers controlled the fate of children, that this night would be one of the latter.

As he'd watched, several of the cops gathered around a woman they'd let through the barricade. After a few minutes, one stepped away from the group, said a few words in his radio, looked around, then headed for Alec.

Alec pushed off the car, hoping they'd found something.

"Agent Donovan, you need to hear this," said the young officer when he got closer.

"What is it?"

"That woman over there"—he nodded back toward the group he'd just left—"claims she saw the kidnapper."

Alec frowned. As soon as Chelsea's mother had reported her disappearance, the park had been blocked off. Everyone in the vicinity had been questioned. That had been five hours ago. "Where's she been?"

"Said she just heard about the missing girl on the news."

"But she saw something? And now she's here?"

Most people with information about a crime were uncertain about what to do and used the "800" tip line. Those who showed up rather than called were usually of the crackpot variety.

"She insists on talking to someone, and Detective Smith is tied up with the search. He said to let you interview her."

"Lucky me." Well, Alec *had* offered to assist and could hardly blame them for taking him up on it.

"Her story's a little out there," said the cop, "but I figure we can't afford to ignore any possible leads."

Alec sensed the slight rebuke, and knew the other man was right. Becoming jaded was one of the dangers of too much time in law enforcement. Sometimes it took a rookie to put things in perspective. "You're right. Let's do it."

They headed toward the knot of officers, and Alec sized up the woman as they approached. Medium height, thin and young, with short dark hair. She wore faded jeans and a lightweight sweater, and for a moment he thought she was a kid. Then her stillness gave her away. She wasn't as young as she seemed, but a woman in her late twenties or early thirties, calm, and with an uncommon air of confidence. Good information or not, this was no nutcase.

She acknowledged him with a brief nod as he approached.

"I'm Special Agent Alec Donovan," he said, flashing his badge. "I'm with the CACU, that is the—"

"I'm aware of the Crimes Against Children Unit, Agent Donovan."

That surprised him. Few people in the general population had ever heard of the CACU. "And you are?"

"Erin Baker."

"This officer"—he gestured toward the young man at his side—"tells me you have information about the missing girl."

"I saw the man who took her."

He'd expected her answer, but the way she said it took him

aback. Calmly. Looking him straight in the eye. "I hope you're right, Ms. Baker—"

"It's Dr. Baker. Ph.D., not medical," she added before he could ask. "I'm on the faculty at Georgetown."

Was she trying to impress him? He'd be more impressed with solid information leading to Chelsea Madden. "All right, *Doctor* Baker." He gestured toward a couple of picnic tables being used as temporary command post behind a screen of trees, away from reporters, onlookers, and the knot of gathered uniforms. "Let's talk."

To the cop beside him, he said, "Come on. I want you to hear this as well."

The young man nodded, and the three of them made their way to the tables. Alec gestured toward one of the benches. "Have a seat, Dr. Baker."

"No, thank you."

"Okay." Alec matched her no-nonsense attitude. "You say you saw the kidnapper." He crossed his arms. "Convince me."

She tilted her head slightly, as if taking his measure before speaking. "I was here in the park, this morning, between nine and ten."

"Doing what?"

"Running."

An interesting choice of words. Running. Not jogging. "Do you run often?"

"Every morning. Usually earlier, around six."

"Go on."

"When I finished, shortly after ten, there was an ice-cream vendor here."

"Odd time to be selling ice cream."

"I thought so, too." She took a deep breath, then folded her arms. "He did sleight-of-hand tricks for the children. And I—"

"Wait. Go back. What was that?"

She looked at him oddly. "Coin tricks. You know, pulling

them from the air or from behind children's ears. That sort of thing. He had quite an audience by the time he started handing out ice cream."

Alec suddenly felt uneasy, not liking the leaps his own thoughts were taking.

"Are you okay, Agent Donovan?"

He came back to himself with a start. "I'm fine. You said he was doing magic tricks . . ."

"Do you know of this man?" she asked.

Only by rumor, and the testimony of a traumatized young girl years ago. No one gave her account any credence. Except Alec. "What else, Dr. Baker?"

She watched him a moment longer, then said, "I knew I'd seen him before, but couldn't place him. Then, when I heard the news about the missing girl, I remembered."

"Where?" He had to force himself to breathe.

"A park in Miami." For the first time, a slight tremor shaded her voice. "The day my younger sister was kidnapped."

Alec's mind raced. Was it possible?

The man she was describing wasn't supposed to exist. He was fiction, a myth in law enforcement circles. No one wanted to believe there was a predator out there, stealing children for profit, getting away with it for decades, too organized, too disciplined to be caught.

"When was this?"

She hesitated, as if wishing he hadn't asked this particular question, but answered, knowing he would. "Nineteen eighty-five."

Alec did the math. "Nineteen years ago?"

"I know how it sounds, but I also know what I'm talking about." There was no hesitation in her voice now. "It was the same man."

"Describe him." He nodded to the young officer, who wrote down everything she said.

She did, describing a fairly average-looking, middle-aged man. Someone you'd see a dozen times in fifteen minutes walking down any city street. When she was finished, she hesitated again, then added, "But it wasn't his looks that were the same." Another brief pause on her part, as if she knew that what she was about to say, too, was weak. "It was his hands."

"You recognized his hands?" It seemed a stretch, but then everything about her story was a stretch.

"The way he moved them. The magic tricks—" She stopped, as if realizing how crazy she sounded.

A woman sees a man, who reminds her of someone she'd seen nineteen years earlier, on what might have been one of the most traumatic days of her life. And it had Alec thinking about a little girl's words.

He was magic. And I knew he wouldn't hurt me.

But he'd taken her from her family and sold her to others, who would have done more than hurt her.

Alec had to be crazy even to consider taking this woman's claim seriously. Even for him, a man who'd built his reputation on following odd hunches and offbeat leads, this one was a leap. But he knew he had to make it, had to trust the voice that was no longer whispering, but screaming now, that this woman could lead him to more than just Chelsea Madden and Cody Sanders, but to an evil predator who'd stalked the innocent for years.

"Would you recognize this man if you saw him again?" he asked.

"Yes." No doubt in her voice.

He was going to catch hell for this. Especially if his instincts about this woman were wrong.

"Officer"—he glanced at the man's badge—"Lamont, get the name of the ice-cream franchise—"

"Kauffman Farms," Dr. Baker offered.

Alec snorted in disbelief. This woman was full of surprises.

"Get me a name and address of this Kauffman Farms," he said to Lamont. "I need the person in charge." He glanced at his watch. After seven. "And I expect I'll need a home address. Then give Detective Smith a call and tell him I'm going to check out Dr. Baker's story, and that I need you and your partner to come along as backup."

"Yes, sir."

"Oh, and tell him . . ." *Sometimes you have to break the rules.* "Tell him I'm taking Dr. Baker with me." He shot a questioning look at the woman in front of him. His best shot at catching this guy was if she pointed him out. "That is, if she's willing."

She nodded.

Officer Lamont arched an eyebrow but didn't comment before hurrying off to make the calls.

Alec turned back to the woman. "Give me a minute, Dr. Baker." Moving out of earshot, he pulled out his cell phone.

When he had Cathy on the line, he said, "I need everything we have on a woman named Erin Baker. She's a Ph.D. on the faculty at Georgetown. Start there, and then see what else you can find on her, including a 1985 missing child case in Miami."

"Who is she?"

"A potential witness in the Chelsea Madden case, and she seems to be . . ."—*more*—". . . not what she claims. I need to know if she's reliable."

"Any connection to the Cody Sanders case?"

"I don't know yet. It's possible."

"What's going on, Alec?"

He hesitated, knowing that this time not even Cathy would believe him. "I think we've found the Magician."

VI

Isaac Gage watched the chaos he'd created.

The cops had cordoned off all entrances to the park. A crowd had gathered on the fringes, neighborhood gawkers huddled together to swap stories and share theories about the missing girl. A half-dozen uniforms milled about, some pacing the perimeters keeping the natives at bay, while the others stood gulping coffee and resenting that they'd been stuck up here while the real fun was down in the park, with the hunt. As if in reminder of their low status, from deep in the woods along the river, dogs barked as they tried to pick up a scent.

Isaac rarely missed returning to a kidnapping site. It was a small treat, which he figured he'd earned. The risk of someone recognizing him was nearly nonexistent. Watching, he was never the same man as the one who'd executed the abduction. So he allowed himself a brief tour through the lives of the people he had shattered. And he enjoyed the hell out of it.

He knew the criminal psychologists and profilers would have a field day with that little piece of information. They would try to analyze him and predict his next move—as they'd done in a dozen previous incarnations—blaming his misdeeds on an abnormal childhood.

Well, his early years *had* been pretty fucked up, but so had the lives of most of the kids he'd met as his family moved from place to place, courtesy of Uncle Sam. His father had been career army, a hard-drinking, heavy-fisted colonel, who'd taken out his frustrations over his lackluster military career on his only son. Isaac had learned early to disappear whenever the old man was around. Sober or not.

Isaac had no complaints, though. He'd grown up strong, fast, and smart. It had been a matter of survival, and he'd been good at it. Something that couldn't be said for most of the kids who crossed his path now.

Plus the life of an army brat had taught him another skill that had served him well. With each move to a new base, he'd become a different kind of kid: a jock, a brain, a troublemaker and rabble-rouser, or social and popular. Whatever role struck him the first time he walked into a new school, that's what he'd become. It was a game he loved, and it had kept the boredom at bay.

Over the years, he'd perfected the art, developing an uncanny ability to take on different personas and blend in where he didn't belong. People—even children—tended to trust him without question. Therefore, he could go anywhere, be anyone, he wanted. It was a rare gift, and he'd capitalized on it.

Though lately, monotony had begun to creep in, making him restless. No one had come close to identifying, much less catching him, in more years than he cared to count. Not that he wanted to get caught. That was another absurd notion of the pop psychologists. He just expected there to be more of a thrill, more of a challenge, and it had been a long time since he'd experienced either.

Maybe it was time to quit.

It wasn't the first time the thought had crossed his mind. A couple of years ago, he'd bought some property in the western North Carolina mountains. He planned to have a cabin built, maybe build it himself. He'd always been good with his hands, and he expected he could learn the rest. It would keep him busy, keep the tedium at bay. For a while at least.

First, though, he had a job to finish.

As he worked his way through the crowd, toward the police barrier, he caught snatches of conversations.

"I heard the mother left the little girl alone, sleeping in a stroller," said one middle-aged woman to another. "I just don't know what's wrong with young people these days."

"It's no wonder this type of thing happens," said the second woman. "Not that I would ever want anything to happen to the child, but this should be a lesson to the mother."

"The poor thing," said the first woman. "Do you think their marriage will survive it? I heard he's seeing someone on the side."

The second shook her head in mock horror. "Oh, no."

Isaac smiled to himself. He'd provided these people with their evening's entertainment. A child was missing, and they'd come out to watch the show. And they would have the nerve to label *him* the monster?

He moved away from the women. As much as he enjoyed the scene unfolding around him, he had another objective in mind. The girl's parents. Every now and then, he'd get close to the families of his victims, a sweet taste he didn't often indulge. However, he needed to shatter the boredom, the tedium that was threatening to overwhelm him lately. The chances were slim that anyone would connect the man he was tonight with the one who'd taken Chelsea Madden, but it was a possibility that made his contact with the family worthwhile and very, very sweet.

Scanning the scene on the other side of the yellow tape, he

made note of its occupants. Besides the parents, off to the side, huddling together on a park bench away from their overly compassionate neighbors, and the half-dozen or so uniforms, a suit leaned against one of the patrol cars, a cell phone to his ear. A fed? He looked familiar, and Isaac experienced a thread of interest as he recognized the man. It was the agent heading up the Cody Sanders investigation. Donovan.

Isaac hadn't remained untouched for all these years without knowing his opponents. He'd checked Donovan out, and the man had a good closure rate on child abduction cases. Isaac figured it was just luck that they hadn't crossed paths before. Perhaps this final job, if it was his final job, would turn out to be more interesting than most.

As he approached the barricade closest to the cops, he caught the eye of a rookie who stood slightly apart from the gaggle of coffee-drinking veterans.

The boy came right over. "Can I help you, Father?"

It was one of Gage's favorite personas. Put on a collar, and people willingly dropped to their knees. "Actually, Officer, I'm here for the parents of that poor child."

"Are you their priest?"

The kid was sharp. Most cops would have ushered Isaac over without a second question. "No. I don't even know if they're Catholic." Though, of course, he did know. He figured he knew more about the family than they knew about themselves. "But I was close by when I heard the news. I thought they might welcome a man of God."

The cop glanced at the couple. "Okay, Father, I'll ask them."

"Thank you."

The kid approached the distressed parents, looking awkward and uncomfortable. He spoke with them briefly, then nodded in Isaac's direction. The woman turned tear-streaked eyes his way and beckoned him over with one beseeching nod.

Seconds later, Isaac was at her side, holding a rosary between his hand and hers, praying aloud with her for the safe return of her daughter.

By the second set of Hail Marys, however, Isaac realized it wasn't working. There was nothing new here. The scene was one he'd witnessed a dozen times before, the parents no different from others he'd consoled. Even the fed, Donovan, had no interest in him, having barely glanced in Isaac's direction. He wondered if he stood and yelled, *Here I am, I did it,* if they would even notice, or just go on with their pointless search.

Then a spark of interest wiggled down his spine as a woman showed up, approaching the cops. She looked familiar, and he knew he'd seen her recently. He searched his memory, placing her quickly. She'd been at the park this morning, early, among the small group of parents when he'd made his first pass through the park.

He almost smiled, curious, the spark of interest flaring.

Without missing a beat, he continued to add his voice to the mother's while his attention was on the woman as she talked to the uniforms. Whatever she was saying, they didn't seem impressed. Oddly enough, that disappointed him. She was here, so maybe she thought she could help find the lost girl. Yet it looked like they were ready to blow her off.

Incompetence.

No wonder he'd managed to do his work unimpeded for so many years.

Then the rookie, who'd led Isaac to the parents, broke away from the group and headed for Donovan. Not only sharp, the kid was willing to stand against majority opinion. Isaac suppressed a grin. Idealism. A rare gift indeed—though he figured it wouldn't last long. They'd either beat it out of him or drum him off the force.

For tonight, however, he'd have his way. After a brief discussion, he and Donovan crossed to the woman, who held her ground amid the ring of disapproving blue.

The missing girl's mother stopped praying, her attention caught by the scene as well. Her husband stood, his eyes locked on Donovan as he escorted the woman away from the cops, out of Isaac and the parents' line of sight.

"I wonder what's happening," he said. "I'm going to find out."

"Wait, Mr. Madden." Isaac stopped him with his soft priest's voice, though he'd also love nothing more than to listen in on the conversation between the unknown woman and Donovan. "Let the police do their jobs. They'll tell us when they know something."

The man hesitated.

"Please, Tom," said his wife, agreeing with Isaac as he knew she would.

Reluctantly Madden returned to the bench, but neither he nor his wife seemed inclined to pray anymore—which suited Isaac just fine. All their attention was on the spot behind the trees where they caught occasional glimpses of Donovan and the woman, as if their daughter's fate rested on the conversation between the two.

Ironically, they were more right than they knew. Gage might just have to change his plans concerning their daughter. If the woman really did know something.

They waited, five, ten minutes, and again the girl's father lurched to his feet. "I have to do something."

"Please, Tom, wait . . ."

Before he could respond, there was a new and sudden flurry of activity. Donovan and the woman left the sanctuary of the trees and headed toward the unmarked sedan. At the same time, the rookie returned briefly to the cluster of uniforms, calling out to another cop—his partner most likely—and the two of them started toward one of the black and whites.

"I need to find out what's going on," said the father as he started toward the two men.

Isaac caught his arm, barely concealing his own excitement at the prospect of finding out more about the woman and what she knew. "Mr. Madden, please, you're too upset. Stay with your wife, and I'll talk to the police for you."

Madden looked at his wife, who'd followed them both the few steps from the bench.

"Trust me," said Isaac. "I *will* find out who she is." *One way or the other.*

After a moment more of hesitation, Madden nodded. "Okay, Father. Maybe they'll tell you more than they'd tell me anyway."

"I'll do my best." Isaac started toward the patrol car, intercepting the rookie just before he closed his car door. "Officer, I need a minute."

"We're in a hurry, Father."

"Please, you have to tell Chelsea's parents what's going on." *And me. I need to know what I'm up against.*

The cop glanced past Isaac to the couple. "We don't know anything for sure yet. It's a long shot."

"Just tell me enough to give them some hope."

Pressing his lips together, the young cop nodded. "Okay. We may have someone who can identify the kidnapper."

A thrill of challenge raced through Isaac, and he almost laughed aloud. "The woman who was here earlier?"

"Father, I can't . . ." The cop shook his head.

"Okay, you don't have to tell me who she is." Isaac would find that out on his own. "But what about the kidnapper? Do you have a name for him?"

"I'm sorry, until we know more, that's all I can say."

It would be enough. For now. Isaac backed up. "Thank you, Officer. That will help a lot." Isaac knew he could get the woman's name from one of the disgruntled older cops, one of the ones who were certain the fed was on a wild-goose chase.

As he watched the patrol car pull away, Isaac considered his next step. Somehow, the woman thought she'd recognized him. How? And from where? He needed answers, and a few discreet questions to the remaining cops would put him on the right course to finding them. But first, he needed to get rid of the girl.

VII

Erin felt like she'd fallen down a rabbit hole.

Since seeing the news coverage on Chelsea Madden's disappearance, she'd needed all her training and experience to keep herself together. On one level, the incident dragged her back to the days following Claire's kidnapping, and she had to fight the urge to curl into a ball and hide. On the other hand, the possibility that the man she'd seen could have some connection to that nineteen-year-old nightmare kept her moving forward. To the police. To telling them what she saw. To convincing Special Agent Alec Donovan that she knew what she was talking about and wasn't crazy. Something she wasn't entirely certain of herself.

But then, he seemed a little off-kilter himself.

He should have taken her statement and sent her packing. It's what she would have done if someone had come to her with a story as crazy as hers. Instead, she'd sensed his mounting excitement with each question. He knew something of the man she'd seen, and wanted him badly. Bringing her along was his way of ensuring he identified and caught the right man.

With a quick glance, she sized him up. He was a tall, good-looking man with dark blond hair, blue eyes, and strong, even features. Very conservative, very clean-cut, very FBI. Under different circumstances, she might have found him attractive. Though at the moment, he looked tired, strained, his eyes lined with fatigue, his hair slightly mussed from where a hand had been dragged through it. And she realized she'd seen him on the news the night before.

"You're working the Cody Sanders case as well, aren't you?" He'd held a press conference to update the media on the search.

He gave her a quick look. "Yes."

"Is there a connection between the two cases?"

He didn't answer right away. Then he said, "We don't know."

"But you're here instead of in Baltimore, so there must be something."

"I can't talk about the details," he said, his eyes still on the road. "Let's just say there are a few similarities I couldn't ignore?"

She heard the switch in pronouns, from we to I, and realized he considered himself alone in linking the two kidnappings. So, he was a man who worked hunches, which explained why he was willing to chase her crazy story. And made her like him, just a bit, and also made her wonder what kind of man made his FBI career in the Crimes Against Children Unit.

She knew something of the CAC mission, which was to use multidiscipline and multiagency resource teams to investigate and prosecute crimes against children. Since 1997, at least two Special Agents in every FBI field office were designated as CAC coordinators, with the idea of maximizing the FBI's resources and expertise in CAC investigations. It was an important job but hardly high profile. So was Donovan dedicated to helping children? Or was this just a stop on the career ladder, a chit he

needed to acquire before moving on to bigger and more presti-
gious assignments?

It didn't make any difference, she realized, and turned away
to stare out at the dark night outside the car's windows. Either
way, Donovan seemed intent on finding the man she'd seen
today, and to Erin, that's all that mattered.

"You must have been pretty young when your sister was
taken," he said.

She glanced back at him, knowing this was one of the
weakest parts of her story—along with the amount of time that
had elapsed since Claire's disappearance. "I was twelve."

"Did the police question him?"

"I couldn't say." She thought of the days and weeks following Claire's disappearance. And the agony of waiting for news.
That had been one of the hardest parts. The waiting. "They
didn't share their investigation with us."

"But you're sure he's the same man?"

She fought down her impatience. If Donovan didn't already
believe her, they wouldn't be here. "The man I saw this morning was in Miami the day Claire disappeared. Whether he took
her or the girl today"—she shook her head—"I don't know.
But, in my opinion, the coincidence is too much to ignore."

If she told him she was CIA, it might help him understand.
She'd been trained to pay attention, to notice the details that
might mean her survival in some back alley or desert town
halfway across the globe. If nothing else, revealing her Agency
connections would give her more credibility and justify Donovan's investigation of her information.

Breaking her cover, however, wasn't an option. And even if
she could, her Company training didn't account for a nineteen-
year-old memory of something that happened when she was
twelve.

She doubted if words existed that could make sense of that.
Though she could try. She could explain how that entire

day had been seared in her memory; how sometimes at night she would close her eyes and relive every minute, remember every person she'd spoken to; how sometimes she believed if she willed it hard enough, *she* could change what had happened.

Yeah, right, that would work.

Tell Donovan any of that, and he'd turn around in a heartbeat while recommending she get a padded room next to her sister Claire. So Erin remained silent, counting on his interest in the man she'd described to spur him on.

They drove north, following the police car, through McLean and into Great Falls, a deceptively unassuming-looking town of expensive homes on estate-size parcels of land. They passed Great Falls Park and the elementary school, then turned into a residential neighborhood where the houses sat well back from the road amid manicured lawns and mature trees. After winding through the quiet streets, they ended up on a cul-de-sac and stopped in front of a stately, three-story brick home with great white pillars flanking the massive portico.

In actual miles, it wasn't that far from the small house Erin had bought and could barely afford in Arlington, but it might as well have been a different universe.

Evidently Kauffman Farms was doing well.

Out front, a half-dozen cars lined the circular drive.

"It looks like our friend has guests," said Donovan. "Wait here, I'll be right back."

Erin ignored the order and followed him out of the car. "It was your idea to bring me along, so I'm coming."

He looked ready to argue, then obviously thought better of it. Maybe he thought the man she'd seen this morning was inside the overblown house. Or else he just realized she wouldn't be left behind.

"Okay," he said. "But let me do the talking. Having you here isn't exactly Bureau policy."

"I understand."

The police officers who'd followed them stayed with their car while Erin accompanied Donovan to the door. A maid answered and went for her employer only after Donovan flashed his badge. Roger Kauffman appeared a few minutes later, obviously displeased by the unexpected visitors.

Again, Donovan held up his identification. "Mr. Kauffman, I'm Special Agent Alec Donovan with the FBI, and this is Dr. Baker. We need to speak with you for a moment."

"What about?"

"May we come in, sir?"

"This isn't a good time, Officer . . . What did you say your name was again?"

"It's Agent Donovan."

"Well, Agent, I have a house full of company, if—"

"It's important," Donovan assured him.

Kauffman looked past them to the uniforms waiting at the curb. Frowning, he opened the door. "All right, but just for a minute."

As they stepped inside, a rail-thin, middle-aged woman emerged from a formal living room alive with people. "Roger, what's going on here? Our guests are asking for you."

"I'll be just a minute, dear." He shot Erin and Donovan an annoyed look. "I need to speak with these people."

The woman looked unhappy but didn't challenge her husband, who led them into an expensively appointed study and closed the door.

"Now, what's this about?" he asked, not bothering to hide his irritation.

"We're looking for a man who works for you. He was in Jamestown Park this morning, selling ice cream from one of your carts."

Kauffman choked out an abrupt laugh. "My company runs two dozen ice-cream trucks, a dozen hand-rolled carts, and we employ almost twice that many drivers and operators. I have no idea who worked that route today."

"We need a name, Mr. Kauffman."

He shook his head. "Sorry, but I can't help you. I don't keep any records here. Everything's at the office."

"We'll drive you."

Donovan's politeness impressed Erin, who wanted to shove Kauffman up against his mahogany bookcases and tell him they didn't have time for his bullshit. A little girl's life was at stake.

"Not tonight," Kauffman said. "Come in to the office tomorrow—"

Donovan interrupted, his patience obviously stretched to the limit. "Mr. Kauffman. A child was kidnapped this afternoon, and your man is a potential suspect. I need his name and address. And I need it now. So, either you cooperate, or I'll have the officers outside escort you down to the precinct."

"Don't try and intimidate me, Agent." Kauffman drew himself up to his full height. "You have no right. I've done nothing wrong."

"Maybe not," Donovan said, "But at the moment, the only rights I'm concerned with belong to a five-year-old girl."

Twenty minutes later, Kauffman unlocked the main doors to Kauffman Farms and ushered Erin, Donovan, and the officer named Lamont inside. He flipped a switch, and the ceiling stuttered to life with harsh fluorescent light.

The room was cramped. A reception counter crossed the space a half-dozen steps into the room. Behind it, two desks sat sideways, face-to-face. A row of gray filing cabinets lined the wall in back of one, while behind the other was a long table with a fax and copy machine. On the far side of both desks was a large picture window that opened onto the warehouse beyond.

Erin saw ice-cream trucks and carts parked across from a large, industrial freezer. The office might be shut down for the day, but the warehouse buzzed with activity. Laughter and rowdy male voices reached through the glass as men in silly white coats and hats unloaded trucks. One man circulated among them, counting boxes and recording his findings on a large clipboard before the drivers wheeled the merchandise through freezers' open doors.

Erin suspected it was like this all summer, especially on nights like tonight. It was a pleasant weekend evening, maybe the last of the year, and the drivers would keep their trucks out as late as possible to entice people as they enjoyed summer's last fling.

She searched the faces. No one looked familiar, at least from this distance, and she fought the urge to leave Donovan and Kauffman to their files and head out to get a closer look. Unfortunately, Donovan wouldn't appreciate her initiative, and she needed him on her side.

"My secretary takes care of these things," Kauffman was saying as he unlocked one of the metal filing cabinets. "So I might have trouble finding the shift reports." He rifled through one drawer, slammed it shut, then started on a second. Finally, from the third drawer, he pulled out a sheet, glanced at it, then handed it over.

"Okay," he said. "Here's the schedule for the day. It looks like Al Beckwith worked Jamestown Park."

Donovan scanned the sheet. "Any chance he's still here?"

"Could be. Want me to page him?"

"No. We'll go look. But first, I want his personnel file."

Kauffman returned to the cabinet, went through the first drawer again, and returned with a slim folder. "Here's everything we have on him."

Donovan opened the file on the nearby desk, and Erin

stepped up beside him to look over his shoulder. It contained a simple application form, a couple of evaluation sheets, salary information, and a photograph.

"You keep pictures of all your employees?" Donovan asked.

"It's for insurance purposes," Kauffman said, glancing at his watch. "Because our drivers deal mostly with kids."

Erin studied the picture. Beckwith was youngish, a couple of years on either side of thirty. Thin blond hair. Watery blue eyes. And looked nothing like the man she'd seen in the park today.

Disguise, however, was an art. Once you'd mastered it, changing your appearance was as simple as slipping on a new set of clothes.

"Does he do magic tricks for the kids?" she asked, speaking up for the first time.

Kauffman shrugged. "Haven't a clue."

Donovan frowned. "So you don't know if he entertains the kids with disappearing coins?"

"They get paid a salary plus a percentage of what they sell. So, whatever they have to do, they do."

Alec glanced at Erin, a question in his eyes. *Is this the guy?*

"We need to talk to him," she answered.

"Okay." Alec turned back to Kauffman. "I'm going to keep this file, but meanwhile let's take a look and see if Al Beckwith is here."

Kauffman seemed distinctly uncomfortable with the prospect of handing over one of his employees, but agreed. He led them into the warehouse, toward the bevy of men who slowed when they saw him approach, obviously surprised to see their boss here on a Saturday night.

"Is Beckwith back?" Kauffman asked the man with the clipboard.

He nodded across the floor, toward a man unloading one of the handcarts. "Over there."

"Hey, Al," Kauffman called, "there are some cops here to see you."

Beckwith turned, arms loaded, his eyes flicking from Erin and Donovan to the uniformed officer behind them.

Donovan tensed. "He's gonna bolt."

Beckwith dropped his load. The boxes crashed to the ground, splitting and spilling ice-cream bars, as he sprinted toward the back of the warehouse and the gaping loading dock.

"Shit." Donovan and the young cop shot after him, dodging men and vehicles.

Kauffman stood, mouth wide, feigning surprise that Beckwith had run after his loud announcement.

"Is there a side door?" Erin demanded, furious at the man.

"What?" Kauffman looked at her, brow furrowed.

"A side door."

"Yeah, sure." He made a vague gesture to the right of the freezer. "There's a fire exit."

Erin sprang toward it, her path relatively clear compared with that of the men following Beckwith. Slamming through the emergency door, she set off a wailing alarm. She ignored it and raced toward the rear of the building.

As she rounded the corner, Beckwith leapt from the loading dock, with no sign of Donovan or the cop behind him. He was headed for the woods, across a parking lot and litter-strewn field. Once there, they'd lose him.

She increased her speed, her feet barely touching the pavement, wishing she had a weapon.

He saw her coming, seconds before she slammed into him, bringing him to the ground. He landed with a grunt, and she tucked and rolled, back on her feet before he'd gathered enough wits to scramble. Then he jumped up with the energy of youth and fear, but she didn't give him time to regain his balance. Swinging a leg around, she swept his from beneath him. And he was on the ground again, cursing.

Suddenly, Donovan and the uniform were on them.

Erin backed off, letting the cop snag Beckwith's arm and roll him onto his stomach.

"I didn't do anything," Beckwith hollered.

"Then why the hell did you run?" asked the cop as he slapped cuffs on the man's wrists.

Donovan grabbed Erin's arm and pulled her away from the other two men. "What the hell do you think you're doing?"

"Catching your man for you." She yanked her arm from his grasp, irritation rekindling the adrenaline just as it had started to ebb. "Or would you rather have had to track him through those woods?"

"It was a damn stupid stunt," he said, features tight. "You could have been hurt."

"Do I look hurt?"

He started to answer, then stopped, as if suddenly realizing something about her. And he looked her over, possibly for signs of blood. "Where did you learn to drop a man like that?"

"Does it matter?"

Again, he looked ready to argue but stopped himself. Giving her a look that said their conversation was far from over, he turned his attention back to the young cop, who was hauling Beckwith to his feet.

"Read him his rights," Donovan snapped. "Then I have a few questions."

"It's not him," Erin said, disappointment tinging her voice.

Donovan swung back to her. "What?"

"He's not the man I saw in the park." Beckwith didn't move right. He was young and agile, but lacking the grace and control of the other man. And he'd gone down too easily.

"Damn." Donovan dragged a hand through his hair. "Are you sure?"

"Yes." Again, she was expecting him to accept her at her word and knew it was asking a lot.

"Agent Donovan."

His frustration showing, he turned toward the second police officer, jogging toward them from the direction of the cars. "What is it?"

"They found her." The officer stopped in front of them, looking at her first before settling on Donovan. "They found Chelsea Madden."

VIII

FROM HIS WINDOW, Ryan watched the headlights approach the mansion. It was after midnight, well past time for deliveries or household staff returning for the night. That left only one possibility. Trader.

Ryan shivered.

The General had arrived earlier in the day with his usual flourish: a black stretch limousine and four-car diplomatic escort. A short while later, another visitor had arrived. One of the many who often showed up during the General's short stays. A small man, nervous, his eyes darting this way and that as one of the General's men escorted him inside.

Trader, on the other hand, always came at night. Always alone. No one ever greeted him. And his visits were never a good thing.

Although Ryan had been expecting him. The boy, Cody, had already been here longer than most. Three days. It had to be some kind of record. It was past time for Trader to come for him.

Suppressing a stab of guilt, Ryan crawled back into bed and waited for the stomp of feet in the outside hallway, the click of the door opening, and the sound of fear from the next room. He tried not to think about what Cody would go through, where Trader would take him, or who would own him next. There was nothing Ryan could do, no way he could stop what was about to happen.

The kid would learn the hard way the meaning of defiance, and he'd learn it from a harsher hand than Ryan's.

Ryan turned his head sideways to watch the slow progression of time on his bedside clock. Four minutes since he'd seen Trader's car. Five. Seven.

Still, only silence from the next room.

At ten minutes, Ryan sat up. It was taking too long. Trader never lingered. Trader came, he picked up or dropped off merchandise, and he was gone. Usually within fifteen or twenty minutes. Ryan couldn't remember a time when he'd done anything different.

Something else was going on, and it made Ryan nervous.

From under his mattress, he retrieved the key he'd stolen from the housekeeper several weeks ago. Although he suspected she knew he'd taken it, she'd never reported it missing. He liked to think she had a soft spot for him, but more likely she feared the certain punishment she'd receive if the General discovered the loss. At the very least, he'd send her home immediately, without the promised money that made her months in the U.S. bearable.

The staff consisted entirely of the General's countrymen—coarse, hardworking Germanic people, who did their jobs and didn't meddle in the General's affairs. None of them spoke more than a smattering of English, but during the two years Ryan had lived here, he'd picked up enough of their language to communicate. Though he often pretended to understand less than he really did. It suited both him and the silent, stoic servants, who pretended not to know Ryan's function here or even notice him much.

They came here for one reason. To work for a year or sometimes two. No longer. Then return home, with what seemed like a fortune in American dollars.

With that, the General bought loyalty. And silence.

Ryan's loyalty, on the other hand, had always been to himself, to finding a way just to survive. Which tonight meant finding out what was going on. So, key in hand, he stepped out into the hallway.

All was quiet.

The key opened the door to the main section of the mansion. He had full run of the east wing, which housed the kitchens, servants' quarters, and bedrooms for himself and the occasional visitor, like Cody. However, the rest of the building—inside and out—was off-limits.

The one other time he'd dared use the key, he'd explored the General's silent and luxurious rooms. He'd felt daring and brave that night, spying on forbidden territory. His courage had failed him, however, when a maid entered the General's dressing room, where Ryan had been about to check out the contents of one of the closets. He'd slipped inside, barely hiding in time. Since then, he'd never summoned the courage to use the key again.

Tonight, however, he planned to risk it.

Cody had accused him of cowardice, but it wasn't true. Ryan had simply learned to cope in a world that claimed more victims than survivors. Finding out what Trader was up to was just another way to ensure that Ryan kept his place here in the mansion. It had nothing to do with bravery, or lack of it, and he was going to prove it.

As he crept down the back stairs, he willed himself invisible.

He was good at going unnoticed. He'd learned it early, practiced it for years. If you didn't call attention to yourself, maybe no one would see you, no one would call on you or pick you out of a group. Blend into the background, and maybe another child would be chosen.

At the bottom of the steps, he waited before opening the kitchen door, listening. At this time of night, it should be empty, but he wasn't taking any chances. Even here, there would be questions if he was discovered.

Silence.

He cracked the door and peered into a darkness lit only by a low-wattage bulb above the stove. Except for the cook's cat, sleeping on the heating vent, the room was empty.

He slipped inside and eased the door closed behind him.

Okay. So far, so good.

Though he felt anything but good. He took a deep breath, trying to calm his nerves, the slight tremble in his hands, and the thumping of his heart. He had to be crazy coming down here tonight. Whatever was going on was none of his business, and sneaking around could only get him in trouble.

He knew he should go back upstairs.

Instead, he crossed to the door leading to the rest of the mansion. During the day it was open, but at night, once the General was done with the staff, it was locked. Only the house-keeper and butler were supposed to have a key.

Ryan wondered how she'd hidden her loss. Would the but-ler cover for her? In exchange for what favors?

At the door, Ryan hesitated.

Once he went through it, there would be no explaining his actions. It was forbidden territory without the General's express permission, and Ryan shuddered to think of what would happen if he was caught. Especially with Trader in the mansion.

Suddenly, his courage fled. *What was he doing?*

The question struck him with mind-numbing fear. This was so crazy. He'd seen what happened to those who openly defied their owners, and he'd learned his place long ago. Turning, he was halfway across the kitchen to the stairwell before he came to an abrupt halt.

You're a prisoner here, too.

Cody's words. An accusation thrown at Ryan on the first day, then again and again in the days that followed. Cody had kept up his defiance and his demands for Ryan's help. And even though he'd finally started eating, Ryan knew it had nothing to do with surrender. He suspected the kid was gathering strength for some useless escape attempt.

The kid's attitude ticked Ryan off, and along with the anger came a surge of defiance that his rational voice couldn't silence. He wasn't the victim here. Not a prisoner. And he was going to prove it.

Before he could convince himself otherwise, he unlocked the door and was on the other side closing and relocking it behind him. He didn't want one of the staff discovering it open. The whole time, the survivor in him screamed at him to go back.

Ignoring it, he started down the corridor, toward the grand foyer. Except for an occasional dim light, everything was dark, and he kept to the shadows along the wall. Trader would be with the General in his study, where he spent most of his time at the mansion.

Ryan had only been in the room a few times, three or four when called in by the General and once the night he'd done his exploring. He remembered it was large, with dark paneling and heavy leather furniture. A massive stone fireplace dominated one wall, where the General took his evening brandy, a couple of Dobermans at his feet. Big, fierce dogs, they'd watched Ryan with suspicious eyes.

He hated those dogs, and feared them. Almost as much as he feared Trader.

Over the fireplace hung a portrait of a fierce-looking man in full military uniform. The servants claimed he was the General's

father, who'd beat him regularly, then died and left his family
penniless. Ryan figured it was just idle servant gossip. Something to talk about, a way to bring the General down to their
level. The man who owned this house was rich, and Ryan
couldn't imagine anyone having the courage to raise a hand
against him.

Besides, if the stories were true, why would the General
keep such a reminder in his favorite room?

While the question rattled around in his thoughts, Ryan
crept toward the servants' pantry, a long, narrow corridor
stretching behind the length of the study, dining room, and
main parlor. Years ago, servants had used the room to serve the
family. Now the doors that once accessed each room had been
sealed off, and the pantry remained unused and empty. It was a
good place to listen without being seen.

Inside he positioned himself on the floor next to a heating
vent, where he could hear snatches of conversation from the
study. Although the two men were speaking too low for him to
make out their words, he could hear the tone. And the timbre
of Trader's voice. Deep. Low. And menacing.

It sent a shiver through him, making him realize he'd been
very, very stupid. He should never have come down here. What
did he think he'd find or hear that would make any difference
to him? After all, the General had been good to him. Generous.

Two years ago, Ryan's owner had been ready to dump him
on the street. He'd grown too old and become just another
mouth to feed. Instead, the General had taken Ryan in, giving
him a place to live. All he had to do was tend the young ones,
the irregular stream of children that passed through the General's mansion, and follow the rules. Easy enough under most
circumstances. Easier by far than his duties for any of his previous owners. Instead, he'd let Cody goad him into proving his
courage.

Stupid. Stupid. Stupid.

He wished he was back in his room, safe and warm in his own bed. But it was too late now. Because with Trader's voice in his ears, the thought of sneaking back down that long hallway and risking getting caught scared him beyond reason. He'd just have to stay put. And wait. For the General to go to his rooms. For Trader to leave.

So he huddled down, willing himself invisible once again.

Despite his fear, however, the heat, the drone of voices, and the late hour eventually lulled him into a half slumber.

He was little again, and a woman he didn't recognize held him on her lap. She rocked back and forth, her voice calming and familiar.

Hush, little baby, don't you cry . . .

She had a sweet voice, soft and gentle. And she smelled of baby powder and lotion. He knew her, should remember her name . . .

Ryan came sharply awake, the word *boy* lingering in his mind, along with an awareness of the sharp change in the General's voice.

"I don't like this. You shouldn't have brought him here this early. The ambassador does not return home until Tuesday."

"I had no choice." Although they were both speaking louder now, Trader's voice was lower, calmer than the General's. "The boy was a difficult mark. When I saw the opportunity to take him, I did. I might not have gotten a second chance."

They were talking about Cody. Ryan shifted and pressed his ear closer to the metal grate.

"It is all over the news," said the General. "The FBI is involved."

"The media is already bored with the story. It's the girl they're talking about now. This boy is nothing. His mother is alone. A whore. The FBI will soon move on to more important people."

"I hope you are right."

"I am. When the ambassador leaves, the boy will be on that plane."

Ryan sat back, a rush of pity churning his stomach.

He'd had a string of owners, but he'd never been sold overseas. The ones like Cody, though, the pretty blonds and redheads, were worth a lot outside the States, in countries where they were an oddity. Once he was lost in one of those places, no one here would ever see Cody Sanders again.

There was a long pause on the other side of the wall. Then the General said, "He will . . ."

Ryan didn't catch the rest of the sentence. He strained to hear, turning to press his ear against the vent again, but the General was speaking too low.

Suddenly, pain slammed into his temple and sent him sprawling. He groaned and looked up at a dark figure looming over him. The blow had blurred his vision, but he knew . . .

Trader bent down and dug his fist into Ryan's hair, dragging him to his knees.

Ryan tried to speak, to beg.

The next blow ripped across his cheekbone, a heavy silver ring splitting the tender flesh.

Ryan, falling, hit the floor amid flecks of his own skin and blood. He rolled, fear pumping through his veins, and scrambled back toward the wall.

"Get up."

Ryan shook his head, terror hammering in his chest, and tried to sink into the wall.

He was going to die. Here. Now.

Trader took a step toward him, and Ryan whimpered, pushing against the wall in an attempt to stand. He was halfway to his feet when Trader's fist exploded against his chin and put him on the floor again.

He tried to move away, but Trader followed, his booted foot connecting with Ryan's ribs.

"Please." Tears washed his face and mixed with blood.

"You want to die, boy?" Trader kicked him again.

Ryan screamed and curled into a fetal position as a knife-point of agony streaked through his chest. He could barely breathe, much less speak, but he got the word out. "No."

"You could have fooled me. Will I have to repeat this lesson?"

"No."

"Are you sure?"

"Yes." Ryan sobbed . . . the pain. "Never again . . ."

One final kick, and the room blurred and blinked out. Just for a second. Not long enough.

Trader came back into semifocus. "Get back where you belong. If you're here when I return, I'll kill you. Do you understand?" His face loomed large, menacing, and all Ryan could do was sob. Then Trader was gone, as silently as he'd appeared.

Ryan was alone. And alive.

He tried to stand, but the pain in his chest crippled him, bringing him to his knees. He inched toward the door, one hand holding the agony in his side, the other dragging himself along the floor, leaving a trail of blood in his wake.

He had to get out of here. Back to his room. He'd been a fool, an idiot. He knew the rules and he'd broken them. He deserved this punishment, and worse. He should be . . .

Then everything went black.

IX

In his study, General William Neville waited.

The big dog, Daimon, sat beside him, ears forward, body tense beneath his hand. The unpleasant sounds from the next room disturbed them both. They heard the eavesdropper fall, heard him whimper and beg, and the low threat of Gage's voice.

Daimon's chest rumbled.

William stroked the dog. "Easy, boy."

Then silence.

With a sigh, William sipped his cognac. He hated violence. Unfortunately, sometimes the situation required it.

A moment later, the study door opened and closed, and Isaac Gage returned, moving at once to the sideboard, where he poured himself a drink. Bourbon was the man's preference. Very American. At least over the years, William had taught him to appreciate a better brand of the stuff.

Gage threw back the shot, then came over and draped himself into the other wing chair flanking the fire.

"It was the boy, Ryan," William said. "Was it not?" It

could have been no one else. No other member of his staff would dare defy him. Just as only Gage could have picked up the boy's presence in the next room. The man had a sixth sense about such things.

"He's become a liability," Gage said.

"Too bad, it is such a waste." The boy had been good at handling the younger ones. And loyal. "But his age is a problem. Sixteen. Boys become . . . difficult."

A flicker of dark amusement distorted Gage's face. "I've never understood your odd attachment to your servants. Why do you care for this boy, especially after he's defied you?"

William shrugged. "They are like children. No, not children, more like Daimon here. Simple. And while loyal, they are useful." He let his fingers stroke the big animal. "In exchange, I care for them. Until . . ."

"Until they betray you."

"I am not a fool, Isaac." Did he think William would overlook Ryan's disobedience?

"He must be dealt with."

William waved away the suggestion, not wanting to think about it just yet. "I am well aware of what must be done."

He and Gage had had a very long and prosperous arrangement. It was grounded in Gage's unique talents and William's contacts in the international community, but neither required details about how the other managed his side of things. It was safer that way, and less offensive to William's sensibilities.

Besides, they had more pressing problems than the young caretaker.

"I am not happy about any of this, Isaac." It was not like Gage to make a mistake, and now he'd made two. "First you bring the boy here way too early; now this trouble with the Madden girl."

Gage's features tightened at the rebuke. "I explained the situation."

"Yes, yes, you were recognized. So what would you suggest I tell the customer?"

"Tell him there are other girls."

"It is not that easy." Thanks to the Internet and the stupidity of people posting pictures of their children, William's customers could handpick their merchandise. Which was exactly how the Madden girl had been selected. "These people do not take disappointment well."

"Offer him two for the price of one."

"It is not about the money." Not anymore.

There was far more profitable merchandise than children. He'd completed arrangements for one such transaction this afternoon, the final one before leaving the States. As distasteful as he found such dealings, the children were worse. Bothersome and barely worth the trouble. However, supplying one on occasion was a courtesy, a favor for those whose buying power had made William a very wealthy man. He wouldn't risk offending them because of one girl. Or some woman Gage claimed had seen him. The man was losing his nerve.

"Tell me about this woman you say recognized you."

For the first time, Gage looked a bit uncomfortable. "Her name is Erin Baker. She's on the faculty at Georgetown, teaching international relations."

"Baker?" William rolled the name around on his tongue. It had a familiar taste.

"Her sister is Claire Baker. Miami. Nineteen years ago." Gage handed over a slim folder. "I had some trouble getting information on her, but once I found this, the connection fell into place."

William studied the contents of the folder, several old newspaper clippings. "Oh, yes. Now I remember. Little Claire. Blond, blue-eyed, a lovely child." He'd gotten a tidy sum for her. Not as much as he'd get today in the foreign sector. But then, things were different now. "As I remember, the police picked her up in

San Francisco a few years later, during a drug raid. Some minor dealer . . ."

"Roland Garth. He cut a deal with the DA and all charges related to the girl were dropped. He's serving thirty years in San Quentin."

"And we decided the girl was no threat."

"*You* decided. I advised against letting her live."

William frowned in distaste. "She was in a mental institution. Harmless."

"A loose end. And now we have her sister to contend with. She was in Miami the day I took Claire, and somehow she made a connection between the two kidnappings."

"She recognized you?"

"That is what I've been telling you."

It seemed utterly amazing that someone had gotten the better of Isaac Gage. "I didn't think that was possible. She must be a very special woman, indeed. Either that, or you are slipping, my friend."

Gage tensed, leaning forward, his humorless face darker than usual. "Be careful, General. I'm not one of your flunkies."

The big dog growled beneath William's hand. "Easy, Daimon." William stroked the dark fur, fighting a grin. "I am afraid I just stepped on Mr. Gage's ego." He nodded an apology. "Forgive me, Isaac. It is just that in all these years we have been working together . . ." No one had ever identified Isaac Gage. William wasn't sure he knew the man's true identity. Gage was too good at being whoever he wanted. "Well, never mind."

Gage settled back in his chair, and William wondered why he was so touchy, so easily riled. This woman, this Erin Baker, must have struck a nerve. And again, William seemed to know the name, though in a different context, having nothing to do with the child, Claire. He mulled it around in his head, until it fell into place. And with it, another chord of unease.

"You say this woman is at Georgetown."

Gage nodded.

Yes, that was it. "I have met her." Gage's eyes narrowed, and William brushed aside his suspicions. "At an embassy function, I believe. A tall, dark woman. Very thin. Athletic maybe."

"Sounds like her."

An embassy hopper. She might work for the U.S. government—so many of the Americans at such functions did. She could be CIA even. Or a nobody. Just an international-relations academic, as she claimed, looking to hobnob with the rich and influential. Either way, he needed to find out. "So, tell me the rest."

It took Gage a minute to answer, but when he did, his implacable facade was back in place. "The police think she's a nutcase."

"But?"

"There's an FBI agent who's listening to her, the same agent working the Cody Donovan case."

William sucked in a breath. Worse than he'd thought.

"I see you now understand why I had to discard the Madden girl."

"Yes, of course." If Gage was caught, it could come back on William. His position in the embassy would protect him, but only to a point. Especially if the woman was CIA, who played by their own rules. "Obviously, we need to find out more about her."

"I agree."

"But not you." They couldn't risk her spotting Gage again. "You need to stay away from her." William's mind raced through the logistics of what he needed to do. "I will have her watched and will find out who she is before taking any action."

Gage settled deeper into his chair. "Whatever you say. That's your area of expertise, not mine."

William eyed him warily. It was not like Gage to agree so easily, particularly when it came to dealing with a risk like this

Baker woman presented. Normally he would want her dead, and the sooner the better.

"In the end," William conceded, "you may have to eliminate her."

"Both of them. Her and her sister." It wasn't a question.

"For once, I agree with you. But wait until we know more and after the boy is out of the country. I have an eager buyer, and I don't want to have to placate him as well as the girl's buyer." He took another drink, the dark liqueur warming him as it slid down his throat. "When I give you the go-ahead, make it look like an accident. Then her already unstable sister will commit suicide."

With that, he finished the cognac, then patted the dog and stood. He'd had all he could stomach of Isaac Gage for one night. "I assume you will be leaving now."

"Yes."

"I'll be in touch when I know more about the woman." Then, to the dog at his side, "Come, Daimon, it's time to turn in."

"What about the other boy?" Gage asked. "Your caretaker?"

William sighed again. "I am afraid Ryan's outlived his usefulness. He's getting too bold. What a shame." William started for the door. "I hate killing. But business is business."

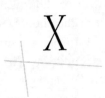

X

ERIN SPENT THE NIGHT chasing sleep.

She'd gotten home around midnight, exhausted and wired. So she'd taken a long shower, standing under the hot water until it ran cold. Only then did she climb into bed.

Still, the thoughts scurried around in her head, refusing to give her any rest.

Once the details of Chelsea Madden's disappearance came out, Erin had looked like a fool. A hysterical bystander who'd jumped to conclusions and dragged an FBI agent halfway across town to interrogate a legitimate businessman. At least that was how Kauffman portrayed the situation, and the detective in charge of the case had bought the scenario. If for no other reason than it got him off the hook.

Chelsea had been found within a mile of the park. Alive.

The official story was that while the girl had been napping in a stroller, her mother had gotten distracted by a younger sibling, a toddler. Chelsea had awakened and wandered off, getting lost and confused. She'd eventually crawled beneath a row of bushes lining the nearby residential street and cried herself to sleep. A passerby spotted her and notified the police.

It had all been a mistake.

The girl was fine, unharmed and safely returned to her family. The man Erin had seen in the park had been selling ice cream. Nothing more, nothing less. Or so the authorities concluded.

Erin wasn't so easily convinced.

There were too many questions left unanswered, too many leaps in logic the police had eagerly taken in order to tie everything up and mark the case closed. Like how a five-year-old little girl managed to get a mile from the park without some adult noticing her. Like Al Beckwith, who'd admitted handing over his ice-cream cart to another man, a friend of a friend, who'd paid him for its use for the day.

No, Beckwith didn't know the man personally, nor did his description sound anything like Erin's. Nor was he the first to rent out his cart in order to take an unofficial day off. And no, neither Beckwith nor the police had located or identified the man who'd borrowed the cart. He'd simply vanished.

Too many coincidences for Erin. Yet the police were okay with it.

Even Donovan had seemed satisfied, attempting to mollify her by claiming he'd check out Beckwith's story once he got back to Baltimore. She didn't believe him. Not that she thought he was lying, but he was in charge of the hunt for Cody Sanders, and that case would demand all his attention. Evidently, the only reason he'd become involved with the Chelsea Madden search was that he suspected a connection between the two cases.

That didn't change what she knew. Or what she didn't.

For instance, she might not know the details of how, but she believed Chelsea had been taken from the park, then abandoned. Why?

Erin didn't have a clue, but she had no doubt of the *who*.

She didn't know his name, and she suspected she didn't even know what he really looked like, but she knew how he moved. Those quick hands, plucking coins from the air, too graceful and skilled for a simple playground magician. And she *would* recognize him again.

For now, though, she wanted sleep, which seemed to move deeper into hiding with each passing hour. She had a long day ahead of her tomorrow. Sunday was the day that she took Janie and Marta to visit Claire, and Erin needed a clear head to deal with her sister. Unfortunately, needing something and getting it weren't always the same thing.

Finally, as the night ebbed toward morning, she resigned herself to the inevitable and got out of bed. She'd go out for an early run. Maybe if she physically exhausted herself, she could still get a couple of hours' rest before going to see Claire.

It was still dark when she stepped outside. A light rain had fallen during the night, leaving the ground coated in a thin layer of mist. The cool air, with its promise of approaching fall, felt good against her skin. Invigorating. She skipped her warm-up walk and started off at a slow jog, feeling her muscles stretch and revive her blurry mind.

She passed silent streets, an air of expectancy hovering over them like the early morning weather. In another hour, the first stirrings of commerce would begin. The paperboys and street cleaners would emerge, the corner bakery would lift its shades, and early weekend workers would head for their jobs.

For now, though, she was alone, her breath coming out in soft puffs, the slap of her running shoes against the asphalt, and the steady beat of her heart. Running. It was the one constant in her life, grounding her in a way nothing else had ever done.

Arriving at the park entrance, she turned toward the water and the path that lined it. Remnants of last night's search littered the playground. Coffee cups and cigarette butts flecked the trampled ground. A stray piece of yellow crime tape fluttered from a tree. The grass had been torn up by too many feet and the bushes beaten back.

Eventually, the park would heal, but it would take more than a cleaning crew. It would take time. Something Erin understood all too well.

Once she turned onto the jogging path, she picked up her pace. Usually, she shared the trail with other joggers and walkers. At this time of the morning, however, she was alone with the silence. And her thoughts.

She knew she should let the whole question of the ice-cream vendor, with his repertoire of tricks, go. No one she knew would understand why she had to pursue this after so many years, why she had to find the man who'd ruined her sister's life and scarred the rest of her family. Especially since everyone familiar with Claire's case believed the man who'd kidnapped her was serving time in a California prison.

Her mother would have called Erin obsessed. But Elizabeth Baker had had her own obsessions, and she'd found her solace in vodka and cigarettes. Marta would accuse Erin of trying to relieve guilt she hadn't earned, but Marta hadn't been in the park the day Claire disappeared. Only Erin had been there. And so she couldn't let it go, couldn't pretend she hadn't seen the Magic Man today.

She had to find her own comfort, her own redemption.

As long as there was a possibility the man she'd seen had had something to do with Claire's kidnapping, Erin had to look into it. She'd find out who he was and what he'd been doing in the park yesterday, and in Miami, nineteen years ago. And if she found out he was the one who'd taken her sister, Erin would make him pay and make sure he never hurt another child, or family, again.

On Monday, she'd cancel classes and go into her D.C. office in one of the Company's many anonymous buildings. There, she had access to a computer network unavailable to her at Georgetown. She would research Kauffman and Beckwith and access the old case files on Claire's abduction. And she'd find the man with the magic hands.

She'd be skating on thin ice using the Company's resources for a personal investigation. If anyone noticed, she'd be reprimanded at the very least, or asked to resign. She could live with either, if it meant putting the nightmare of her sister's kidnapping behind her.

Suddenly, she sensed something.

A sudden chill in the air that set the fine hairs at the back of her neck on end. Then she heard it.

Footfalls. Quick and steady behind her.

She kept going, her mind instantly clear. Focused. Her muscles tight and braced for attack. Her breathing deep and steady. Listening. Another minute. Two. With no sense of the gap closing behind her.

Another runner?

Of course. She was being paranoid. She was seldom alone on this path. She'd let the early hour spook her. Stopping abruptly, she spun around, ready to challenge whoever trailed her. Just as a tall shadow darted into the woods, the bushes trembling in his wake.

Another chill swept through her.

Watching her. Not another jogger, but someone following her. Not necessarily dangerous, though. It could be anyone. A homeless person, finding shelter in the woods. A mugger thinking he'd found an easy mark. Or something, some*one* more.

She waited, reminding herself she was far from defenseless. She'd faced down dangerous adversaries before, and not just in the demo ring at Langley. She could handle herself. Yet she kept seeing hands, fluid, competent hands that could kill as easily as they pulled a coin from a child's ear.

Nothing.

No more sound. No movement. He was still there, though, just out of sight, hidden by the dense undergrowth. She could feel his eyes on her, heavy and menacing, and for the first time in her life, she understood the sensation of skin crawling. She considered calling out, confronting him. Taking the offensive.

At least he'd no longer be behind her.

"Are you afraid to face me?" She put all the bravado she could muster into her voice, all the arrogance she'd learned from five years around men with elevated testosterone levels. "Is that why you hide in the bushes?"

No reply.

Except a wave of amusement that drifted on the air.

She was hallucinating. If someone was still there, he was probably more frightened of her than she was of him. And she certainly couldn't feel something like amusement across the yards of space separating them.

Don't be a fool.

With clarity, the thought struck her. And she knew she was not imagining any of it. If she'd been in Baghdad or Cairo, she wouldn't question her instincts. She'd sense the danger, accept it, and deal with it. Here, in the suburbs of D.C., however, she was second-guessing herself.

It could get her killed.

So she shut down her hesitation and listened to the gut feeling that told her to get out of here, back to the park. And home. With no weapons and no clear idea whom she was up against, she'd be an idiot to hang around.

The only question remaining, was how?

She'd just passed the two-mile marker. An easy run, except *he* was between her and the trailhead. The other direction would be worse. Six miles, with the water to her right and the woods to her left. She'd run herself into a dead end.

That left her only one option. To go back the way she'd come. With her back to the water, she retraced her steps while scanning the brush for any hint of movement. Each footfall brought her closer to where she'd seen the shadow leave the path, until she was within a couple of yards from the spot. Six feet. An easy distance for an attack. She steeled herself, knowing it would be a fight for her life.

None came.

Then she was past it, her eyes still scanning the bushes for another yard as she edged farther and farther away. Two yards. Three.

She turned and started for where the trail returned to the park, suppressing the urge to give in to the fear rippling through her and run full out. In case he followed her, she needed to conserve her strength. After a minute or two with no further sound or movement, she slowed down more. At the one-mile marker, she began to breathe easier.

Then she sensed it again. Closer this time. Heavier.

She broke into a run, heading for the park. Though she knew it was a mistake, letting the fear take over. Crippling her. Voiding her years of training. Making her weak. But as she rounded the last curve, the bright playground equipment visible in the dim light, she picked up even more speed. Though no sound came from behind her. No sense of danger. Until . . .

She stopped cold. Terror gripped her insides as a dark figure stepped out in front of her. Tall, broad shoulders, powerful, and moving purposefully toward her.

XI

Isaac could have killed her.

It would have been so easy, so sweet. She'd been mere feet away, standing there, her courage leaking from her like blood from an oozing wound. She'd tried to hold it in, tried to stop the flow, but her efforts failed. In the end, fear had drained her, made her weak.

Oh, she would have fought. And from what he'd discovered about her in the last few hours, it would have been an interesting encounter.

The information he'd given to Neville about her had been easy enough to uncover. He'd gotten her name from one of the cops at the park, and from there it had been a piece of cake to discover her address, occupation, and her sister, Claire. After leaving Neville, however, Isaac had dug a little deeper into Erin Baker's life. The martial-arts training was an interesting twist, but not unusual. That she'd excelled at them, however, notched up his interest a bit. Still, she wasn't a killer. She lacked that instinct, which would forever put her at a disadvantage. So he would have prevailed, taking her life and the threat she posed all in one move.

Unfortunately, her death would cause a stir neither he nor Neville could afford at the moment. Time was what they needed and what kept her alive. Time to let the whole Chelsea Madden incident die down. And time for the feds to give up and forget about Cody Sanders.

Besides, she was far too interesting a subject. She presented him with a challenge he hadn't experienced in too long. He didn't understand how she'd recognized him. What was it she'd seen in the two men, the two personas, that had caught her eye? He wanted to know, and until then, he wouldn't kill her.

So he'd just watched, taunting her. Because she'd sensed his presence, and that, too, made her special. Unique.

Now, as he cut back through the woods to reach the playground before her, he thought about his meeting with Neville. For once they'd agreed on what needed to be done, if not on the how or why.

Neville hadn't a clue about the real threat Erin Baker presented. Though he understood the danger to himself and had come to the same conclusion about her background as Isaac. She was NSA. Or CIA. It was the only thing that made sense. She'd fallen off the radar for a full year after earning her doctorate, then surfaced in Cairo for two more. It wasn't exactly your standard career path for an academic. What Neville didn't understand was that this was not about her government connections. This was personal. It was about her sister. And that made her all the more dangerous.

Neville had sent men to watch her. Isaac had seen them, parked a discreet distance from her house, close enough to watch, far enough not to be spotted. Not fools. Competent, efficient men who would watch her movements and report back. They weren't, however, in her league. They would underestimate her—her skill and her determination—and she'd bring them all down.

So Isaac would do things his way, despite Neville's orders to the contrary. Just as he'd done with the Madden girl. He'd let her go because killing her would have lent weight to Erin's story. Missing or dead, they had a crime. Alive, they had a hysterical witness. As it was, the sleeping child had no recollection of the missing hours she'd spent in the back of his van. He'd dropped a chloroform-soaked cloth over her nose and mouth before taking her from the stroller. It had kept her sleeping, and ensured she had no memory of him.

He reached the edge of the playground and settled in to wait. Erin wasn't that far behind him, running now, her long legs eating up the dirt path along the river.

Despite his resolve to do otherwise, he considered again the expediency of killing her now. He could take her quickly, then disappear. Neville wouldn't be happy. But then, Isaac didn't take Neville's orders.

XII

ALEC SAW HER brace herself, her body settling into a defensive posture. He'd learned a lot about Erin Baker in the last six hours. She'd been training in the martial arts since she was twelve and held three black belts: tae kwon do, aikido, and kenpo. Which explained the incident with Beckwith last night. The kid hadn't stood a chance.

Alec stopped walking, hands up, palms out. "Easy, Dr. Baker. It's me, Agent Donovan."

She didn't let down her guard, though she eased up a bit. "What are you doing here?"

"I need to talk to you."

"And so you stalk me in the middle of the night?"

"I'm not stalking you, and it's almost—" He started forward but stopped when she tensed again.

"Were you following me along the path?"

"What?" He looked behind her, toward the dark water, and reached for the weapon beneath his jacket. "No."

"Someone was, if not you—"

"It wasn't me." He moved up beside her, the .38 automatic in his hand now, and scanned the surrounding trees. The darkness was giving way to morning, but too many shadows lingered with too many places a man could hide. "You told me you ran early, so after checking your house and finding you'd already left, I came here to wait for you to finish. Did you see him?"

"Only a shadow." She took a deep breath and seemed to shake off a chill. "He's gone now."

He realized she was spooked, and from what he'd seen so far, she wasn't a woman who spooked easily. "Are you okay?"

"I'm fine." She noticed the gun in his hand and laughed abruptly. "It was probably nothing." Though she didn't sound like she believed it.

"Maybe." But then, maybe not. Especially if his suspicions were correct and they'd hit a nerve last night. In that case, she shouldn't be running alone, no matter how many black belts she held.

"I think it would be best if we talk somewhere else," he said, slipping his weapon back into its holster. "There's an all-night diner a block over. Is that okay?"

She nodded and started for the park entrance, but he held back, studying again the now-empty dirt path and the rim of bushes framing it.

Was he out there even now? Watching them?

With a shiver of his own, Alec turned and caught up to her.

They walked in silence, and he could almost feel her settling back into the coolheaded woman he'd met the night before. It wasn't until they'd put the park a full block behind them that she finally spoke.

"So, what does the FBI want with me?" she asked.

"Not the FBI. Me."

She threw him a glance, a spark of surprise in her eyes. "Agent Donovan, are you hitting on me?"

He actually felt himself blush. The thought appealed to him more than he'd admit aloud, more than was prudent under the circumstances. He was looking for a kidnapper, possibly a serial kidnapper. He couldn't afford to be distracted by a woman, even one as intriguing as Erin Baker.

"No," he said, and realized that didn't sound right. "I mean . . ." He shook his head, clearing the inappropriate thoughts. "I just have some questions about the missing girl."

"There is no missing girl, remember?" Her voice held a touch of sarcasm. "She was found under a bush."

"But there *is* a missing boy." He pulled a manila envelope from his inside jacket pocket and withdrew a picture of Cody Sanders. Offering it to her, he said, "He's been gone five days now."

She refused the picture. "As I recall, we've already had this conversation. I told you I watch the news, and you suggested there might be a connection between the two kidnappings."

He was about to tell her a lot more, probably more than he should. But he needed her help. "Then you also know we're running out of time. The longer Cody's missing, the less chance we have of finding him alive. Or ever."

She stopped and turned to him. "What does this have to do with Chelsea Madden? Or me?"

"You believe someone took her yesterday, don't you?" He slipped the picture back in his pocket. "Then left her for us to find?"

She didn't comment. Why should she? She'd made her opinion clear enough to the police the night before. Calm. Rational. Totally sure of herself. She'd told them they were making a mistake.

"And you think it was the man you saw in the park who took her?" Alec added. "The same man you saw in Miami nineteen years ago."

"Even if you don't buy my story—and I really can't blame you for that—there are still too many coincidences to write off Chelsea's disappearance." She started walking again. "You need to be looking for someone who had a motive for taking her and then letting her go."

"I agree." He snagged her arm and stopped her. "Cody Sanders was seen in Cross Street Market the day he disappeared." It was the break in the case Alec had been waiting for, ferreted out by the locals who knew the area much better than his agents. "He was talking to a middle-aged man, balding, soft around the middle." He saw her understanding, the recognition that he'd just described the man she'd seen in the park. "No one knows how long the man's been hanging around the market. A week? A month? But we can't find him now."

He released her arm. If he hadn't caught her attention yet, he'd have her with the next piece of information. "The one thing everyone does seem to remember is that the man played the shell game for quarters."

She went very still.

"You do know what the shell game is, don't you, Dr. Baker?" She nodded, but he explained anyway. "It's a sleight-of-hand game played with shells and a ball. The dealer puts the ball under a shell and mixes them up. To win, the player needs to identify which shell hides the ball."

They'd reached the diner, but neither of them seemed inclined to go in. "If the dealer is good," Alec said, "if he has very quick hands . . ."

"Then he seldom loses." She took a deep breath, looked away for a moment, then seemed to accept some unseen burden. "The same man I saw performing magic tricks in the park?"

"It's possible."

"And the man in Miami, the day Claire disappeared?"

"A long shot, but again, possible. Along with a dozen or more kidnappings over the past twenty or so years. That's why I'm here, why you and I need to talk."

The early morning, with its wakening sounds, settled between them. A street-cleaner pushed its bulky weight along the curb. A city garbage truck stopped and started in the alley alongside the diner, the gears of its belly cranking and creaking as stiff steel arms lifted and emptied a full Dumpster. And a few Sunday-morning commuters straggled onto the streets, heading for the district.

"Why would he do it?" she said. "Why grab Chelsea, then let her go?"

"Because someone—you"—he paused, letting his words sink in—"recognized him."

She was so still. It was an extraordinary ability, one that seldom came naturally to the human species and was even beyond the skill of most professionals. And he had to wonder how she'd acquired it. "But that's only one of the remaining questions," he said, referring to her question about Chelsea's release, though it applied to his thoughts about Erin as well. He gestured toward the diner. "Come on, I'll buy you coffee and tell you the rest."

They claimed a back booth. Other customers had begun drifting in, bleary-eyed, for coffee or a quick breakfast after a late shift or before an early one. A girl in her late teens, with nine silver hoops marching up each ear and three in each eyebrow, poured coffee.

After the waitress left, Erin wrapped her hands around the white ceramic mug but didn't drink. "Okay, tell me what you know about the Magic Man."

"Is that what you call him?"

She shrugged.

"In law enforcement circles, he's known as the Magician." Alec swallowed the hot coffee, wondering just how long the caffeine would keep him going before he crashed. "Except most don't believe he exists."

"But you do."

"Three years ago the Coast Guard stopped a ship, the *Desert Sun*, off the California coast. The manifest indicated the ship was transporting engine parts to various Middle Eastern ports." He hesitated, leaned forward, and lowered his voice. "What they found were children." He could still see those faces, the fear marring their young features, and it churned the anger inside him. "Twenty-two of them."

Her eyes filled with horror, though her expression remained blank. She was good at hiding her emotions, except her eyes. They spoke volumes, and he heard every word. She was thinking of families, tormented by a child's loss. It was something too close to her, a pain she understood too well.

That's why he needed her help.

"The kids had been kidnapped one by one during the previous twelve months, from all different parts of the country. Most fit a certain general physical and socioeconomic profile." He took a moment, gathering his thoughts. "Blonds. A few redheads. All light-skinned and most from low-income families. Many of the older ones, the nine- to twelve-year-olds, had been classified as runaways."

"Why have I never heard anything about this?"

"It was hushed up and deemed classified so the information wouldn't leak out." He leaned forward, lowering his voice even further. "Think of the outrage if the general public thought American children were being sold overseas. No one would wait for a declaration of war. There would be killing in the streets, with every mosque from here to California as prime targets."

"What happened to the children?"

The waitress returned to refill their coffee, and he waited until she'd left again. "None of them had been physically harmed, but they were hospitalized for observation and counseling before being sent home."

"And so the FBI could question them."

"We wanted more than a crew of sailors who manned the ship. Or even the ship's captain." He sat back, feeling the caffeine start to work on his nerves. "Unfortunately, the children weren't much help. Most were too young or too traumatized to tell us anything we could use."

"Most?" She was quick, her mind leaping ahead of him. "There were exceptions?"

"One. Her name was Suzie, and she told us about the man who'd kidnapped her."

"The Magician?"

"I was working out of the L.A. office at the time and was called in to help with the interviews. Suzie was a precocious ten-year-old who'd been snatched from a fairgrounds a month earlier." She was a feisty little redhead, with a sharp tongue and a bad attitude. A survivor. If he ever had a daughter, he'd want one like Suzie. "She claimed the man who abducted her did magic tricks."

He gave her a moment to take it all in, finishing his coffee, while she still hadn't touched hers. "Would you like something else?"

She shook her head. "No, this is fine. What came of the girl's testimony?"

"Not much. None of the other children could verify Suzie's story, and the man was never found or identified." He shrugged. "The case is still open, but it's been dormant for years. As for the Magician . . ." He paused again. "It wasn't the first time we'd heard of a child abductor who did magic tricks. There have been random reports of him going back twenty years."

"But no one really believes he exists?"

"I'm not sure I believed it myself, until that interview. You see, the Magician has become something of a myth, like the big one who got away. Anytime we fail to find a lost child, it's easy to blame the man no one else can catch either."

It sounded lame, like an excuse made by lazy cops and field agents, the very people meant to protect the Suzies and Codys of the world. But, it was more defense than anything else, a way to explain and somehow deal with their failure to always protect the innocent. "Then today, when you showed up with your story . . ."

He watched Erin work through it, analyzing his words. Cathy had done a full background check on her, but nothing she'd found explained the woman in the booth across from him.

Erin Baker was more than she claimed.

"So, who took the fall for the *Desert Sun?*" she asked.

"The captain. He claimed he masterminded and executed the entire plan with help from his crew. It seemed unlikely, but with nothing else, he was all we had." Alec turned over his hands, a gesture of helplessness and frustration. "Besides, he wasn't an innocent, he knew he was running a slave ship."

"What about the ship's ownership?"

"A shell corporation, which we eventually traced to this man." From the same envelope holding Cody's picture, Alec drew out another and pushed it across the table. "General William Neville."

She studied the picture without touching it. "I know him. He's attached to the German embassy."

"And you know this because you're a professor at Georgetown?"

"Don't start playing games with me, Agent Donovan." She slid the picture across the table. "We both know you had me thoroughly checked out. Yes, I do the embassy circuit. I'm a professor of international relations, and it usually helps to know something about the subject you teach."

"Is that why you spent two years in Cairo?"

"If I wasn't interested in foreign cultures, I wouldn't be in this field."

"You're not going to tell me who you work for, are you?"

"You already know."

He didn't press her, though he knew she was skirting the truth. "Okay, so you've met General Neville."

"I was introduced to him once, that's all." She sat back. "He's not the Magician." Again, she was so sure of herself.

"No, but he might be involved." He slipped the photo back into its envelope and returned both to his jacket pocket. "Do you know anything about Neville?"

"Very little." He could sense her pulling away from him, reining in her interest. "My expertise is in Middle Eastern cultures."

"Neville's old-world aristocracy. His father was a high-ranking officer in Hitler's SS who lost the family fortune during the war."

"But Neville is wealthy."

"He's also brilliant and ruthless. Over the past thirty years, he's built a business empire whose interests are worldwide and diversified. And one of those interests is a small shipping firm."

"Which owned the *Desert Sun*."

"Exactly. He was, of course, questioned, but with his diplomatic attachments and the captain's claim of operating on his own, we couldn't pin anything on him." Alec thought about it, holding in the anger that threatened to rise up whenever he thought about Neville and how he'd sidestepped responsibility for running a slave ship. "But yeah, I think he's more than involved."

"And his connection to the Magician?"

He scooted forward, feeling the frustration of something just beyond his reach. "I'm chasing threads here, Dr. Baker, and they may not connect. But that little girl was taken by a man who lures children with magic tricks, a predator who has been operating with impunity for years. And she ends up on one of Neville's ships." He leaned back. "Now I have a boy, a street-smart kid who's not going to fall for much. He's not getting into a stranger's car or helping a guy unload a van. But the day he disappears, he's seen with a man who plays the shell game."

He forced himself to relax. "Seems to me there could be a connection."

"Or none at all."

He sighed and dragged a hand through his hair. That's exactly what Cathy had said, what he knew his superiors would say if he ran this theory by them. He wasn't chasing leads, he was chasing phantoms. "I'm desperate, Dr. Baker." And he couldn't ignore the instincts that had so often led him to find the lost, even when he knew there was very little logic to back him up. "If we don't find Cody Sanders soon, we're not going to find him ever. And the man with the shell game is our only lead."

She looked away, out the plate-glass window, where night had given way to morning while they'd talked. When she spoke, she kept her eyes on the street and seemed far away, distant. "This is all very interesting, Agent Donovan, but—"

"Alec, please call me Alec."

She turned to him, then hesitated. "Agent Donovan"—she emphasized his title, denying his request to use his first name—"you've got to be breaking a half-dozen Bureau rules telling me all this."

He couldn't deny it. "At least."

"So why? Just because you think I can help identify the Magician, *if* you ever find him?"

"First, I need you and Beckwith to work with a police artist, to come up with a composite sketch of the man you saw yesterday."

"Okay." She nodded. "But that's not why you're here. You could have sent anyone to ask me for that."

"You're right." He leaned forward. "I need to know whether I'm on track, or if everyone else is right and I've lost my senses. You say you'd recognize him if you saw him again. That's great, but if your sister—"

She reared back. "Whoa, wait a minute. Leave Claire out of this."

"I can't. She can help."

"Claire can't help anyone. Not even herself."

"Just hear me out. You were right earlier; I pulled a file on you last night. I know your sister was found in San Francisco four years after her abduction."

"Then you also know the man they found her with is serving a thirty-year prison sentence."

"Yes, but on charges unrelated to your sister."

"He's still in prison. What difference does it make why?" Except it did bother her, he could tell. When it came to her sister, she wasn't as good at masking her reactions. "He said he found her on the street and gave her a place to stay."

"You don't believe that."

"I don't know what to believe, Agent Donovan, because my sister refused to testify at his trial. At first we thought she'd eventually talk about her ordeal, at least to the doctors. Finally we realized it wasn't that she wouldn't tell us, she couldn't. She doesn't know who kidnapped her or what happened to her during those four years. And the rest of us . . ."

"Don't want to know."

She recoiled as if slapped. "That's not true. I'd give anything to see the man who took her punished."

"Then help me." He leaned forward and grabbed her hands. "It's been fifteen years, if she can just tell us something about the man who kidnapped her, anything, even verify that he did magic tricks. That's all I need." It would help him convince his superiors to give him the manpower needed to run with this.

She pulled her hands from his and buried them beneath the

table. "Aren't you listening to me? She doesn't remember, she's blocked it out."

"Maybe she just doesn't want to remember."

"What's the difference?"

His back was against the wall. He hadn't been able to find out nearly as much about Claire Baker as he'd found about Erin. Just that she'd had serious problems since the cops found her during a drug raid on the West Coast fifteen years ago. She'd gone home to her family, but she'd been damaged in unseen ways, and had run away within a month of her homecoming. It was a pattern that had repeated itself throughout her adolescence, along with attempted suicides. Over the years, she'd been in and out of three psychiatric hospitals. But her condition and treatments were protected by doctor-patient privilege that not even a desperate FBI agent could violate. He'd been hoping that with Erin's help he could get to the woman whose secrets might lead to Cody Sanders.

"She's a cutter," Erin said, reading the question in his silence. "When she feels threatened, she uses sharp objects to make herself bleed. And any little thing can set her off." She laughed abruptly, bitterly. "They tell me it's a survival mechanism. Do you believe that? It's her way of keeping herself from committing suicide."

Alec felt Erin's pain and frustration reaching across the table and wrapping around them both. Claire Baker had lived a nightmare, was still caught within its grip, and Erin was unable to do anything about it. He suspected that helplessness wasn't an emotion that sat well with her.

He didn't know what to say. He'd seen such pain before, on the faces of parents waiting for news of their children, and had never had the words to ease their burden. So the silence settled between them, awkward now that she'd refused him. And he felt Cody Sanders slipping, fading away into that no-man's-land of lost children.

No.

Alec wouldn't give up yet. He had one more avenue to pursue, one more person who might know something.

Then Erin stood abruptly. "I have to get home. Janie's waiting."

"Oh, yes, Claire's daughter. You came back to the States to raise her, didn't you?"

She stiffened. "That's none of your business."

He took one more stab at reaching her. "This isn't about you or me, Erin." He purposely used her first name, forcing her to accept this as a human plea. "Or even about your sister, Claire. It's about a young boy. Cody Sanders. And preventing what happened to your sister from happening to him. All I want you to do is talk to Claire. Soon. Today. Tell her what you saw, and ask her to help us find Cody."

She was shaking her head.

"Just think about it," he insisted, handing her his card. "Call me day or night."

She stared at it for a moment, and he thought he'd gotten through to her. Then she pulled a couple of bills from her sweatshirt pocket and tossed them on the table.

"I'm sorry. I can't help you."

XIII

PAIN WOKE HIM.

He'd been dreaming of lavender fields, stretching as far as the eye could see. The tiny blossoms blended together, a rippling blanket of multihued greens and purples covering the earth, their scent a balm to his senses. It was a pleasant dream, filled with sweetness and promise, and he longed to linger within its borders. But a dull, insistent ache pulled at him, wrenching him from the gentle world of dreams to one of harsh light and nightmares.

Ryan opened his eyes, disoriented. He lay atop a bed, naked except for a rough blanket that smelled of stewed meat and onions. Nauseated, he shut his eyes again, reaching once more for the scent of lavender. But it was gone.

Along with the oblivion of unconsciousness.

Instead, hot sunlight streamed across him, disturbing him as much as the unfamiliar blanket. He always shut the drapes before sleep—an old habit, its origins lost somewhere in his past.

He pushed up, half rising before a streak of pain ripped

open his chest and dropped him back to the mattress. Then he couldn't move, could hardly breathe, as the agony ricocheted through his insides, and he had to bite his tongue to keep from screaming. Seconds turned to long torturous minutes, and only after it ebbed a bit did he remember.

Trader.

Standing above him, anger darkening his features. And something else, something stronger and more terrifying than the anger: pure hate.

Ryan shuddered, reliving the surprise blow that had sent him reeling, and the feel of his skin ripping open. He could smell the heat of Trader's breath as he hissed his warning. And his savage boots, slamming into Ryan's side.

With a groan, Ryan touched his chest, where wide bandages bound his rib cage. Closing his eyes again, he barely kept sobs of fear at bay. He should be dead, would be except . . .

How had he gotten back to his room?

Slowly, he pushed himself to a half-sitting position, careful not to jar his body and send another wave of devastating agony through it.

The details he'd noticed on first waking took on new meaning. Someone had found him and carried him back to his room. But who in this house of wordless servants had that kind of courage? Who had dared risk the General's—and Trader's—anger to help him, a boy they barely knew existed?

Ryan had no friends in this place, no one who cared whether he lived or died. Yet someone had helped him. And that person or persons had done more than carry him to his room. He or she had removed his clothes and taped his ribs, covered him, and left food, water, and aspirin for the pain he'd face when he awoke. The idea warmed him in a way he'd never known and helped ease his fear.

Suddenly, he noticed the time. Almost noon.

He needed to get a tray to Cody. None of the household

staff would dare enter the boy's room, and Ryan couldn't risk another dose of the General's wrath by shirking his duties.

Forcing himself to move slowly, despite his mounting panic, he swung his legs to the floor. Then waited as a wave of pain passed through him. If he was lucky, the General had already left the mansion, or at the very least hadn't bothered to ask after his young houseguest and caretaker.

First, Ryan took the aspirin, four, because he needed to make it down the stairs and back again, and he doubted two of the painkillers would do the trick. Then he ate, taking a lesson from his charge, to build up his strength, even though food was the last thing he wanted right now. He dressed in loose-fitting clothes to conceal his bandaged ribs while avoiding the mirror and its reflection of his ruined face. There was nothing he could do to hide that damage, so what would be the point in torturing himself by looking?

Besides, by now the entire staff would know what had happened.

The trip down to the kitchen was difficult, but even worse were the minutes he spent gathering Cody's lunch. No one spoke to him, or even acknowledged him. Though he felt their eyes, their thoughts, on him. To them, he was already dead. And very soon he'd stop walking around.

With the tray in hand, he reentered the back stairwell. Closing the door behind him, he waited, catching his breath and steeling himself for the long upward climb. It wasn't as bad as he'd expected, though. Maybe the aspirin had kicked in, or the movement eased his aching muscles. Or maybe it had more to do with the anger building inside him.

Damn them all. He wasn't dead. Not yet.

As he opened Cody's door, the boy said, "It's about friggin' time. I—" He broke off midsentence when he caught sight of Ryan's face. "Hey, man, that looks really bad."

Ryan actually smiled, relieved that at least someone was

willing to acknowledge him, even if it was to tell him he looked like a punching bag. "I've had worse." A lie, but one meant to ease the other boy's concern.

"Really?" Cody seemed awed.

Ryan half laughed and handed over the tray. Then he went to the mirror to take a look for himself. The entire left side of his face was swollen and mottled in shades of red and purple. His cheek, ripped from cheekbone to lip, had been treated with some kind of yellow ointment and pulled together with butterfly bandages. And both eyes, black, made him appear like a character from a horror movie.

"It does look pretty bad, doesn't it," he said, stating the obvious.

"Yeah." Cody raised his eyebrows and nodded, but didn't ask any more questions as he set the tray on the table in front of the cold fireplace and sat on the floor. "Roy hits me sometimes."

Ryan eased into one of the chairs beside the table. "Who's Roy?"

"My mom's boyfriend." Cody dug into the food, shoveling it into his mouth, his manners a far cry from the days he refused to eat. "Her current one, anyway."

"Where's your dad?"

Cody shrugged. "Don't know. He took off a long time ago, but Mom says we're better off without him." He seemed to think about that for a minute, then added, "I don't know, though, we haven't got much money and she's always . . ."

"What?"

"Never mind." Cody shook his head. "Don't you guys ever have normal food here?"

Ryan looked at the thick beef stew and hearty bread. It was one of his favorite meals, and he'd brought Cody a double serving since he'd missed breakfast. "I don't know what you mean."

"You know." Cody eyed him like he was from another

planet. "Like hamburgers. Hot dogs. French fries." He rolled his eyes. "Man, I'd kill for a Whopper about now."

Ryan grinned, amused. In a way, he was from a different world than Cody. Though one of the maids had been a fast-food junkie and snuck it in occasionally. She let Ryan try some once, but he hadn't been impressed. The meat was thin and rubbery, the bread soggy, the potatoes laden with grease. He just didn't get it.

"The General's not big into Whoppers," he said.

"Well, it just proves your General's an idiot."

Ryan laughed, then stopped abruptly because the action hurt his chest. He'd never heard anyone speak badly of the General. No one Ryan knew had the nerve. "He's not my General." Not after last night, when he'd let Trader nearly kill him. "How come your mom lets Roy hit you?"

Cody glared at him. "Hey, she does the best she can."

Ryan lifted a hand, winced, and dropped it again. "I'm sorry, I didn't mean anything by that."

Cody gulped down another spoonful of stew. "Well, she tried to stop him once, but then he started in on her. So, I figured it was better to keep him hitting me instead of taking it out on her. Since, you know, women aren't so strong."

Ryan was amazed. It would never occur to him to take a beating for someone else. In his world, survival meant keeping a low profile and out of the way of flying fists. "How did you do that, get him to hit you instead of her?"

Cody chuckled. "Roy's not too bright. I just keep egging him on until he can't stand it no more. He forgets all about Mom and starts in on me." He tore off a piece of bread and shoved it in his mouth. "Of course, he's got to catch me first. And I'm real fast."

Ryan grinned, thinking he might enjoy watching Cody get the better of this Roy. "So, if he's so bad, why doesn't your mom just kick him out?"

Cody shrugged. "It's not that easy."

Ryan thought about their situation: the guards, the dogs, Trader. "Yeah, I guess it never is."

"How about you? What's your mom like?"

"I don't remember her." Ryan settled back in his chair, feeling tired again. He needed to rest, time for his body to heal. Only he expected he didn't have much time left.

"She dead?"

"I don't know. They took me from her when I was younger than you."

"And you haven't seen her since?"

"Nope."

"Man, that sucks."

Ryan hadn't thought about his mother for years, but Cody was right. It sucked. "I remember she was real pretty, with long black hair. And she used to sing to me."

Hush, little baby, don't you cry.

The words floated in his mind. A snatch of memory. Too elusive, too distant, to catch.

"My mom never sang to me," Cody said. "But she used to take me to the movies every Saturday. That was"—he rolled his eyes—"before Roy moved in."

"You miss her, don't you, Cody?"

"Yeah. I guess I'm just used to her and all. And well, I want to see her again. I don't want to forget her, like—" He suddenly looked a bit embarrassed.

"Like me?"

"Sorry."

"It's okay. Look, Cody." Ryan eased forward in his chair and lowered his voice. "If I can find a way to get us out of here, are you willing to make a run for it?"

"Let's do it."

"Not now. I need a day, maybe two." Ryan wasn't even sure how he was going to get them out the door, much less past the dogs and the guards. Plus, he had no idea where they were or where they'd go once they got away from the mansion. "If we're caught, it will be bad." Then there would be Trader to deal with, and he wouldn't just hurt Ryan this time. And he had no idea what would happen to Cody. "Really bad."

"I don't care. I don't want to grow up never seeing my mom again."

"Okay. Be ready, then, and I'll come for you when I can."

As he left Cody to finish his meal, Ryan realized some people would say he was crazy. He no longer cared. All he knew for sure was that he was sixteen and he wasn't ready to die.

And he wanted to see his mom again, too.

XIV

SUNDAYS WITH CLAIRE were always an ordeal.

From one week to the next, Erin never knew what to expect. Often Claire was sullen and irritable, or simply refused to see or speak to them. That was hard enough on Erin and Marta, but devastating to poor Janie, leaving her confused and hurt.

Even on her good days, though, Claire was unpredictable. She might be wildly silly and childlike, playing games with Janie as if they were peers instead of mother and child. Or Claire might remain quiet and thoughtful, gracing them with her presence and a few words, but hardly noticing her daughter.

Either way, Janie was usually fussy and demanding afterward, and Erin came to dread their weekly excursions. According to Claire's doctors, however, she needed regular contact with her family. They said it grounded her and aided the healing process.

Their concerns were validated when Erin had to cancel one of their visits in early spring. She'd been called to a last-minute meeting at Langley and didn't want Janie and Marta going alone to see Claire. As it turned out, that decision had been a mistake.

Claire called the house and, getting Janie on the phone, accused the little girl of not loving her. By the time Marta claimed the receiver from the sobbing child, the damage had been done. But Claire wasn't finished; she continued to berate the older woman, alternately sobbing and ranting, accusing Erin of heartlessness and desertion.

Erin had been furious when she'd first heard about the call. Janie had been through enough. She didn't need her mother berating her about things she couldn't help. Then, after a long talk with Claire's doctor, who'd put her under watch in case she hurt herself, Erin had calmed down.

Claire, after all, wasn't well and hadn't been for a very long time. Her official diagnosis was Post-traumatic-Stress Disorder, or PTSD, stemming from severe childhood trauma. But Erin suspected not even the doctors really knew how those years of abuse had damaged her.

Still, Erin worried about Janie and how her mother's illness affected her. How did you explain to a seven-year-old that her mother behaved irrationally because she'd been kidnapped as a child, because years and her innocence had been torn from her life? It was a horror story no child should have to hear, much less live with, and Erin couldn't inflict it on Janie.

So all her niece knew was that Claire was very ill and lived at the hospital, where the doctors were trying to make her better. And after the phone incident with Claire, nothing got in the way of their weekly visits. Not even the Company.

Today, Erin felt more on edge than usual. Her encounter with Alec Donovan had left her unsettled. After leaving him at the diner, she'd gone home, showered and changed, then headed down to the police station to work with the sketch artist. It had taken a couple of hours, but he'd come up with a remarkable likeness of the man she'd seen. Now, if the authorities could just locate him, they might also find Cody Sanders.

She told herself she'd done her part. The rest was up to the FBI and police. Still, Donovan's request buzzed in her head, whispering that there was one more thing she could do to help. Except the last thing she wanted was to ask Claire about the fateful day nineteen years ago when she'd disappeared from a Miami playground.

Claire had never spoken about her ordeal, about the kidnapping or her missing years. Not to Erin or to their mother. Not to numerous psychiatrists or mental health professionals. Not to anyone. Whatever she'd endured during those years was locked in her damaged mind. But the physical exam after she'd finally been brought home told them enough about what she'd been through, about the monster who'd taken her, about the abuse, physical and emotional, that she'd suffered. Fortunately, according to her current set of doctors, Claire didn't remember what had happened to her. She'd blocked out the memories because they were too painful.

Erin had never quite believed that explanation. In her opinion, everything Claire had done since the police had found her indicated she did remember, but couldn't put words to the memories.

Despite that, Claire had been steadily improving over the last year. After their mother's death, Erin had moved her sister to Gentle Oaks, a psychiatric hospital on the outskirts of Fredericksburg, about an hour south of Arlington. It had taken the bulk of their mother's life insurance to keep Claire there, but the facility was world-class and well regarded.

So Erin didn't want to risk whatever progress Claire had made by picking at a subject that could tumble her sister back into the abyss. She had Janie to consider, and no matter how

Erin felt about her sister's ability to mother her daughter, Janie loved Claire.

When they arrived at Gentle Oaks, they found Claire outside, sitting under a tree. She seemed lost in her own world, wearing a loose cotton dress of soft blue that emphasized her pale skin and hair. From a distance she looked young and beautiful. And fragile.

"Mommy!"

Claire turned, a smile brightening her face, and spread her arms. Janie rushed into them, nearly knocking Claire to the ground as she pulled the child onto her lap.

"Did you miss me?" Claire asked as she buried her face in curls so like her own.

Janie giggled and squeezed her mother's neck. "This much."

"Is that all?"

Janie tightened her hold, scrunching her face in an expression of effort. "And this much, too."

"Ooh, that's a lot." Claire laughed, a high, tinkling sound.

"Did you miss me, too?" Janie asked.

Claire untwined the small arms from her neck and leaned back to look into Janie's face. "Of course."

"I made a picture. Want to see?"

"I do, but first help me up."

Janie climbed off her mother's lap and pulled her hand as if helping her to her feet. By then, Erin and Marta had reached them, and Claire gave Marta a warm hug. "Are you taking care of my baby?"

"With your sister's help," Marta answered.

Claire brushed the comment aside. "Oh, I doubt that." Then, offering her cheek to Erin, added, "She's not exactly the maternal type."

"It's good to see you, too." Erin gave Claire a perfunctory kiss, sensing the accusation—never spoken—but always there, just beneath the surface of Claire's words. She was here because Erin had failed her all those years ago. "And I manage to find a maternal moment or two when needed."

"Did I hurt your feelings?" Claire looked surprised. "I didn't mean to. You're just so good at everything else . . ."

"Come, let's sit down," Marta said, diverting them. "I packed us a nice lunch."

Claire brightened and turned back to Marta. "I'm ready." She looped her arm through Marta's and started toward a nearby picnic table beneath a sprawling oak, its leaves just starting to turn. In another week or two, it would wear its full fall regalia. For now, though, only a smattering of yellow tarnished its summer cloak.

Erin followed with the promised basket of goodies, and Janie skipped alongside.

While Marta started unloading the basket, Janie pulled at her mother. "Can I show you my drawing now?"

"After we eat," Claire replied absently, still focused on Marta. "Did you bring my favorite?"

The little girl's face clouded.

"Janie is becoming quite the artist," Erin said, upset by her sister's lack of interest.

Claire met her gaze, irritation and understanding sparking her eyes. "Of course she's a good artist, she takes after her mother."

"Then I'd think you'd take the time to look. She spent a lot of time—"

"Enough," Marta said. "Janie, come help me set up lunch."

Janie looked from Marta to the two sisters, then nodded and climbed up onto the bench.

Erin bit her tongue, angry with herself for losing her patience. Just being around Claire was a trial, making Erin act like the twelve-year-old child who'd once lost her baby sister rather than a grown woman. She knew better. She was the adult here, the one in control of all her actions. Yet she always managed to let Claire get to her, especially when it came to Claire's lack of maternal instincts.

"Marta made fudge," she said, smiling an apology. It was Claire's favorite.

After that, lunch was uneventful. Claire ended up looking at Janie's picture of her school as they ate, letting the girl explain and point out all the details of the building. When they finished, Janie turned back a page of her sketchpad and pushed it toward her mother.

"Now you draw, Mommy."

Claire flushed, obviously pleased. "Okay. Do you have your pencils with you?"

Janie produced the box of precious pencils.

To anyone watching Claire work, there was no doubt where Janie had gotten her talent. Claire sketched the graceful stone building that looked more like an expensive boarding school than a psychiatric hospital, added the stately oaks, and filled in the finely manicured lawns. Unlike Janie, whose attention to detail marked her drawings, Claire used broad strokes, which gave her work an otherworldly appearance.

Erin experienced a moment of sadness at the waste of Claire's talent, and guilt over her own part in that waste. What would Claire have done, what would she have become, if a stranger hadn't plucked her out of that Miami park nineteen years ago?

While Claire focused on her drawing, Marta and Janie went in search of the ice cream that was always available to patients and their guests during Sunday visiting hours. Erin watched Claire for a minute or two, her thoughts slipping to Cody Sanders.

Like Claire before she'd been taken, he had his whole life in front of him. Erin wondered what talents, what gifts he possessed that might be lost if the authorities never found him.

What damage would his kidnappers inflict on him? If he even survived. Would he end up in an institution like Claire, or become a monster himself? And if *she* had the power to stop any of those fates, how could Erin turn her back on him?

With that question weighing on her mind, she made a decision she hoped she wouldn't regret.

"You'll never believe what I saw yesterday," she said.

Claire didn't seem very interested. All her attention was focused on the sketch coming alive under her hand. "Hmm."

"An ice-cream vendor, performing magic tricks for the kids in the park."

Claire's shoulders stiffened. "Really."

"Do you remember that in Miami?"

"No." Claire's hand moved faster, adding the concrete walkways that crisscrossed the grass.

"Sure you do. He came to the park near our house a couple of Saturdays. He wore that bright orange Hawaiian shirt, and we giggled and called him a snowbird."

"I said, I don't remember."

Erin let the silence settle for a minute, then pushed on. "Mom gave me money for ice cream the day you disappeared. I think you ordered a Creamsicle."

Claire turned on her, angry and frightened. "Why are you talking about this?"

"I just thought it was an interesting coincidence, that's all."

"Did you?" Claire shut the pad and started putting away the pencils, her hands trembling. "I think it's time for you to go now."

Erin ached for her sister, for making Claire think about things she preferred to keep buried. But as Donovan had pointed out, there was a young boy's life at stake.

"Claire, you have to help me. This man in the park yesterday, he looked an awful lot like the man we used to see in Miami. Please." She clasped Claire's hands, tried to steady them with her own. "Was he the one who took you?"

Claire yanked her hands free and stood abruptly. "I need to go in now."

Erin followed and grabbed her hand again. "Could it be the same man? There's a missing boy, and he's running out of time."

Claire pulled away. "I don't want you here."

"Claire, please—"

She covered her ears and backed away.

"What's going on here?" From behind them, Marta hurried forward and wrapped her arms around a distraught Claire. "What did you say to her?" Marta snapped as she glared at Erin.

Erin turned and saw Janie, who hung back, eyes wide, staring at her mother. She held two ice-cream bars: a partially eaten Fudgsicle and a Creamsicle, still in its wrapper. On the ground beside her were two more in wrappers, which Marta had dropped in her rush to Claire.

Guilt raced through Erin, but she squelched it. She hadn't meant to hurt her sister, but she knew she'd ask her questions again if it meant a chance to help Cody Sanders. She could do nothing to change what had happened to Claire all those years ago, but Erin might be able to prevent the same horrors from happening to him. And whether Claire realized it or not, she'd given Erin the answer she needed.

"I'm sorry, Claire." She raised a hand to her sister, who huddled closer to Marta and buried her face against the older woman's shoulder. *For everything that happened to you.* Erin backed away.

"I think you better go out to the car," Marta said.

Erin nodded.

"Janie, go with your aunt. I'll take care of your mother and be out as soon as she's settled."

Janie reached up and took Erin's hand, and the two of them walked silently across the grass toward the parking lot. They waited beside the car, neither speaking. Erin thought she should say something to Janie, at least to apologize for ruining their visit, but she couldn't. Not without explaining about Cody Sanders. And Janie didn't ask, a sad testament to her mother's illness.

About a half hour later, Marta finally joined them.

Stepping forward, Erin asked, "How is she?"

Marta frowned, then seemed to deflate, as if only her anger at Erin had given her the strength to handle Claire, and now that was gone. "She'll be okay. The doctors will keep a close watch on her for the next twenty-four hours, just to make sure she doesn't . . ." Marta glanced at Janie. "To make sure she gets some rest."

"I'm sorry this always falls on you, Marta."

The older woman shrugged, evidently resigned. "There are sweet compensations." Marta reached down and stroked Janie's cheek. "I'm not going to ask what you said to her, but I know whatever it was, you meant well."

Erin smiled tightly and slipped an arm around Janie's shoulder.

"Maybe we should cancel our trip to Miami," Marta said, glancing nervously back at the building. "I hate to leave you alone when Claire is not feeling well."

"No," Erin said. "Go. You've been planning this for months, and you both need to get away for a couple of days. I'll check in on Claire. Besides"—she squeezed Janie's shoulder to let her know she was kidding as she said—"I'm going to be very busy next week and don't need the two of you getting in my way."

Marta hesitated. For a year she'd dealt with Erin's job and its unusual demands, but nothing Erin had ever done for the Company had touched Claire or Janie. To Marta's credit, she didn't ask many questions. This time, however, she had just one. "Is there something going on that you are not telling me?"

It was uncanny how this woman could sense Erin's thoughts. Of course, she'd known Erin since she was in diapers. "Nothing I can't handle. Now, I need to make a couple of calls, then I'll take you and Janie home."

Marta hesitated again, then held out a hand to the little girl. "Come on, sweetie, let's sit in the car."

Erin moved away from them and pulled out her cell phone. Her first call was to an old friend at Langley, Sam Anderson, a brilliant analyst and computer whiz, who owed her from their days together at the Farm.

She dialed the secure line, and he picked up on the second ring. Somehow it didn't surprise her that he was in his office on a Sunday afternoon. "Sam, it's Erin Baker."

"Oh, the master spy, or should I say *mistress* spy? Or is that *spyess*."

"Cute." Erin shook her head at Sam's antics. "Look, I need you to do something for me."

"I am your slave, my lady."

"I need three files pulled. ASAP. And I want you to bring them to me this afternoon." As a covert officer, Erin rarely went to Langley. Its location was too well known and too well watched. "We'll meet in the usual place."

"Man, you don't ask much. It is Sunday, you know."

"So what are you doing answering your phone?"

He laughed. "Yeah, well . . ."

"It's important, Sam."

"Okay, then." Suddenly, he was all business. "Let me have it."

"I need everything you can find on a Roland Garth. He's doing time at San Quentin. I'm particularly interested in his arrest information, what deals he cut with the DA, past criminal activity, that kind of thing."

"I don't know, Baker, this doesn't sound like something you should be messing with."

"Sam, I'm in a hurry."

He sighed audibly. "Okay. What else?"

"I also need information about General William Neville. He's attached to the German Embassy."

"That sounds more like it. You gonna recruit him?" Recruiting foreign "agents" to share information about their governments was a covert CIA officer's primary function.

"If I tell you that—"

"You'll have to kill me, right?" He laughed at the old joke.

"Well, no, you *do* work for the Company."

"Right." He sounded disappointed. "Okay, General William Neville."

"Also, get me an invite to the reception at the German Embassy tomorrow night." This wasn't exactly in Sam's job description, but if she asked one of the assistants who usually made such arrangements, there would be too many questions. Hopefully, Sam wouldn't get insulted.

Obviously, he didn't. "Gotcha. And the last file?"

She glanced back at the car, where Marta and Janie waited, then moved farther out of earshot. "I need all the information you can find on a kidnapping that occurred in 1985."

"What country?"

"Miami."

"I know it seems like a foreign country sometimes, but let's get real, Erin."

"Sam, I'm serious."

A heartbeat of silence, then he said, "Baker, what are you doing?" All the amusement had left his voice.

"Just do it, Sam, okay? Early June 1985, a seven-year-old girl was taken out of Glades Park. I want police reports, interviews, everything you can put your hands on in the next twenty-four hours."

"You got the kid's name?" He still didn't sound thrilled about this.

She hesitated, knowing she was about to reveal a piece of herself she'd kept carefully hidden from most of her colleagues at the Agency. But she needed Sam's help if she was going to get what she needed in time. "Claire Baker."

Silence.

"Sam?"

"What's going on here, Erin?"

"Please, I really need you to do this."

She could almost hear him thinking, weighing what he owed her against her request. As a CIA officer, she had no business investigating a criminal case within the United States, and she certainly shouldn't be looking into something as close to home as her sister's kidnapping. At the very least she was risking her career, and she was asking Sam Anderson to climb out on that limb with her.

Finally he said, "I owe you that much. But if I do this . . ." He paused, but when he spoke again, the humor was back in his voice. "You've got to have dinner with me."

She laughed. "It's a deal. My treat. I'll bring my niece along, okay? She's seven and loves pizza."

He groaned. "Never mind." Obviously, Sam didn't do the kid thing. "Okay, let me get working on this, and I'll see you in a couple of hours."

"Thanks, Sam. I owe you."

"Forget it." Then he was serious again. "I just hope this doesn't come back to bite you."

"Me, too." She pushed the disconnect button, took a deep breath to brace herself for the second call, then pulled out a business card and dialed.

He picked up on the first ring. "Donovan."

"It's Erin Baker."

Silence.

She could almost picture him. His sandy blond hair in disarray from dragging his hands through it. His shirt rumpled, tie loose, and his eyes bloodshot from too many hours without sleep.

"Can you arrange an interview with Roland Garth?" she asked.

"You talked to your sister." It wasn't a question.

"Can you arrange the interview?"

"It's already done. I've got a four-thirty flight out of Dulles."

She looked at her watch. Damn. It was already after two. That didn't give her much time. She'd have to call Sam back and get him to bring the Garth file to Dulles. She could read it on the flight west. And she would need a ticket. They were inching farther out on that limb, and she was going to owe Sam Anderson more than a pizza.

"Okay, I'm ninety minutes away," she said. "I'll meet you at the airport."

"Wait a minute, you're not going."

She ignored him. "Give me your flight information."

"You're a civilian. My SAC would have my badge if I took you along."

"Then don't tell him. You seem to be willing to break the rules when it suits you."

"Give me a reason I should break them this time?"

"I'm going to a reception at the German Embassy tomorrow night. The ambassador is returning to Berlin, and this is a farewell party. I expect William Neville will be there, and I plan to talk to him. But I want to have a conversation with Garth first."

From the other end, more silence.

"Donovan?"

"Your sister confirmed my theory?"

"Not exactly. I tried talking to her, but she shut down and kicked us out." Erin glanced at the car, where Marta was soothing a distressed Janie. "Like most cutters, Claire hurts herself to release stress or hide from some horrific pain. Well, now she's under watch because her doctors think I may have triggered an incident."

"I'm sorry."

"No, you're not." Erin sighed and looked away. "And neither am I. That boy . . ."

For a moment, neither spoke. Then Erin said, "She does remember, though. At least the man in the park. The one selling ice cream and doing magic tricks. I could see it in her eyes just before she shut down."

"Are you sure?"

"That's why I'm coming with you to interview Roland Garth. If you refuse me, I'll make a few calls of my own. And trust me, Donovan, I will get in to see him." She paused, giving him a moment to digest her words. "I want the man who took my sister from me. And Garth's going to tell me how to find him."

XV

Isaac watched them drive away.

They'd walked right past him without ever looking his way. Erin, Claire's daughter, and the older woman who hovered over them all. He'd been standing by the reception desk then, giving the woman behind it his current name and the time of his appointment, when Erin and the girl went out. He'd been early, so he'd moved to the window and studied the two of them as they waited for the older woman.

He had to admit, he was disappointed at Erin's lack of interest. Granted, he was a different man from the one she'd seen in the park yesterday. He stood straight and lean, his hair with a touch of genteel gray, suited and groomed to perfection. Nothing at all like the paunchy vendor he'd been the day before, or the pious priest of the previous night. Yet he'd expected some flicker of recognition. She had, after all, remembered him after a span of nineteen years.

"Dr. Holmes."

Isaac turned toward the receptionist. "Yes?"

"Dr. Schaeffer will see you now."

"Thank you." Though he would have preferred staying by the windows until Erin and the others left, he followed the frumpy woman down the hall to the administration wing. He would see them all again soon. But first, he'd deal with Claire.

They entered a large corner office, and another suit, with the smile of a consummate politician, greeted him. "Dr. Holmes, it's so good to meet you." He took Isaac's hand firmly. "I'm Robert Schaeffer, director of Gentle Oaks. I've been following your work on post-traumatic stress for years, and I can't tell you how honored I am that you've chosen to visit our facility."

Isaac smiled tightly, in the manner befitting a world-renowned jackass and the real Jacob Holmes. "I've heard you've done interesting things here as well."

"Yes, yes, well, we do our best. Would you like some coffee or something?"

"No, nothing. Thank you. I only have a few hours before my flight."

"Well then, let's get on with the tour."

The pompous man escorted Isaac around the building, blabbing on about his supposedly innovative programs. Group therapy. Art therapy. Pet therapy. It was all a bunch of nonsense in Isaac's mind, but he nodded and agreed, asking a pointed question or two. He was, after all, a bit of an expert on the subject of mental illness himself.

Even more boring than the treatments Schaeffer espoused were the physical facilities themselves and all the special touches he claimed gave his patients a sense of home. Isaac almost laughed aloud at that one. If what these people needed was a home environment, they'd have been better off staying in their own. It would be a hell of a lot cheaper.

"This is all very interesting," Isaac said, not trying to hide the impatience in his voice. Holmes was one of the world's leading authorities on Post-traumatic Stress Disorder and didn't need to be polite. "But I'm really more interested in some of your patients."

"Oh, of course." Schaeffer's smile broadened: obviously so taken with his esteemed visitor that he didn't even notice the rebuke. "I have several interesting residents at the moment. A young man, a veteran, who seemed fine for the first few years after the Gulf War, then—"

"No, no veterans, Doctor. I've treated more than my share and there's nothing new there."

"Well"—Schaeffer seemed a bit taken aback—"there is Tara, a rape victim."

Isaac brushed that suggestion aside as well. "What about the woman you wrote about last year?" It was a miserable little piece Isaac had almost missed in his research, but he had found it. "The victim of child abuse. I think you called her Lady X."

"Oh, yes." Schaeffer brightened. "Very interesting case. She was kidnapped when she was seven and held for four years. You read my article?"

"I'd like to meet her."

Schaeffer hesitated. "I'm not sure that's such a good idea. She's had a rather difficult day." He moved closer, confiding in a colleague. "Family visit and all. We have her under a suicide watch."

Isaac almost smiled. So Claire Baker was suicidal.

He'd risked a lot to come here and find a way to eliminate her without arousing undue suspicion, and the means had fallen into his lap. He wouldn't kill Claire, he'd let her do the task for him. All he had to do was get in to see her.

"If this is a bad time"—he glanced at his watch—"I need to be heading back to the airport. This has been"—Isaac paused, searching for the right word to convey his disappointment— "Interesting."

A flash of dismay crossed Schaeffer's features. "Well, I guess it can't hurt for us to take a quick look."

Isaac lifted an eyebrow. "Only if you're certain. I wouldn't want to interfere with any of your treatments." He put a touch of sarcasm in his voice.

"No, no, I'm sure it will be fine," Schaeffer claimed. "This way."

As Isaac followed Schaeffer, he experienced a twinge of unexpected excitement. He'd never met one of his children all grown up, and he wondered if she'd recognize him. If not, he planned to remind her.

He knew her immediately, of course, as Schaeffer escorted him into a brightly lit room. Same bright golden curls. Same blue eyes. Wide now. Filled with horror. And recognition.

This time he couldn't suppress the smile. "Hello, Claire."

XVI

ALEC WASN'T HAPPY about Erin coming with him.

Whether Roland Garth had actually abducted Claire Baker or not, she'd been with him when the police found her. During his fifteen years with the Bureau, Alec had seen too many people come apart when faced with the victimizer of a loved one, and although Erin seemed remarkably composed, her sister was her Achilles' heel.

She shouldn't go anywhere near Garth.

Unfortunately, Alec didn't think he could stop her. He had a feeling she didn't make idle threats. She *would* somehow get in to see Garth with or without his help. At least if he was along, he could control the situation. Or attempt to.

Plus, traveling with her to California and back gave him time to talk her out of an even crazier notion: approaching William Neville.

They had nothing on Neville except suspicions. And with his money and connections, Erin could only get herself into trouble. If Neville's hands were clean, she could trigger an embarrassing political situation. And if he was dirty? Well, that would make things even more sticky. Alec doubted she'd get any information from him. Instead, she would become a target and damage whatever chance they had of finding Cody Sanders.

So Alec was relieved when she showed up outside the departure gate just five minutes before the steward planned to close the door. She carried an overnight bag and looked harried and disheveled in jeans and a white oxford shirt, her short dark hair windblown, her cheeks flushed from running. With a nod, she acknowledged him, but stopped to talk to a tall, gangly man who'd been hanging around the gate area.

Alec couldn't hear what they were saying, but the man was clearly agitated. Erin shook her head repeatedly and stuck out her hand. With obvious reluctance, the man gave her a large envelope, then threw Alec a look meant to maim as Erin headed over.

"Thought you weren't going to make it," he said.

"Disappointed?"

"Nope." He led Erin over to the desk. "I have a feeling we're all a lot safer if I keep an eye on you."

She laughed, the first time he'd heard it, and it made him smile. Under different circumstances, he would enjoy getting to know this woman.

They spent another couple of minutes checking in and changing Erin's seat assignment, something he'd arranged while waiting, despite the full plane. Then he threw one final glance into the waiting area before following her down the Jetway. The other man had left.

"Who was that guy?" he asked as they took their seats.

"Jealous already, Agent Donovan? And we hardly know each other."

He didn't know how to respond to that. It wasn't the first time she'd used a throwaway line to divert one of his questions.

So he kept quiet and buckled his seat belt. Sooner or later, he'd find out the truth about Erin Baker. He was a patient man.

Then, as the plane taxied down the runway, she said, "He's my assistant."

She was, of course, lying. Getting past airport security without a ticket these days—especially in any of the three D.C. area airports—was no small feat. Alec suspected it would take a bit more than a plea from someone trying to deliver an envelope to their boss at a boarding gate. It was just another indication that Erin Baker wasn't exactly what she claimed.

Alec let it go again, this time just until the plane was airborne, when she pulled a file from the envelope given to her by the man at the gate, and opened it.

"Your assistant has access to confidential court documents?" he said, seeing the heading of the top sheet. "California court documents?"

She didn't look up from her reading. "He's not really my assistant."

"No kidding." Alec made no attempt to hide his sarcasm. "So, when are you going to tell me the truth about who you work for?"

"You know the truth."

"Oh, I don't think so, Dr. Baker. I know only part of the truth."

Ignoring that, she said, "I need to know something about Garth before going in there."

It was far from an explanation, but it was a start. It was honest. So he let her read, taking each page when she'd finished with it and reviewing it himself. He'd scoured the FBI files on Garth, but it couldn't hurt to look it over again. Maybe see something new. And it wouldn't surprise him if she'd gotten hold of information his files lacked.

When Erin finished reading, she pushed back in her seat and closed her eyes. "He really is a lowlife, isn't he?"

"Yeah."

"And they gave him a deal." She shook her head, her eyes still closed. "Hard to believe."

"I expect since none of the girls would testify, the district attorney thought it better to get him off the streets than risk him beating all the charges in court."

"You're probably right." She sounded tired.

"You didn't know much about him before this, did you?"

She hesitated. "No. My mom shielded Claire, and consequently me, from his trial. And everything else having to do with Claire's abduction, for that matter. She wanted us to forget it ever happened."

"Do you blame her?"

"No. But it wasn't possible. Our lives had been thoroughly turned upside down twice in a very short period of time. First when Claire disappeared, then when she came home. We'd lived for four years wondering what had happened to her, or if we'd ever see her again." She paused, and he imagined her steeling herself against the painful memories. "I never would have admitted it at the time, especially to my mom, but I thought Claire was dead. And it was my fault."

"*Your* fault?"

She turned her head against the headrest and gave him a bitter half smile. "I guess that part wasn't in your files."

Evidently, he was missing a lot of information about Erin Baker. Something, he realized, he'd really like to change. Something he shouldn't even be thinking about. Not now when all his focus needed to be on finding a missing boy and a serial kidnapper known as the Magician.

"I was supposed to be watching Claire the day she disappeared, but I couldn't be bothered." She turned away, to stare out the small window. "I wanted to spend the day with my friends. So I bought her an ice cream and told her to get lost. And, well"—her voice broke, but she regained control quickly—"she did."

Alec squelched his automatic impulse to assure her of her innocence. Her sister's kidnapping was not Erin's fault. No matter what she'd done or not done that day. Unfortunately, he knew nothing he could say would do any good, or change her mind.

He'd seen it a hundred times with family members of missing children. All the *what if*s and *if only*s. They never led anywhere, never changed a thing, but they seemed to satisfy some innate need to put the blame somewhere, on some*one* more concrete than a nebulous stranger. The only problem was it also tended to destroy marriages and sometimes whole families. At the very least it damaged the person taking the blame upon him- or herself. And he had to wonder what it had done to Erin Baker, what it had shaped her into, what she'd become underneath that tough exterior.

He'd like to take her hand and offer comfort. Just the simple human contact. But that, too, like his earlier thoughts, was inappropriate. Besides, he doubted she would allow it.

"Then the call came from the Family Welfare Office in San Francisco," she said, obviously unaware of the directions his thoughts had wandered. "And everything changed again.

"We were so excited, numb almost with joy. Mom and I flew out to San Francisco to bring Claire home, but she was different."

He could imagine. He'd seen Claire's smiling second-grade class picture. And he'd seen the snapshot of the girl found in San Francisco four years later. It was hard to tell she was the same child.

"I'd braced myself for Claire being older, taller, and I would have easily adjusted to that. But she was broken. In some ways we could see, but in ways we couldn't, too." She paused again, taking a deep breath before continuing. "Only we didn't know it right away."

"I'm sorry, Erin."

She smiled tightly and looked at him, embarrassed, he guessed. "You're sorry." She let out a half laugh. "I'm the one who should be sorry. You didn't sign up to listen to me whine."

"Forget it." He shrugged. "It gives me a better idea why you're so intent on seeing Garth."

"Yeah, well, while my mother was alive, the focus of her life was getting Claire better. Now . . ." She shrugged. "I just figure it's time someone looked into making the man who took her pay."

She fell silent then, and, after a bit, pushed back as far as her seat would go and shut her eyes.

"It's a long flight," she said, her voice reverting to that of the cool, standoffish woman he'd met yesterday. "I'm going to get some sleep. Since you look like you haven't slept in a week, Donovan, I suggest you do the same."

William was on his way back to Washington when the call came in on his secure line. His assistant answered, nodded, then handed over the phone. He knew before a word was spoken that it was about Erin Baker.

"General, I have some information about the woman." Even on a supposedly secure line, his men would be careful about using names.

"Go on."

"She boarded a nonstop flight to San Francisco about an hour ago."

"Alone?"

"No, she met a man at the airport. Tall, blond. A suit. Possibly a cop of some kind, could be a fed."

Donovan. They were going after Garth. William would have to get someone in California to meet the plane. And take care of Garth. Whatever he knew, it was too much. "Okay. Anything else?"

"Before getting on the plane, she talked to another man in the gate area. No identity, but we're working on it. He gave her an envelope of some kind. Didn't look happy about it. So we followed him when he left the airport."

"And?"

"We lost him in McLean."

"You lost him?" William had no patience for incompetence.

"He turned into Langley, General."

William let out a breath he hadn't realized he'd been holding. She'd met someone from Langley. "Which means . . ."

"Yes, sir, that would be my guess."

"Erin Baker is CIA."

The nonstop flight from Dulles took almost six hours, getting them into San Francisco a little after seven Pacific Time. Then it had taken another hour and a half to get a car and make the drive to San Quentin State Prison. So it was almost nine by the time they stepped into the chilly half-light of the prison, and a heavy iron door clanged closed behind them.

Alec glanced at Erin, and caught the brief flash of emotion in her eyes before she shut it down. "Are you sure you want to go through with this?" he asked. "This is the man who held your sister hostage."

"That's exactly why I need to be here."

Alec understood, better now than he had before leaving D.C. Still, he'd tried to change her mind on the drive from the airport. Not that it had done any good. He might as well have been talking to a wall. "Let's do it, then."

The warden wasn't happy about their showing up so late, but a quick call to Quantico had overcome his resistance. They were on a manhunt for a child abductor, and the investigation couldn't wait for a more appropriate hour.

They followed a uniformed guard down a long, sterile corridor, their footsteps echoing off solid walls. The place smelled of men and sweat, anger and fear, and the scent of disinfectant attempting to mask it all. They passed a small squirrelish man with a mop, who watched them without lifting his head from his work. Other than that, they saw no one.

At the end of the hallway, the guard ushered them into a stark conference room, containing four chairs and a rectangular steel table, all bolted to the cold concrete floor. Two small windows, set high, were black holes in the dingy space, while the ceiling drenched them in green fluorescent light.

Erin shivered and rubbed at her arms.

Alec sympathized. The room made even the harshest of police interrogation rooms seem warm.

They sat, and Alec opened his briefcase, pulling out a carton of cigarettes and a yellow notepad. A few minutes later, the door opened again, and a different guard escorted Garth into the room. He wore leg and wrist irons, and the guard shoved him into the lone chair across from Erin and Alec, released one of his hands, and cuffed the other to an iron ring on the table.

Garth's eyes flicked over Erin, then dismissed her.

Too old, Alec suspected, and the thought made him want to pummel the creep. "Thank you," Alec said to the guard.

"We'll be right outside if you need us."

Alec nodded, waiting until they'd left before turning his attention to Garth.

"I'm Special Agent Alec Donovan," he said while resting his hand on the carton of cigarettes. "I have some questions."

"So? Why else would you be here?"

Alec tossed a single pack of cigarettes to the inmate. "As a gesture of goodwill."

Garth snatched the pack, but took his time opening it and lighting up. After his first long drag, he said, "So, what's the FBI want from me?"

Alec took out a picture of Claire, the way she'd looked the

day the police found her in this asshole's den—much older than her twelve years. "Recognize this girl?"

Garth shrugged. "Can't say that I do."

"But you can't say that you don't, either?"

In answer, he took a deep drag of the cigarette and blew it out in Erin's direction. "Who's the woman?"

"I'm Dr. Baker," Erin answered, though Alec had specifically forbidden her to speak. Not that he expected her to take his orders. Or anyone else's, for that matter.

"A shrink?"

"Tell me about the girl," Alec said, reclaiming Garth's attention.

He shook his head. "Nothing to tell."

"She was found in your house the day you were busted."

"How about that."

"She was twelve, and the oldest of three girls living with you."

"Crazy kids. Must have broken in."

"You cut a deal with the DA." Alec scooted forward in his chair. "He dropped the kidnapping charges in exchange for a guilty plea on the drug charges."

"See, you remember more than me."

Alec snorted in disgust and sat back, feigning resignation. He was tired and irritable and not in the mood for games. Garth, on the other hand, seemed to thrive on them. Well, Alec was about to blow him out of the water.

"You like little girls, Roland?" Alec smiled, one man to the other, sharing a secret.

Roland grinned, but shook his head. He wasn't admitting to anything. "Do you?"

"How would that information go over here?" Alec asked. "If say . . . the rumor got out somehow?"

Not real quick on the uptake, Garth frowned. But once he got it, he responded every bit as strongly as Alec had hoped.

"Hey, look at her." Garth shoved the picture back across the table. "She don't look like no little girl to me."

"Then you do remember her."

He backed off, considered, then came to a decision. "Yeah, yeah. I remember her."

"Did you grab her?"

"Hell no. Just like I told the cops, I found her on the streets, gave her a place to live."

"Out of the goodness of your heart?"

Garth shrugged. "Something like that."

"Yeah, we heard this story before, and I'm not buying it." Alec leaned forward again, arms on the table. "Now I'm going to ask you again. Did you grab her?"

Garth hesitated, his eyes flicking to Erin again before coming back to Alec. "Why should I tell you anything?"

"I already answered that question."

"And this don't change nothing?"

"I don't give a rat's ass what happens to you, Roland. All I want is the man who grabbed this girl. You give me that, and I walk out of here a happy man. So, did you grab her?"

"No. I bought her."

Alec's stomach tightened, and he fought the urge to look at Erin. Nothing in her file of abstract facts could have prepared her for hearing those words from Garth.

"You *bought* her?" Erin asked, her voice cold. Hard.

This time Alec had to look at her, but what he saw surprised him. Instead of the face of an outraged sister, he saw a stoic facade, a look almost of detachment, as if Garth was talking about something distasteful but unconnected to her.

Recovering quickly, Alec turned back to Garth. "Who sold her to you?"

Garth backed up, hands in the air. "No way in hell, man."

"Look, you've already got your deal from the DA. All I want is the man who snatched this girl off the streets."

"I said, no way."

Alec waited, knowing his silence would eat at the inmate faster than words. Garth already knew the consequences of denying Alec. Now he'd just have to decide which fate was worse.

"Besides, I don't know who grabs them. I got her from a . . . you know . . . middleman."

"How?"

"If I tell you that, I'm dead."

"If you don't, I expect you're dead anyway." Pedophiles were the lowest of the lows, even in prison. "I expect you'll become some big guy's whore. If you last that long."

"Okay, look, all I did was place an ad."

"Where?"

"Different papers, depending on the time of year. *The New York Times* in the winter. Miami in the summer."

Alec leaned forward. "Tell me about the ads."

"I tell them what I want, and they deliver."

"You advertised for a twelve-year-old girl?" Erin asked in that same emotionless voice she'd used earlier.

"Hell no." He glanced at her, licked his lips, nervously.

"A puppy. A bitch if you want a girl. Months to years. And different breeds, depending on what else you want." He focused again on Alec. "I want a seven-year-old girl, I advertise for a seven-month-old bitch."

"So, you advertised for this girl?" Alec didn't know how Erin was doing it. He could barely keep his own disgust under control. "Then what?"

"I get an answer, time and date of where to pick her up. And where to leave the payment. I never see the guy who delivers her." He turned his hands palms up. "That's the truth."

Alec leaned back, thought, then shoved the yellow pad

across the table. "Okay. I want the codes. I want to know when and where to advertise."

"Hey, it's probably all changed. It's been fifteen years, and it's probably done on the Internet now."

"So, tell me how to do it. How to tap into this network."

"I can't—"

"Oh, I expect you can." Alec shoved back his chair. "You write down what you remember. Then tomorrow I'm going to have a couple of agents in here to go over it with you in detail."

Garth started to object, but Alec spoke right over him. "If your information turns out to be good, then we got nothing else to talk about. If not . . ." Alec shrugged and pushed to his feet. "Then have a nice life. I expect it will be rather short."

Outside, the California night was cool and damp.

They stood in the prison parking lot, Erin's back to him as she leaned against the rental car to steady herself. She hadn't said anything since they'd left Garth and the prison walls.

"Are you okay?" he asked, mentally kicking himself for bringing her along. He should have found a way to keep her away from Garth.

"I could kill him." Her voice was shaking with anger. It was the first show of emotion he'd seen from her, and he could only guess what it had taken for her to keep it inside.

"A bitch. He advertises for a bitch and gets a little girl. What kind of monster—" She broke off, her entire body trembling. "I really could have killed him, you know."

Alec took a step toward her, but she held up a hand to ward him off. "No. Don't."

He waited, giving her the space she needed. Though it was hard. He suspected Erin had been handling everything alone for a very long time and could use someone to lean on for a change.

It bothered him that he wouldn't mind being that person, and that she'd probably never allow it.

Finally, she took a deep breath and turned around. "I'll be okay."

Alec wondered if that was even possible as he watched her pull herself together, hauling in her emotions until she held them once again under tight control. Although he admired her strength, he had to wonder what such denial was doing to her physically. It couldn't be good.

"It looks like this was a wasted trip," she said. "Nothing we found out here is going to help you find Cody."

"You're right, it won't help Cody." They'd investigate Garth's information, but it would be a lengthy process. "But it might help another child. So, not wasted." Though he had to admit he'd been hoping for something more, something that would lead them directly to the Magician and Cody Sanders. "Come on." He nodded toward the car. "Let's get going." They had reservations on a red-eye back to the East Coast.

He'd left Cathy running the investigation in Baltimore and had checked in with her when they'd first landed. They'd hit a wall. So far, they'd gotten nothing more at Cross Street Market, no other sightings or information about the man seen with Cody Sanders. Nor had anything come of the sketch of the man Erin had seen in the park. Alec hated to admit how much he'd been counting on Garth giving them something else to go on. So he needed to get back, to see if he could find some other way to breathe some life into the search.

Only from now on, Erin Baker was out of it.

He waited until they were on the road, heading for the airport, before bringing up the subject of William Neville.

"Erin, you can't go to that embassy party tomorrow night."

"Really." She sounded distracted, like she wasn't even listening to him. Or at least not taking him seriously.

"Neville is dangerous."

"So am I."

He ran a hand through his hair, frustrated with her stubbornness. "Look, I know you've had a lot of martial-arts training, but that doesn't mean you're a match for a man like Neville."

"I'm also a pretty fair shot."

He glanced sideways at her, unable to believe they were having this conversation. "And you're going to walk into the German Embassy with a gun."

"They wouldn't let me through the front door."

"This isn't funny." She was an infuriating woman, using throwaway lines to distract him from the real problem.

"I'm not laughing."

"Then forget the embassy." He'd find another way to get to Neville.

"Look, Donovan, I'm the only one who can do this. The FBI can't walk into a foreign embassy and mingle with the natives. But I can. I know embassy protocol and I know the people. And I'm not going to do anything stupid. I'm just going to talk to the man."

"And say what?"

She shrugged. "I won't know that until I see him."

"This is crazy, Erin. You're a civilian."

"That's where you're wrong, Donovan. I do know what I'm doing. And I'm no more of a civilian than you are."

XVII

"Where is he?" Donovan's disembodied voice came through clearly to the receiver in Erin's ear. It, along with the wireless transmitter embedded in the pendant around her neck, kept her tied to him.

"He'll be here," she answered, when in truth, she was beginning to worry about Sam. Though she wasn't about to admit that to Alec Donovan.

Sam had promised to meet her with an invitation to the German Ambassador's going-home party, and he was forty-five minutes late. It wasn't like him. Sam was meticulous to a fault in all things, including punctuality.

She glanced in her rearview mirror and pretended to touch up her makeup while watching the street. She'd parked several blocks from the embassy, where Sam was supposed to meet her.

There was no sign of him.

"I'm going to give him a few more minutes," she said.

There could be any number of reasonable explanations. He

could have been called in on an emergency at Langley. Or it could be as simple as heavy traffic and a dead cell-phone battery.

"I don't like this," Donovan said.

"Neither do I."

Normally, she'd be on the guest list, and the physical invitation, though expected, wouldn't be required. Until yesterday, however, she hadn't planned on attending this particular function. Without an invitation, she'd have to find another way in, an idea that didn't exactly appeal to her. Slipping past armed guards and through service entrances wasn't the easiest thing to pull off when dressed in a cocktail dress and three-inch heels.

"Then let's call it a night," Donovan suggested.

"Feel free to leave anytime you want."

Which she knew he wouldn't do, not as long as she was determined to go inside. He wasn't happy about her approaching William Neville. Even after she'd practically admitted she was CIA, Donovan had tried talking her out of attending the embassy party. Eventually he'd realized that nothing he could say would change her mind. For better or worse, she was in this. So he'd commandeered a communication van and technician to monitor her.

Doing this, she suspected, gave Donovan the illusion of maintaining control. Something Erin understood all too well. Of course, she didn't even want to think what his superiors would say if they knew he was using FBI equipment to monitor a CIA officer within a foreign embassy. That was his problem.

She was breaking a few rules herself.

So she'd agreed to wear a transmitter and receiver. Not that she needed Donovan's permission to go after Neville. But if it made him happy to monitor her, she could live with it. After all, it wasn't the first time she'd worked on a tether.

She glanced at her watch. Fifty minutes. Sam wouldn't stand her up if he had any other choice, and that was what worried her. She'd talked to him this afternoon, and he'd been onto something. Only he'd refused to speculate until he was certain. Now she wished she'd pushed a little harder.

When she'd gotten home after her quick trip to the West Coast, she'd called him immediately to set up a meeting. Even though it was early on a Monday morning, she knew she'd find him in his office. Sometimes she wondered if he even had a place to go home to, or whether he camped out in his sterile ten-by-twelve cubicle.

As she'd expected, he'd been waiting for her call. They'd once again met in a parking lot, a Wal-Mart this time, and he looked like he'd slept in his clothes. If at all. He'd gathered information on Claire's kidnapping, but it was digging into William Neville that had him really excited.

"The guy's a regular Midas," Sam said, talking a mile a minute while handing her reports she didn't even try to read with him in the car. "He inherited a small, floundering shipping company, the last remaining asset of his family's dwindling fortune. And he managed to build it into a thriving business, profitable enough that he could diversify and buy up other companies, primarily in emerging markets. He's into mining in South America, technology companies in Southeast Asia, and banking in Eastern Europe.

"Oh, and he's expanded his shipping interests to support it all. Over the last thirty years, he's amassed a respectable empire."

Erin nodded. That was pretty much what Alec Donovan had told her. And nothing new.

"Now hold on." Sam pulled off his glasses and polished the lenses. "I can tell you're not overly impressed. But just wait. The shipping company. Well, my sources claim Neville made it viable by running slaves up the African coast." He grinned from ear to ear. "Can you believe it? He's a modern-day slaver."

Erin wasn't smiling.

"Of course, that's not a good thing," Sam hurried to say. "It's horrible, despicable. But who knew?"

"What about now, Sam? What's he into now?"

"Well, on the surface he looks clean, though ruthless. You don't want to take this guy on. If he comes after your company, you'd best just hand over the keys. That's not a crime, but if you dig deep enough, you have to wonder. Once a ruthless bastard, always—"

"Sam."

"He's got connections to Saudi Arabia and Iran, which again in itself is not incriminating, but . . ." He shook his head and started gathering up his files. "It's still too early to say. A guy like this Neville shields himself behind so many layers, it takes time to peel them all away. And I've had"—he glanced at his watch—"not quite twenty-four hours. So I don't want to speculate. I can't afford to be wrong on this. Give me a few more hours, and I'll give you the best I can."

"Just tell me what you suspect."

"Tonight. I'll bring your invitation to the embassy party and turn over whatever I've found."

After that, he'd refused to say any more. And she'd let him get away with it. She'd gone home to get some sleep and read the files he'd put together before the evening.

They were particularly disturbing.

One didn't think much about slavery in the modern world, but evidently it was alive and well. Mines in Brazil, brothels in Thailand, and farms in India were all manned by slave labor. Even in Western Europe, the UK, and U.S., household slaves numbered in the thousands. According to Sam's research, the number of slaves around the world ran into the millions, with some estimates as high as 200 million. A staggering and frightening statistic.

And William Neville had ties to all of it.

Now, pulling out her cell phone for the second time in

fifteen minutes, Erin dialed Sam's office in Langley. As before, no one answered. Then she tried his cell phone and home number. Still nothing.

Something was wrong, and a part of her wanted to go looking for him. The other part, the one trained to think of the mission first and foremost, reminded her that Sam wasn't a child. He'd gone through the same year of CIA training she had, and could take care of himself. But of course, he couldn't. He was an analyst, who'd barely squeaked through the Agency's physical training, and then only with a great deal of help. Still, if it came down to getting a lead on Cody Sanders or looking for Sam, all her training told her that Cody was the priority.

So she was back to finding another way into the embassy.

"I'm going in." Ignoring Donovan's objections, she climbed out of the car. She'd decided to bluff her way through the front door rather than find a less direct route. After all, she was well known within the embassy circuit. If she was lucky, someone would vouch for her. So as she got closer to the embassy, she fell in behind other formally dressed guests making their way toward the building.

Just as she was about to head for the door, however, a threesome—two men and a woman—rounded the corner, coming from one of the side streets bordering the embassy, where guests were left to their own devices to find parking. They looked awfully young for embassy hopping. Then she recognized them.

"Cassidy." She approached the young man she'd put on the mat in Bill Jensen's class at the Farm. Slipping her arms around his neck, she said, "I thought you'd stood me up."

The look on his face was pure shock, for about half a second. Then he grinned and put his hands on her waist. "I'd have to be a fool to do that."

She let him pull her just close enough to give him a peck on the cheek. "I need to get inside."

"Oh, I imagine we could work out something."

She flashed him a smile and pulled back. "Don't push your luck."

She turned then and greeted the other two, pulling their names from her memory. "Sheila and Chad, isn't it?"

"Hi, Erin." And she had to give the woman credit for remembering to use her first name. Using last names was pretty much taboo within the Agency, particularly in the field.

As a training exercise, recruits from the Farm were sent to embassy parties under the guise of State Department personnel. For those who ended up as field officers, it was good practice for what would become a regular activity. Evidently, Cassidy thought Erin was part of the practice, and the other two weren't going to question him.

It worked for Erin.

So she draped herself on his arm and said, "Shall we go in?" They made their way into the embassy, where Cassidy handed his invitation to one of the tuxedo-clad butlers in the foyer. Erin squeezed Cassidy's arm and continued to smile, as if she was just thrilled to be included.

Once inside, Cassidy turned to her, checking her out from head to toe. "Well, I didn't expect—"

She extricated her arm from his. "Thanks, you just redeemed yourself. Now don't go getting into any trouble. I'd hate to have to come rescue you."

Cassidy winced. "Very cute."

"Yeah, I know." She kissed him on the cheek again, then nodded toward the reception line, where the ambassador and his wife stood with key staff members to greet other Washington elite. "Now get on with whatever you're supposed to do here. I'll see you later." And she walked away.

To Cassidy's credit, he didn't ask questions or try to stop her. He and his two companions moved off to introduce themselves to the embassy staff.

"I'm in," she said, after taking a glass of champagne from a passing waiter.

"If you make it out of there in one piece, I expect an explanation," Donovan replied.

"Explanation?" She sipped the champagne and scanned the crowd. She'd been working the D.C. embassy parties for a year now and recognized many of the faces. She'd also studied files on the most promising potential foreign agents and the most volatile embassy personnel. General William Neville hadn't been on either list.

"Like who just waltzed you through the door," came Donovan's voice again.

"Oh, that." She had no intention of enlightening Donovan about other CIA personnel. "Sure, whatever you want to know."

She worked the room, stopping occasionally to smile or say a word to an acquaintance. She'd become a common face to these people, so no one questioned her presence. Neville, on the other hand, didn't frequent many embassy functions outside those given by his own ambassador. And she couldn't be certain he'd show up tonight.

She'd just entered one of the smaller rooms, a gallery of some kind with portraits lining the walls, when a familiar male voice stopped her. "Erin? Is that you?"

She turned toward the approaching man. "Hello, Sebastian."

He gave her a quick kiss on the cheek. "I didn't expect to see you here tonight."

"I decided to come at the last minute."

"And snuck your name on the guest list." He grinned. "Tsk. Tsk."

His name was Sebastian Cole, and although she'd spoken to him a number of times in the last year, she hadn't figured out where he fit in the scheme of things. The Agency had very little on him. He was the son of a wealthy New York banker, with more time and money than direction. So he'd made Washington his home and the embassy circuit his social scene.

Of course, none of that meant a thing. He could be anyone, working for any government. Even her own.

"Actually," she said, "I came with a date."

He arched an eyebrow and glanced around, as if looking for the missing man.

Erin laughed. She couldn't help but like Sebastian. Where others might find him sarcastic and cynical, she found his irreverent wit and charm refreshing. "He's around somewhere."

"Obviously not a love match, then, but a convenience."

"Something like that," Erin said, tasting the champagne, the cool bubbles sweet on her tongue, and scanned the crowd for Neville.

"Well, you look particularly lovely this evening."

Erin refocused on Sebastian. "Thanks."

Learning to dress and behave like a socialite had been a hard lesson for her. She'd have preferred facing down a gang of thugs in a dark alley any day. But the embassy parties required that she look and act the part, so she had a separate wardrobe she called her embassy gear, a half-dozen cocktail dresses and gowns. Tonight she wore one of her best, a beaded black Versace that clung to her like a second skin. She'd wanted to catch Neville's eye, and even if she hadn't yet spotted him, it was nice to know she'd pulled off the charade once again.

"Sebastian, would you do me a favor?" She moved in closer, where no one else could hear.

"Oh, I do love secrets."

She slipped an arm through his. "There's someone I want to meet."

He slapped his hand against his chest. "And here I thought I was your only love."

"Sebastian, you're gay. Remember?"

"Oh, yes, that could be a problem." He gave her a dazzling smile, and she thought, What a shame. He really was too good-looking for words. "So, who is the lucky man?"

"General Neville. Is he here?"

"Ooooh. You do have good taste. Handsome, in a very stoic sort of way. Lots of money." He nodded toward the main reception area. "He just arrived a few minutes ago. Come, I'll see that you get acquainted." He took Erin's arm and led her toward the door, but as they crossed into the next room, he added, "There's one thing you need to remember about the General, Erin."

She looked up at her escort, aware of a new seriousness to his voice. "Which is?"

"He's the direct type." He met her gaze, all the humor she'd come to associate with Sebastian Cole gone. "Your best bet is to come at him straight on. If you dance around him, he'll eat you alive."

She hardly had time to assimilate the information before they arrived at General William Neville's side. "Oh, General, we've been looking for you," Sebastian said.

Neville was surrounded by a group of men, and Sebastian was once again the silly man she'd grown fond of. "There's someone here you just have to meet." He released Erin's arm. "This is Dr. Erin Baker, she teaches at Georgetown. An expert, I hear, on international relations. Just your type of thing."

Neville smiled, though it was one of the coldest Erin had ever seen, and extended his hand. "We've met."

Erin took his offered hand. "I didn't think you'd remember."

"How could I forget such a lovely woman?" His compliment held no warmth.

"I'm sure you're surrounded by women of all sorts, General."

He shrugged, the flattery not affecting him, then turned to the other men and said, "We'll talk later."

Sebastian took the hint to move off, too. "Well, you two get acquainted," he said. "I'll be around if you need me."

Once they were alone, Neville said, "So, to what do I owe the pleasure, Ms. Baker? Surely you didn't get that buffoon Cole to make introductions just to flatter me."

"I have no intention of doing that, General." She hesitated, considering her strategy, then decided to follow Sebastian's advice and take the direct route. A man like Neville, who'd built a business empire on the ruins of a dwindling family fortune, would possess a certain amount of arrogance. He probably believed himself above the law. If she could play on that, she might learn something. "I wanted to talk to you about another matter entirely."

"Which is?"

"I was doing some research a while back and came upon some interesting information about you."

"Really?" His look remained polite.

"It was by accident, actually. My area of study is Middle Eastern cultures, and I was looking into imports and exports from Saudi Arabia." She watched for a reaction, even something as small as a shift in his eyes, and saw none.

Again, she questioned her strategy. If they were wrong about Neville, or even if they were right, this could be a mistake. Confronting him was a gamble, putting Donovan's investigation at risk. So if she was going to back off, now was the time. One more sentence, and it would be too late.

On the other hand, they needed to know if Neville was involved with Cody's disappearance, and at the moment, they had only a loose connection to a slave ship and the Magician, and a lot of circumstantial evidence linking him to slave markets around the world. She had to risk it. Because until they were certain, they were wasting time looking at Neville.

"I came across a ship confiscated by the U.S. government,"

she said. "About three years ago." She waited a moment before continuing, as if giving him time to remember. "The *Desert Sun.*"

He didn't even blink. "You are telling me this because?"

"The ship belonged to one of your companies."

"Oh, I see." He glanced around the room, as if losing interest and watching for someone more engaging. "I have many companies, Dr. Baker."

He was good, carefully controlled and not easily rattled. Too controlled, maybe. As if he had something to hide.

She pushed a little harder. "The *Desert Sun* was transporting kidnapped children from the U.S. to Saudi Arabia." She paused, to give her next words weight. "It was a slave ship, General."

He sighed and turned back to her, a spark of something in his eyes. Anger? Or just annoyance at an unpleasant conversational partner? "And you, being an outraged American, want to know if I had anything to do with it."

"I'll admit, that was my first question." Erin sipped at her now-warm champagne, taking her time, attempting to unnerve him a bit. He was, she could tell, an impatient man. "So I did a little further research and found the FBI asked you the same question."

"And no doubt you discovered they determined I had nothing to do with that ship's dealings. The captain was operating completely on his own."

"Actually, I don't believe that's what happened at all." Another nudge. Dangerous. But necessary. "I think they just couldn't prove your involvement."

"I'm not quite sure what you're getting at, Ms. Baker." She saw the anger then, hard and cold in his eyes. "Are you a policeman, then?"

She shrugged. "I wanted to hear your side of the story."

"Well, now you have." He turned as if to move away. "Excuse me."

"Are you so anxious to get away from me, General?" She couldn't let him escape. Not yet. She was more convinced than ever that he was no innocent. Yet he still hadn't told her anything she could use, and she needed that. *They* needed something to go on.

"Not anxious, just bored."

"Or guilty."

He turned back to her slowly, then moved in close, his presence suddenly menacing. "I have to wonder why you are approaching me about this. You must realize that if I was involved with this . . . slave ship . . . as you call it, that initiating this conversation would be a very dangerous strategy on your part."

She met his cold stare. He didn't frighten her. Or so she told herself. "Is that a threat?"

"I never make threats, Ms. Baker. Besides"—he stepped back, putting space between them again—"I was not involved, so there is nothing to fear."

She shook her head. "You see, that's the problem. I don't believe you, General." Innocent men didn't make veiled threats. "I don't think there's anything that goes on in that particular company without your knowledge."

"Well, Ms. Baker—"

"It's Dr. Baker," she corrected.

He snorted and shook his head. "You know, one thing I find particularly unpleasant about you Americans is your tendency to overeducate your women."

She crossed her arms. "And that's a problem?"

"I think other cultures have a better hold on it. Women belong at home, raising our children."

He was attempting to turn the tables on her, rile her as she'd done him. Not a bad strategy, but it wasn't going to work. "Would you prefer we wore veils and acquiesced to regular beatings as well?"

His expression darkened again. "You are meddling in things that are not your concern."

"Who said anything about meddling? I was simply going through some old documents."

"Good evening, Ms. Baker."

She had one final card to play, a risky one. One that could lead them to Cody Sanders. Or cost him his life. But unless she played it, the boy would be dead anyway. "Tell me one more thing, General."

He stopped, caught by her despite himself, but didn't turn.

She moved up closer, where she could speak without being overheard, and stepped off the edge. "Where are you keeping Cody Sanders?"

XVIII

Ryan placed his hand over the sleeping boy's mouth.

Cody's eyes flew open, filled with alarm.

"It's me," Ryan whispered. "We're gonna get out of here. Tonight."

Cody's brow furrowed.

"I'm going to take away my hand now. You need to be very quiet."

Cody nodded, and Ryan released him.

"I thought you wanted to wait a day or two," Cody said. "Until you felt better."

"I changed my mind." Tonight was their chance. If they waited, who knew if they'd get another. "The General left this afternoon, and there's no telling when he'll be back."

"But you're in pretty bad shape. Will you be okay?"

Ryan wasn't used to someone worrying about him, and his response came out harsher than he'd intended. "I'll make it. Besides, if we don't get out of here now, they'll send you away, and you'll end up somewhere far worse than here." *And I'll be dead.*

"Where? Where will they send me?"

"Don't know for sure, but I promise they won't speak much English there."

The boy shivered, the first sign of real fear Ryan had ever seen from him. "What do they want with me?"

"Don't ask stupid questions. Now, are you coming or not?"

Cody looked momentarily hurt by Ryan's abrupt answer, but he recovered quickly and pushed off the bed. "I'm right behind you."

"Get some clothes on." Ryan crossed the room to the door, pressed his ear against the wood, and listened for anyone in the hall.

Silence. As he'd expected.

Getting Cody out of this room was the easy part. None of the household staff came up here, especially at night. He understood all too well why. What they didn't see, they didn't know about or talk about to others. So it was easier just to remain blind. It was the same view Ryan had always taken, and a part of him wished he'd never opened his eyes. It was too late for second thoughts, however, and the dull ache around his ribs was a reminder. Just in case.

It took Cody less than a minute to get dressed. "I'm ready."

Ryan looked at the younger boy, at the determination and fearlessness in his eyes. The kid had more guts than brains, but he didn't deserve the life Trader and the General would give him. No more than Ryan deserved to die because he'd broken one of their stupid rules.

Motioning for Cody to hang back, Ryan stepped into the hall. It was empty. He opened the door wider, and Cody joined him. Ryan didn't expect to run into anyone this time of night. Not inside the house, anyway. It was the outside that worried him.

"What about the dogs?" Cody asked, as if reading his mind.

"I drugged their food." While looking for more aspirin in the supply pantry off the kitchen, Ryan had spotted the rat poison on the floor with the cleaning supplies. It had struck him right away what he had to do. To get away, they needed to get past the dogs. No matter what it took.

The idea of hurting an animal—even one of the General's hated beasts—turned Ryan's stomach. But what choice did he have? Besides, he rationalized, the dogs were a lot bigger than rats. Maybe the poison would only make them sick. So he'd dumped a fistful into an old rag and shoved it into his pocket. Later, when he was down picking up Cody's dinner tray, he'd mixed the poison into the dogs' food.

"I only hope I gave them enough," he said, as much to himself as Cody.

They followed the hallway to the back stairs leading down into the kitchen. As he'd done the night before, Ryan paused on the bottom step, listening for sounds from the room beyond before opening the door.

Silence.

He opened the door, and they slipped into the quiet room. Unlike the night before, however, he headed toward the back hallway, past the servants' quarters. He made a shushing motion to Cody, and they crept down the hallway, stealing by the closed doors. If anyone was going to hear them, it would be here.

Once again, their luck held.

They made it to the door, and Ryan unlocked it as quietly as possible. Then he eased it open, pulled Cody outside, and shut it again, making sure to relock it. They stood on the broad back porch, where the kitchen help received deliveries. Beyond, he could see the wide expanse of lawn bordered by dense woods.

"Now what?" Cody said.

"We hope the dogs are asleep." Cody didn't need to know about the poison. "If they are, all we need to do is make it through those trees. There's a stone wall we'll have to scale, then a road on the other side. After that, I think it's another couple of miles to the main road. We'll get a ride from there." Not that he'd ever dreamed he could do such a thing. But once, when he'd accompanied the cook to the market, he'd seen a lone hitchhiker along the road, begging for a ride with his thumb. He and Cody could do that.

"You know where we are?"

"Not really, but I listen to the servants. And they talk about the area around the mansion."

"And if the dogs aren't asleep?"

Ryan shrugged, trying for a nonchalance he didn't feel. "They know me." Not that it would make any difference. They'd tear him apart as quickly as any stranger. But again, it wasn't a detail Cody needed to know. "I'll try to hold them off, and you keep running. Okay?"

Cody nodded, more eager now than frightened. Evidently he smelled the freedom and nothing much else mattered. On the other hand, Ryan was scared enough for both of them.

Together, they made their way down the back steps into the night. Taking a deep breath, Ryan looked at the younger boy and said, "Run."

They started across the lawn, the chilly air slapping at their bare faces, the damp grass slippery beneath their feet. Ryan felt each stride ripple through his center, the pain taking on a rhythm of its own with each jarring footfall.

He told himself to ignore it. Whatever pain he felt now was nothing compared to what he'd experience if Trader caught them. So Ryan pushed through it, forcing himself to concentrate on reaching the forest ahead of them.

Halfway across . . .

He could make out the individual trees and the low bushes that would hide their escape. They were going to make it. Almost there . . .

Out of the corner of his eye, he saw the flash of movement. Silent. Fast. Four-legged. Heading straight for them.

Ryan slipped.

Cody slowed and grabbed his arm. "I thought you drugged them."

Ryan regained his footing and shoved the boy toward the woods. "Keep running, get to the trees—"

The dog struck, knocking Ryan to the ground with one powerful leap, the impact smacking the air from his lungs. He wanted to yell to Cody to keep going, but Ryan had no breath. All he could do was wrap his arms around his head to protect it from the snarling jaws.

"Get away from him," Cody yelled, and Ryan lifted his head to see the kid charge the dog with a stick, bringing it down hard against the animal's back.

The dog swung around and lunged for the younger boy.

Ryan threw himself forward, grabbing the animal's rear quarters just before it caught Cody. "Get out of here," he yelled as the dog turned furious jaws on him, snapping and sinking sharp teeth into his arm.

Ryan screamed. Darkness threatened to drag him down as he fought for consciousness. He had to keep the dog away from Cody. It would tear the smaller boy apart.

Suddenly, the animal released him.

Through a haze of pain he saw Cody jabbing the dog again with the stick, angering the already vicious animal, who snarled and growled with barred teeth.

"Are you crazy?" Ryan hollered.

"Get up, I can hold him off."

"No . . ." Ryan tried to stand to get the dog's attention. Too late. The dog jumped toward Cody.

And died in midair, a bullet ripping a hole in his side.

Ryan collapsed in a haze of red pain. "Go, run," he said, but Cody was at his side, staying there until the guards pulled him away. Ryan's last thought before everything went dark was of rat poison. Obviously, he hadn't used enough.

XIX

"Is she crazy?" Alec's control snapped as he listened to Erin accuse Neville of holding Cody Sanders. "What the hell is she doing?"

The technician at his side looked up. "Sir?"

Alec shook his head, realizing he'd spoken aloud. "Never mind."

He pulled in his anger, his frustration. Although it would serve him right to have rumors that he'd lost it running through the team. He had to have been crazy to go along with Erin's scheme. Of course, she was going in whether he'd agreed or not, and there would have been no way to stop her. "Damn it," he muttered, catching another nervous glance from the technician. "Is she leaving?"

"Sounds that way."

It was about time. He needed her out of there before she could do more harm. Then he'd have to figure out a way to do damage control.

For a few minutes, they listened as Erin made her way

across the crowded reception, with a word or comment to people as she passed. She was so damn calm, so unruffled, it nearly set him off again. Didn't she realize what she'd done? She'd put Cody's life in danger, and for what? If it was some damn ego thing, he'd find a way to bring her down. He didn't care about her connections or whom she worked for.

Then everything got quiet, the only sound her heels against concrete. "I'm out," she said, "heading for my car."

"I'll meet you there." *And you'll have a hell of a lot of explaining to do.* Alec removed the earphones. To the technician he said, "Make up a tape of everything here and send it over to the command post in Baltimore. Tell Agent Hart I'll check in a couple of hours." He started for the rear door.

"Agent Donovan?"

He looked back at the technician.

"What are we doing here, sir?"

Alec sighed. "I wish I knew." He'd have some fast talking to do when this got back to headquarters. Meanwhile, he needed to find out just what Erin Baker was up to. With a nod to the technician, he climbed out of the van.

Outside, fall had staked its claim on the night. The temperature had dropped at least twenty degrees in the last couple of hours and the wind had begun to stir. Considering Alec felt ready to punch something, the coolness was a welcome respite.

Erin had sworn she was just going to talk to Neville. Well, she'd gone way beyond that. Alec wondered if she'd purposely lied to him, or whether she was just incompetent. No, one thing the woman wasn't, was incompetent. Careless. Reckless. Crazy. But not incompetent.

He climbed into his car, parked two blocks from the van and a half block behind Erin's car, and waited, watching for her in his rearview mirror. She came into sight shortly, a lone woman in a silky black slip of a dress and crazy high-heeled shoes.

How hard would it be to take her out?

With a nod, Neville could send someone after her. And it wouldn't be a lightweight screwup like Al Beckwith. Neville would send someone who knew his way around troublemakers, and he'd need nothing more than his bare hands.

The thought had Alec loosening the .38 beneath his jacket.

No one approached her, however, as she passed him without acknowledging his presence and climbed into her car. She pulled away from the curb, and after giving her enough time to disappear in traffic, Alec followed.

They'd agreed to meet on the mall, Erin coming in from the west end near the Lincoln Memorial and Alec from the east and the Washington Memorial. After finding a parking spot, he made his way along the path skirting the reflecting pool, its dark water glassy in the moonlight.

She'd arrived first, but he didn't recognize her right away. She'd covered the sleek dress with a belted all-weather coat and replaced the sexy heels with a pair of practical flats. She'd donned a pair of glasses and carried a slim briefcase, which sat near her feet. Relaxing on a bench across from the Korean War Veterans Memorial, she looked like any other federal employee after a particularly grueling day. As a disguise, it wasn't foolproof, but it worked for the casual onlooker. Not many people would connect her with the sophisticated woman who'd just left the German Embassy.

He dropped down onto the bench beside her, his anger stirring again now that she was near. "Do you want to tell me what that was all about?"

"Neville's involved."

He snorted. "You have proof?"

She leaned over and pulled a file from the briefcase at her feet. "Read this."

Using a small penlight, he spent the next ten minutes studying the three sheets inside the folder. The first was a detailed list of William Neville's early business holdings in Thailand, Brazil, India, and Africa. It included purchase and sale dates of companies, locations, and primary products bought, sold, or produced. It was more detailed than the file Alec had pulled on the man and his dealings.

The second sheet was a summary of the major slave markets around the world: Brazil, Bolivia, India, Thailand, Africa. How slaves were obtained. How they were used. It hit Alec hard, coming at him from left field. It wasn't a problem he'd ever thought much about, but according to this, it was serious and widespread.

The third sheet brought the first two together: William Neville and the slave market. Though the evidence was circumstantial, the connections were all there, pulled together by a brilliant analytical mind.

"Where did you get this?" The documents were unlabeled.

"The same place I got the information on Garth." Then she seemed to understand Alec's dilemma. "Look, Donovan, I have access to information you don't, especially in the international arena."

"Obviously." He wasn't going to ask again whom she worked for. If she decided to tell him, fine. Otherwise, he could make his own guess. The training, the years overseas, her access to information not even he could get to, and her familiarity with the diplomatic world, it all added up. She was CIA. He'd bet his life on it. He only hoped he hadn't bet Cody's as well.

"Okay, I understand why you think Neville's involved, but there's still no proof." He needed more. Cody needed more than some analyst's theories. "And nothing, really, to link him to the boy."

She looked at him for the first time, her eyes filled with a dangerous glint that was unmistakable. "There's the *Desert Sun*, the Magician, and a little girl named Suzie."

For a moment, Alec didn't respond. He understood her anger and frustration. All his instincts and experience, gathered over fifteen years with the Bureau and eight hunting child abductors as a CAC coordinator, told him there was a connection. That somehow William Neville was the key, the link that would lead them to the Magician and Cody Sanders. Neville, however, was a foreign diplomat, attached to the German Embassy, which gave him a certain amount of immunity. But even if that could be circumvented, there was a little thing called due process that neither he nor Erin Baker—no matter whom she worked for— could ignore.

"I wish that were enough," he said, and meant it. "But it's all conjecture, and it doesn't explain why you put everything, including Cody, in danger by verbally attacking Neville."

For a few long seconds more, she held his gaze, defiant. "It was a calculated risk, to learn if Neville was involved."

His anger rose up, hot and furious, and he barely kept his voice down. "What right had you to make that call? There's a young boy's life at stake."

"You don't think I know that?" Her temper matched his, the memory of her sister's loss haunting her eyes. "But we have nothing but guesses here." She tapped the folder in Alec's hand. "If Sam's wrong, if *we're* wrong about Neville, we'd be wasting time going after him. I pushed, purposely, to get a reaction from him."

For a moment, he couldn't speak, unable to believe she'd taken such a foolhardy risk, endangering not only Cody, but herself as well. Yet he couldn't help but admire her logic, and her courage. "So did you?"

"Enough to *know* he's involved. No doubt."

She was always so sure of herself, so confident. He wondered if the CIA had given her that, or whether she'd possessed it when she came to them. Either way, time would render her either a hero or a screwup as far as Cody was concerned. Alec could only hope, and pray, she'd end up the hero. Meanwhile, she'd put things in motion he couldn't stop, and he needed to deal with it.

"If Neville has Cody, he'll move him now."

"And we can watch him."

Again silence fell between them. A few hundred feet away, the seven-foot-tall, stainless-steel soldiers of the triangular "field of service" that was the centerpiece of the Korean War Veterans Memorial, rose in soft illumination against the night sky. In a way, Alec would have rather fought in such a war than the one he currently waged. One where he knew the enemy, and the route to victory, though hard, was clear.

"So where does that leave us?" she asked.

Nowhere.

To be honest, Alec admitted, there never should have been an *us* in this investigation. He'd taken a chance that this woman could help him find a child, and he didn't know whether it had been the best decision he'd ever made or the worst. Not her fault. His. Now it was time—past time—she was out of it. He'd take her suggestion and make Neville his priority, but other than that, he needed to move on and attempt to find Cody Sanders without any more detours.

Before he could put words to the thought, however, she turned to him. "How do you do this?" she asked.

He glanced at her, not sure what she meant.

"How do you spend your life looking for lost children?" she clarified.

"Oh. That." He sighed and leaned back against the hard wooden bench. "Sometimes, I'm not sure myself. But"—he shrugged—"someone has to do it."

"But doesn't it . . ." She hesitated, as if searching for the right word. "Doesn't it eat you alive?"

He studied her, thinking of the sister she'd lost and his own thoughts about getting out of the CACU. "Yeah, it does."

She turned away again, letting the silence settle between them for a few minutes, and he thought she was done with her questions. Then she said, "Did you always want to be an FBI agent?"

He laughed shortly and shifted again, drawing one leg up to fold over the other. "Actually, it was pretty near the top of things I did *not* want to do with my life."

"Really?" She threw him another glance. "What was at the top of that list?"

"Cop. I was not going to be a cop."

It was her turn to laugh, and he realized again that he liked the sound of it. "How come?" she asked.

"You really want to hear this?" He wondered what had sparked this sudden interest.

She nodded. "Tell me."

So he did, because maybe they both needed a momentary distraction. "You see, I come from a whole family of cops. And it's a big family. My dad and all three of his brothers were cops, and their dad before them. And of my five brothers, three are cops. Then there's my sister, Emily, who's the meanest one of the whole damn bunch."

"I like her already."

He grinned. "Yeah, you would." He thought of his sister, the scrapper, who'd held her own against her six brothers. She and Erin Baker would be a dangerous combination. "She'd like you as well." And he'd like to introduce them. If circumstances were different, if they'd met at another time, another place, he'd like nothing better than to take her home to his family. "Anyway, I swore I'd never be a cop."

Erin shook her head, a bit sadly. "I can't imagine having a family like that."

"Let me tell you, it can be hell." His smile broadened despite himself. He loved his family. No doubt. But sometimes they drove him crazy. "Or the best damn thing in the world. Depending on which day you ask me."

"Okay. So you didn't want to follow in your dad's footsteps."

"Nope. Not me. I wanted to be just about anything else."

"So what happened?"

He looked at her, again gauging whether she really wanted to hear this.

"Go on," she said.

"College happened. I was planning on majoring in math. I was going to be a teacher." He laughed again, embarrassed. He didn't like talking about himself. "Can you imagine me trying to corral a bunch of rugrats every day?"

She smiled. "Actually, I can."

He skated right by that and went on with his story. "I had a roommate who talked me into taking a criminal psychology class. I needed an elective, and the rumor mill had it that the course was an easy A. Besides, I figured I'd been listening to this stuff all my life. How hard could it be? So I took it."

"And you fell in love with it."

"Nope. I absolutely hated it. I just barely squeaked by with a C, and I couldn't for the life of me figure out why." He reached up to shove the hair off his face. "It was the same old stuff I'd been listening to all my life. Though, I admitted that when my dad and uncles talked about the streets and the creatures who inhabited them, their descriptions were a bit cruder than those given to first-year psych majors.

"Anyway, I was really upset with that C. So I went and saw the professor, and he told me I had a bad attitude and knew a lot less than I thought I did. He said that if I'd paid attention, or read the book, I might have learned something."

She laughed again.

"So I took the second course in the sequence, just to prove the SOB wrong."

"And did you?"

"Not exactly. That's when I pretty much discovered that there was a whole lot more to this than chasing down bad guys and throwing them in jail." He paused, remembering his own youthful stubbornness and determination to avoid his father's world. "I still had no intention of going into law enforcement, but by the time I finished school, I had enough credits for a minor in criminal psychology. Then I couldn't find a teaching job."

"Sounds like fate stepped in."

He let out an abrupt laugh. "That's one way to put it. That entire summer my dad kept harping at me to apply to the police academy. Until one night at the dinner table, when he wouldn't let up, I told him I wasn't applying for the police academy because I planned to take the entrance examination for the FBI." The declaration had escaped that night, surprising him as much as anyone else at the table. "That shut him up."

"I'd think that would have made him happy."

"Ha. How little you know cops. I was going over to the enemy, and Dad didn't talk to me for months."

"But you went ahead with it?"

"I had no choice. Everyone was expecting it."

She laughed lightly, shaking her head. "I love it, you ended up working for the FBI because of—"

"Because of my big mouth."

She looked away again, but this time she was still smiling. Then her cell phone beeped.

Pulling it out of her pocket, she flipped it open. "Yes?"

He watched the one-sided conversation, and the slow drain of color from her face.

"Where have they taken him?

"Yes, I know it. I'll be there shortly." By the time she pushed the disconnect button and slipped the phone back into her pocket, her face was white.

"What is it?" Alec asked.

"There's been an accident." She stood. "It's Sam. He's at Walter Reed Hospital."

XX

"THE DOCTORS SAY he could wake up at any time."

Erin turned toward the voice. A tall, distinguished-looking man she'd have known from his pictures, even if she hadn't seen him at Langley, stood in the door. Associate Deputy Director for Intelligence, Thomas Ward.

"Or," he went on, "he may never wake up at all. He's hovering somewhere between a four and five on the Glasgow Coma Scale, caused by a severe trauma to the head. Since the lowest possible grade on the GCS is a three, he's in pretty bad shape."

Ward stepped forward and offered his hand. "I'm Thomas Ward, Sam's boss."

Erin took his hand, maintaining her cover despite her certainty that Ward knew exactly who she was. "Erin Baker. Sam and I went to school together." Not exactly a lie, if you considered their year at the Farm a school. She glanced back at Sam, silent in the bed. "What happened?"

Ward hesitated, then nodded toward the door. "Coffee?"

She followed him out and down the hall to a bank of vending

machines. He bought and then led her farther down the hall to a set of glass doors leading to a terrace. "Let's talk out here."

Outside, the wind bit, making her wish for more than a trench coat over her thin dress.

Director Ward, in nothing more than a suit jacket, seemed unaffected. "Sam's car skidded off an embankment and ended up nose first in the Potomac, near Chain Bridge."

Erin's throat tightened. "When?"

"Around seven thirty."

A wave of nausea rolled through her, and she reached out to brace herself against the back of a nearby chair. Sam had been on his way to meet her.

"Fortunately, there was still enough traffic that someone saw it happen. A kid home from boot camp. He went in after Sam and pulled him out of the vehicle. Otherwise he might have drowned."

Erin shivered. "How did he lose control?"

"I've spoken to the police on the scene," Ward said. "They believe it was a hit-and-run. Sam's rear bumper was crushed . . . Someone hit him hard."

Erin watched his face, willing her own to a stillness she didn't feel. His remained calm, but there was a spark of anger in his eyes that was for her as well as the driver who'd hit Sam. So far, Ward had carried on the pretense, but once they were inside the walls of Langley, she suspected he'd take off the kid gloves and she'd feel the full wrath of a CIA Deputy Director.

For now, however, she needed all the available information about Sam's accident. "And what do *you* think, Mr. Ward?"

He hesitated, surprised perhaps that she hadn't cringed from his thinly shielded anger. Then he said, "I think someone purposely ran him off the road."

"I see." Erin sipped at her coffee, the hot liquid doing nothing to dispel the cold kernel of anger growing inside her. Sam must have found out something that had someone running scared. Either that, or someone had struck out at her through Sam, before she'd even spoken to Neville. As a warning? Or to punish her? And in either case, who? The Magician?

"You were supposed to meet him this evening," Ward said, without a question in his voice.

It was pointless to deny it, though she shrouded her answer in pretense once again, hoping it would at least protect Sam's job. "We had a date."

"Have you been seeing each other long?"

"Off and on for the past couple of years."

For several long minutes, he said nothing else, but when he finally spoke again, the charade and kid gloves were off. "I'm not sure what's going on here, Dr. Baker, but I won't lose Sam to some . . ." He hesitated, about to say something about her CIA position, perhaps, then thought better of it. "To some *woman's* undue influence. He's too valuable."

"No, sir, I don't blame you."

"Then I expect this to be cleared up within the next forty-eight hours. And I want a full report in my office at that time."

"Yes, sir."

"Until then, I think it's best if you stay away from the hospital." A command, wrapped in a suggestion. Then the sham of civility fell back into place, though the edge in his voice was not as easy to eliminate. "For your own safety, that is."

"Of course." She left him there, dropping her half-empty cup in the trash can on her way back inside and passing Sam's room without going in.

She couldn't blame Ward for his anger, nor could she deny that she was at fault for Sam's condition. It hurt her heart that she'd gotten him involved, exposed him by having him meet her outside Langley. Nothing she could do would ever make up for that. But she was trying to save a young boy's life, and catch a monster in the process. Sam wouldn't want her to apologize for that.

Outside, she found Alec Donovan waiting for her. Gratitude settled over her, and she almost smiled. When she'd gotten the call about Sam, Donovan had offered to drive her to the hospital. She'd refused, perfectly capable of getting herself the less than ten miles to Walter Reed. Despite that, he'd followed her. And waited. It was a stupidly old-fashioned, gallant gesture, but at the moment, she couldn't think of a kinder one.

She walked over to his car and climbed into the front seat. "Someone ran him off the road on his way to the embassy," she said, again feeling the weight of her responsibility for Sam's condition.

"How bad is it?" She heard sympathy in Donovan's voice.

"The doctors don't know yet." Her elbow on the door, she leaned her head against her hand. "He's in a coma."

"This isn't your fault, Erin. Sam knew the risks."

She looked over at him, another rush of gratitude sweeping through her. It was almost her undoing, almost unlatched the control she'd held on her emotions, her fear for Sam, her anger at Neville and whoever was helping him steal children, and her frustration because it seemed she could do nothing about either. "Yes, he did." Although that didn't make her feel any better, and she barely kept the tears at bay.

Sam was a trained CIA officer, though his skills had never extended to the more physical requirements of the Agency. But he knew to keep his head down. Suddenly she let her anger drive out the fear. It was a more familiar and thus safer emotion. "How the hell did anyone even know about Sam? He spends his days in front of a computer screen, for God's sake."

"Could they have traced his search?"

She shook her head. Langley's security was the best in the world, and no one was better at covering their tracks than Sam Anderson. "Not a chance."

"Then they must have spotted you together."

She peered out into the darkness. He was right, it was the only way. "They've been watching me."

"You said someone was following you along the river yesterday. When you were running."

She looked at him, a new fear leaping out at her. She'd forgotten about the shadowy presence in the park, had written it off to an overactive imagination. But it hadn't been her imagination. They knew where she lived.

"What about your niece? And the woman who cares for her?" Donovan asked, his mind making the same jump.

"They left for Miami this morning." And Erin would say a million prayers of thanks for that small bit of luck.

"Check on them, and have someone keep an eye on them."

She nodded, frightened now in a way she hadn't been moments earlier. If anything happened to either Janie or Marta . . . But no, she wouldn't allow her mind to follow that path. Miami was another world, and Marta was well loved in the tight-knit Little Havana community.

"I'll call and have them stay down there a few extra days. And Marta knows people." As did Erin. She'd make another call after talking to Marta, to a contact she'd made when she'd first come home from Cairo. An ex-Agency officer who freelanced in Miami. She'd have him keep an eye on her family, just to make sure.

"They'll be safe." Though she didn't know who she was trying to reassure. Donovan, or herself.

She fell silent then, considering her next move.

"What about you?" he asked.

She needed to find out what Sam had discovered, what someone had driven him into the Potomac to keep quiet. "I have to get some rest before I can think clearly."

He glanced at her sideways. "You can't go home. Do have someplace else in mind? Somewhere they won't find you?"

"Yes." She'd go into her Agency office. She could sleep there if needed, but more important, she could retrace Sam's steps.

"What about Neville's men?" he asked.

Funny, how they'd both stopped questioning the General's involvement. "Now that I know they're out there, I can lose them."

"Yeah." He glanced away. "I expect you can."

"What about you?" she asked, wondering why he wasn't playing the gallant anymore, trying to protect her and keep her out of this. Maybe he'd finally realized she could take care of herself. Either that, or he understood that she wouldn't be scared off no matter how many objections he raised.

"I have to get back to the command center in Baltimore." He ran a hand through his hair. "I expect they're wondering what happened to me by now."

"Neville's men could be following you, too."

He shrugged. "My movements are no secret. I'm the agent of record in the Cody Sanders investigation. If they want to follow me, they're welcome."

"Be careful."

He smiled, and it warmed her heart. "Always."

"Okay, then," she said, and reached for the door handle.

He stopped her with a hand on her arm. "You'll let me know if you find anything."

"Sure." And she would. Because she had every intention of finding the Magician and his link to Neville.

"And you'll be careful, too," Donovan added.

She smiled. "In case you haven't noticed, Alec . . ." It was the first time she'd used his given name and it felt odd. "I can take care of myself."

William was already in a foul mood when he heard about the boys' escape attempt. He'd just left the embassy, taking the call in his limo as the driver navigated through the D.C. traffic toward Georgetown.

The caretaker, Ryan, had tried to run with the Sanders boy. Such foolishness. They'd set off the silent alarm when leaving the mansion and didn't even get halfway across the back lawn before Daimon took them down.

Which was what really angered William.

His dogs had paid the price for Ryan's insolence. The bitch lay dead from rat poison, and the guards had had to shoot Daimon before he tore the Sanders boy apart.

Ryan would pay dearly for the dogs. And for his disloyalty.

William had given the boy a place to live when no one else would take him. Otherwise, he would have ended up on the streets, whoring or selling drugs to survive. William had saved him from either fate, and this was how he'd showed his gratitude.

William should have let Gage kill the boy the night before. It would have been cleaner and easier on all of them. And Daimon and his bitch would still be alive.

Now the boy would suffer. William would make sure of it.

It would have to wait, however, another forty-eight hours, until Gage returned to the mansion for the Sanders boy. William had considered contacting Gage and sending him out to take care of Ryan tonight, but had decided against it. It would serve no purpose other than to soothe William's anger. Better to keep a low profile and let things proceed on schedule. Especially with the Americans and their inept CIA watching his every move.

He'd never much cared for Americans. They were poorly behaved children, wielding their strength like a bully's club. Yet like any other bully, they had to be handled carefully to avoid falling victim to their muscle.

His encounter with Erin Baker had been particularly distasteful. The woman's arrogance was topped only by her stupidity. He could have killed her with nothing more than a word, and her government would do nothing. They would not even acknowledge her, except to put a star on a wall and claim it a fitting memorial. She was a fool. And it would cost her her life.

Fortunately, he didn't have to tolerate her or her country much longer. Just another forty-eight hours and he'd be on his way home. Maybe forever, this time. Cody Sanders would be on his way to his new life, and both Erin Baker and Ryan would be ending theirs.

XXI

ERIN SHOULD HAVE SPOTTED a tail.

It was a critical skill for covert officers. Without it, you risked not only your own life, but that of your foreign agents. So the Agency dedicated six weeks of training to equip their officers with the skills necessary to spot and evade surveillance. After that, there were simulations and fieldwork that improved on the basics and kept you sharp. Erin had excelled at both.

Since returning to the States, however, she'd been lax.

She wasn't running agents here, and she hadn't thought to watch for someone following her. Though she should have. She'd sensed someone on the trail behind her Sunday morning. That should have alerted her and made her more conscious of her surroundings.

Well, it wasn't a mistake she intended to repeat. Now that they'd woken her up by hurting Sam, she'd give them a taste of her dust.

As she approached her car, she saw the small reflective tape on her bumper. For someone who didn't know better, it would look like part of her license plate. For those following her, it was a means to keep tabs on her at night. It set her car apart from all the other taillights. Not very original. Or effective, if a subject happened to notice—as she had. They'd have been better off planting an electronic homing device on the underbody. The mistake, however, would allow her to continue the charade awhile longer. She'd lose them before they even realized she'd spotted them.

Without touching the tape, she climbed into her car.

She'd parked on a side street, just off Constitution Avenue near the west end of the mall. Pulling out, she headed east on Constitution toward Seventeenth Street, where she turned left, heading toward Dupont Circle.

Her final destination was her office in one of the Agency's nondescript buildings. Sam had been working on something he hadn't gotten a chance to share with her, and she needed to find it. From her office, she could access the CIA mainframe and hopefully retrace his steps. First, though, she'd lose the tail, and Dupont Circle was a good first step.

Traveling north on Seventeenth, she passed the White House grounds and the old Executive Office Building, which looked like a brightly lit wedding cake. She crossed Pennsylvania Avenue, and as she neared K Street, where Seventeenth turned into Connecticut, traffic picked up.

She was closing in on one of Washington's prime nightlife areas and the people who came with it. So she remained in the right lane, slowing occasionally, much to the dismay of those behind her, as if looking for an address. On Dupont Circle, she did the circuit twice before exiting on Massachusetts Avenue, heading south.

If the driver on her tail was any good, he was still with her, and if he was really good, he might even suspect by now that she knew he was behind her. She was going to assume the latter, because it was always safer to overestimate your opponent.

When she reached Fifteenth Street, she took a right and crossed first M Street, then L, while watching for K. It was time to get rid of her car, and her destination was Georgia Brown's, a restaurant that specialized in low-country cuisine and Southern hospitality in the heart of Washington, D.C.

She'd gone there once with a colleague from Georgetown and had made note of its centralized location for future reference. It would work well tonight, and when she spotted it, she turned in and pulled up to the valet stand. Grabbing her heels, she slipped them on, then shoved her flats into her purse before turning over her keys and going inside.

"I'm meeting someone who's already here," she said to the hostess, and walked toward the back of the restaurant. She breezed through the kitchen door, again pretending she had every right to do so, and within minutes was out the rear door and back outside, on foot this time.

Switching her shoes once again, she headed back toward Connecticut Avenue, then up toward Dupont, grateful for the flats, which made walking so much easier. Though they wouldn't help her with her next move, where she needed to become one of the night crawlers who frequented the clubs in the area. Thus the heels in her purse, waiting to be slipped back on at the right moment.

She had numerous clubs to choose from. Her first choice, Club Five, was loud, crowded, and perfect for what she intended. Unfortunately, it was closed on Mondays, as were quite a few others, so she'd have to try her luck someplace else. At least she'd have less trouble getting in someplace than she would on the weekend.

In the end, she went to MCCXXIII, called Twelve Twenty-three, a trendy spot on Connecticut Avenue that catered to the ultrachic. She had no trouble getting in dressed as she was, but she could only hope that the crowd wouldn't be too slim or too full of themselves to help a woman in distress.

Taking a seat at the bar, she scanned the crowd for potential targets—someone about her size and coloring, but a bit out
of sync with the glitzy crowd. Someone trying to fit into the designer set while dressed in JC Penney. The first criterion was
easy to satisfy, the second was no more than an educated guess.
If she approached the wrong person, this wouldn't work and
she'd have to leave and try somewhere else.

Two women seemed like good candidates, both with groups
that were drinking and dancing heavily. It was just a matter of
waiting for one of them to head for the ladies' room. So Erin ordered a glass of wine, smiling at the bartender to make sure he
would remember her, and waited.

After about fifteen minutes, one of the women climbed out
of her booth and headed for the ladies' room. This was Erin's
chance. She looked over her shoulder toward the front door,
then quickly paid for her drink and followed the woman.

Once inside the ladies' room, she draped her coat on the
couch and fiddled with her makeup, letting her hands shake just
a bit. By the time the other woman emerged from the stall, Erin
was nervously adjusting her clothing and looking distressed.

"Great dress," said the woman, eyeing the beaded black silk.

"Thanks, it was a gift."

"Not a bad gift." The woman pulled out her lipstick and
touched up her mouth. "What is it?"

Thank goodness for the D.C. crowd and designer recognition. "Versace."

Erin could almost see the other woman trying to figure out
if the dress was an original or a knockoff. "Looks like you got
yourself a nice sugar daddy."

Erin shrugged while rummaging through her purse. "Damn,
I left my cigarettes at the bar." She turned to the other woman.
"I hate to ask you this, but do you smoke? I could really use a
cigarette about now."

"Sure." The woman pulled out a pack and handed it over.

Erin's hands shook as she took one, then tried to light it and failed. "Damn," she said again, and let her voice choke on the word.

"Here." The woman took the lighter and lit the cigarette. "Are you okay?"

Erin took a deep drag, then let it out. She started to nod, just as the tears slid down her face. "Not really." She turned away and headed for the separate lounge area while wiping furiously at her eyes.

The woman followed. "What is it? Can I help?"

"Thanks, but I don't think so."

"Try me."

Erin hesitated, not wanting to appear too eager to tell her story. "My boyfriend, I mean my ex-boyfriend, just showed up. I don't think he saw me, but if he did . . ." Her hand trembled as she brought the cigarette to her mouth again.

"What? You're with another guy?" The woman shrugged. "He'll get over it. They both will."

"No, nothing like that. I'm alone." Erin dropped down to the couch. "We just broke up, and well, he didn't take it very well." She sucked in more smoke. "I'm afraid of what he'll do if he sees me here."

"Afraid?" The woman sat down beside her. "Will he hurt you?"

Erin felt a twinge of guilt about lying to this woman, whose concern seemed genuine. She held out her arms, showing off the bruises, gone purple and yellow, she'd gotten courtesy of Bill Jensen's testosterone junkie at the Farm. "That's why I left him."

"Son of a bitch." The woman draped an arm over Erin's shoulders. "What can I do to help?"

"I'm not sure, but I need to get out of here without him seeing me."

"What about the back door?"

"I thought of that, but if he sees me and follows me out there . . ."

"Then you'll really be all alone, in an alley." The woman thought a minute, then said, "Come back to my table with me. I'm with a whole group of friends. He won't dare bother you if you're with other people."

"I can't do that. I don't want to get you or your friends involved."

"No, it's okay, really."

Erin shook her head. This wasn't the way she wanted the interaction to go. "You don't know him. He won't hesitate to cause a scene or even pick a fight. No, I just can't . . ."

"Can I call someone—"

"Wait, I have an idea." Then, "No." She shook her head again. "Oh, never mind."

"No, what? If I can help."

"Well . . ." Erin paused, again hesitating to ask a favor. "What if we exchanged clothes?"

The woman backed off, shocked, again eyeing Erin's dress.

"He'll never recognize me in that outfit. It's just not . . . me."

"I couldn't do that."

"Oh, please." Erin grabbed the other woman's hands. "The dress is an original, and this is only the second time I've worn it. You can have it."

"I can't, it has to be worth a mint."

"If you hate it, you could sell it. You could probably get a lot, I don't know, maybe a—"

"No." The woman pulled her hand free. "I mean I can't take it from you."

Erin met the other woman's gaze. "*He* gave it to me."

"Oh." For a moment, neither spoke, a silent understanding running between them. "Still . . ."

"Please." Erin opened her purse and pulled out her wallet. "I'll pay you, and I'll send back your clothes, too."

The woman put her hand on Erin's wallet. "I don't want your money."

"Then you'll do it?"

"Oh, hell, why not? When will I ever be able to afford a dress like that?"

Erin's eyes filled with tears. "Thank you."

Within minutes, Erin was dressed in the other woman's clothes. A short leather skirt, red, that exposed more than it covered, and a white short-sleeved sweater.

"It looks better on you than me," said the woman. "But you still look too . . . polished. Let me do your face."

The woman pulled a makeup case from her purse, and by the time she'd finished, Erin looked like a different woman. Instead of the sophisticated socialite who'd just left an embassy reception, she looked like a party girl, her eyes transformed with heavy liner and dark shadow, her lips with bright red lipstick, and her hair moussed into stylish disarray. Erin liked it. It made her feel . . . young. And free.

"Wow," Erin said, deciding the woman would do well at the CIA. "You're good."

The woman grinned. "It's not bad, is it."

"Not bad at all." Erin primped a moment longer, then put away the last of the makeup. Picking up her coat, she handed it over. "You'll need this, too."

"But—"

Erin held up a hand to stop her protest. "I can't take it. It's a dead giveaway."

The woman shrugged. "Okay."

"You know," Erin said, "I don't even know your name."

"It's Susan," she said, grinning and suddenly looking a lot younger. "Though my friends call me Suzie."

"Suzie. That's a great name." And more appropriate than she'd ever know. "Well, Suzie, you may just have saved a life tonight."

XXII

THE COMMAND CENTER was quiet, empty. Except for Cathy, who sat alone at the large conference table, reports and pictures spread out in front of her.

"Hey," he said.

She looked up, her eyes dull and tired. "Hey yourself."

He dropped his slim leather file folder onto a chair and sat on the edge of the table. "Where is everyone?"

"I sent them all home to get some sleep."

"Good idea." And he should have been the one here to do it. "You look like you could use a few hours yourself."

"There's an epidemic of that going around."

"Yeah." He ran a hand through his hair, feeling the weariness deep in his bones. "Anything new?"

"We've run the composite sketch from Erin and Al Beckwith through our database, and come up with several known sex offenders in the area who fit the general description. We're bringing them in."

He leaned forward. "That's good."

She folded her arms and took a deep breath. "None of them looks real good. So unless this pans out, we just have more dead ends."

"Me, too."

She leaned back in her chair, looking up at him, then reached under a stack of papers, pulled out a computer disc, and slid it toward him. "I listened to it."

He sighed. It was a digital copy of the tape they'd made at the German Embassy. "I figured you would." And it was an indication of just how exhausted she was that she hadn't torn into him the minute he'd walked through the door.

"She's CIA," Cathy said without preamble.

Alec slid into the chair opposite hers. "I suspected as much. How do you know?"

She crossed her arms. "I have my sources."

"And they admitted Erin works for the Agency."

She shifted, glanced away. "No. But they didn't deny it, either."

Which he knew was as close to an admission as they'd get. But he didn't know whether to be relieved or disturbed by the information. On the one hand, it meant Erin was fully aware of the dangerous situation she'd created, and she could take care of herself. On the other, there could be levels to this thing he couldn't see.

"Alec, you're in over your head," Cathy said. "She's using you. Heck, for all we know, the Agency may be using you."

It was a real possibility. He could be playing an unwitting part in one of the Company's wild schemes or missions. They weren't known for sharing their information or plans. Not even with the FBI. But it didn't feel right to Alec. "I don't think so." His gut told him this was about Erin's hunt for her sister's abductor, not the Agency.

"You're too close to it," Cathy said. "To her. You can't see it, but it's pretty obvious to everyone else."

"Everyone else?"

She looked suddenly uncomfortable, guilty. Then she squared her shoulders and met his gaze head-on. "I've been talking to Schultz at headquarters."

"Shit." Schultz was Alec's supervisor.

"I'm sorry," she started, "but . . ."

"You're sorry." He should have seen this coming. That didn't make it any easier to take. "You went behind my back to Schultz and you're sorry." They'd been a team, partners, and they'd always stood together against the desk pushers who pulled their strings.

Her temper flared; she read his thoughts as if he'd spoken them aloud. "This has nothing to do with my loyalty to you. This is about trying to find a little boy, while the best damn investigator in the whole FBI is burned out."

"You told him I was burned out?"

She straightened in her chair, clearly reining in her anger. "I told him that in my opinion it was a possibility that you've been overworked. Yes."

"Did you consider that I might be onto something?"

"Yes. Until I heard that tape, I was willing to give you the benefit of the doubt. But when I found out you'd gone behind my back to put a wire on a CIA officer and send her into a foreign embassy to harass a member of the German diplomatic staff . . ." She held out her hands, palms up. "What was I supposed to think?"

"Erin would have gone in whether I put that wire on her or not."

"Then you should have walked away."

"I couldn't. She might have learned something."

"But she didn't."

He sighed and looked away. "Other than she's sure Neville's involved, no."

"What would you have done in my situation?" she asked, her voice pleading for understanding.

He didn't reply, because they both knew the answer.

"Look, Alec, you've got great instincts. More than that, you're a friend. But I had to do what I thought was best for the investigation, for Cody Sanders. I had to get things back on track before they pull the plug on us."

He looked at her.

"You've been taken off the case. You're to report to Quantico in the morning."

This, too, he should have seen coming. He probably wouldn't have waited this long to relieve her if the situation had been reversed. That didn't mean he planned to play along.

"I'm not going to Quantico," he said.

She looked surprised, but he held up a hand to stop her before she said anything else. "You say I have good instincts. Well, you're right, and those instincts have been telling me that William Neville is up to his stiff, German neck in this thing."

He opened his case and pulled out the files Erin had given him on the Mall. He hadn't planned on drawing Cathy any further into this than he already had, but now he had no choice. He needed her cooperation, if not her help.

"Read this," he said, and handed her Sam's report and analysis.

Cathy took the papers, warily, and he waited until she'd gone through them before speaking again. "I know that's not proof, but there are a hell of a lot of coincidences." Neville's ties to the world slave markets cast a new light on his ownership of the *Desert Sun*. And there was Erin's "assistant," Sam.

"The man who drew up that report was hospitalized this evening. He's in a coma."

"An accident?"

"Someone drove him into the Potomac."

"Neville?" He could see from her expression that she, too, was beginning to recognize the puzzle pieces, still scattered, but somehow part of a whole.

"What do you think?" Now, if Alec could uncover some connection to a man who used magic tricks to lure children, he might be able to find Cody Sanders.

"Neville leaves the country in forty-eight hours with the German ambassador," he said. "Give me that long."

She could hardly take her eyes off the reports and spoke without looking up. "What are you going to do?"

"Neville has an estate near Middleburg. I'm going to start there."

She looked up, alarmed.

"I'm just going to go out and take a look around," he assured her.

"What about Schultz?"

"Tell him I've gone AWOL and you can't find me."

He could see her sharp mind weighing his suggestion.

"You go on with your investigation," he said. "Bring in the matches to that sketch and put them on a lineup. Find out if any of them have alibis. I just need to be free to follow up on this. And I can't do it once Quantico gets their claws in me." He paused, letting her digest his words before playing his trump card. "As you said, this is about finding a little boy, and possibly a serial kidnapper. If I have to break a few rules to do it, so be it."

"It could mean your career."

"Versus Cody's life." He shook his head. "There's no contest there."

She studied him a moment longer, then sighed. "Okay, Alec. I never saw you. You have forty-eight hours."

XXIII

IT WAS NEAR MIDNIGHT by the time Erin finally got to her office. Located in a commercial complex on the outskirts of D.C., it was just another featureless, boxy building among numerous others. The Agency had dozens of such places, where their people could operate discreetly outside Langley.

The sign on the door said CANTON CONSULTING.

A key opened the outer door to the reception area. Then, once inside, Erin had thirty seconds to enter her security code and thumbprint on the door to her inner sanctum. Otherwise, an alarm would go off somewhere within Langley, and Agency officers would be all over this place within minutes.

She was only one of several officers who used this particular site as their contact point to Langley. The reception area was the hub for five individual offices. When Erin needed something, she went through the silent, efficient woman who manned the reception desk.

Erin had no idea what to label the other woman. Secretary? Receptionist? Assistant? Watcher? Whatever title she put on herself, she must have a high security clearance to spend her days in this place of secrets.

As for the others officers, they, like Erin, kept to themselves, not even acknowledging one another's presence. She imagined they all had their own undercover assignments, and it was safer for everyone to guard the lines of silence.

Tonight, the first thing Erin wanted was a shower. Her skin crawled with the memory of her conversation with Neville and the certainty that he'd had her followed. Because, despite the lack of proof, she knew he was behind both those trailing her and Sam's accident. Fortunately, each office came with a fully stocked private bath. The Agency never knew when an officer would need a secure location, or when she did, how long she'd have to stay.

Stripping, Erin stepped into a shower. She'd have the clothes cleaned and sent back to Susan in the morning, with a note of thanks. Erin wished she could do more. The woman had provided Erin the means to lose Neville's men, and it had worked beautifully.

She'd waltzed out of the club, a little bit sexy, a little bit drunk, and no one had given her a second glance. More important, no one had followed her. She'd waited, hidden in a doorway a block away, watching the entrance for any sign that she'd been recognized. Only when she was certain that no one had spotted her did she go on. Still cautious. Still aware of the shadows around her.

She turned up the hot water, scrubbing at her skin.

Sam.

No matter how many times she told herself she'd had no choice, or that he, too, was a trained CIA officer, or that a little boy's life depended on their finding the link to Neville, she couldn't shake the ache of knowing she'd put Sam in harm's way. He was in a coma because she'd drawn him into this. Maybe if she'd gone through channels, if she'd approached her supervisor with what she knew—and what she didn't—Sam would be safely ensconced in front of his Langley computer right now.

Of course, the powers that be would never have let her go forward with her suspicions. She was too close to it, they'd say as they passed the investigation to someone else. Or shuffled it away to molder in some forgotten file.

She switched off the hot water, letting the icy water pummel her.

It was time to stop second-guessing herself. If Sam recovered, she'd do whatever was necessary to clear his name in all this. For now, she had a little boy to find and a madman to bring down.

After getting out of the shower, she pulled on a pair of black jeans and a turtleneck and headed for her locked weapons' drawer.

As a rule, she didn't carry a gun, and since returning to the States, she hadn't needed one. She kept a couple here, just in case: a 9mm Beretta and a .22-caliber Ruger she'd picked up overseas for backup. She slipped the Ruger into her bag and left the Beretta on her desk for when she left the office. The night was far from over, and the next time she went out, she was going armed.

She booted up her computer and waited for the CIA logo to appear. Once it did, she accessed her secure e-mail. Sam had agreed to copy her on everything he'd uncovered, sending her electronic duplicates of the information she'd passed on to Donovan. What she hoped, however, was that Sam had also sent her the information he'd refused to share with her this afternoon.

As she'd hoped, *three* notes from Sam waited for her in her in-box. The first contained the files documenting Neville's connections to the slave trade, along with a detailed breakdown of Neville's worldwide holdings.

She couldn't help but question how quickly Sam had uncovered this information. He was good, but the CIA employed lots of good analysts. Why had no one zeroed in on Neville before? Or had they? Without going through channels, she had no way of knowing.

So for now, she filed away the possibility that the CIA was onto Neville and scanned his list of holdings, her eye drawn to a highlighted section titled *U.S. Holdings.* Two pieces of property were listed: a house in Georgetown and an estate outside Middleburg, Virginia, about fifty miles west of D.C. She noticed that Sam—ever efficient—had made a note to himself in the margin to get floor and security plans for both.

Erin opened the second note and smiled. Sam had included the layout for both properties, with a message that the security systems had probably been enhanced. And without examination of the property or the name of the systems' installer—which she was not likely to obtain since Neville probably used one of his own countrymen, who was by now no longer within U.S. borders—it would be high risk to assume she could circumvent Neville's security.

Sam had read her mind. And, of course, she would take his concern to heart. Even if she didn't follow his advice to back off. Taking a look at Neville's properties was definitely near the top of her to-do list.

That left the third note, which she noticed hadn't come from Langley but had been forwarded through Sam's Langley address. It was from Sam, however, transmitted from some kind of mobile device. Sent at seven twenty-six. Minutes before he'd been forced off the road.

She choked back a sob and opened the note.

Erin. Look at Mid-East connections. Gotta go. He's after me.

Erin leaned back in her chair, reading and rereading the brief message. So he'd known someone was following him. Did he also know his life was in danger? How could he not? He understood better than anyone that Neville was dangerous. Yet Sam hadn't shied away. He'd still come out to meet her and had managed to get off a note to her with one of Neville's henchmen breathing down his neck. A brave man. Even more so because his job shouldn't have included the danger she'd come to accept with hers.

Mid-East connections.

In Sam's early search, there had been no hint of this. Not that he'd shared with her. Except the information about the *Desert Sun*, which had been on its way to the Mid-East. A very loose connection, considering Neville had no recorded holdings or regular dealing with any Middle Eastern country. That must have been the piece Sam hadn't wanted to speculate about. So what bearing did that have on Neville's interest in the slave trade? Or did it? Was it a completely separate piece of his empire? A deeply hidden, dirty piece?

She'd heard the rumors about Americans and Europeans disappearing into the Middle East. Usually women. Also, more than rumor, she knew that after marrying into a culture so unlike their own, Western women sometimes found themselves and their children unable to leave countries like Iran or Saudi Arabia. Erin had helped one such woman flee.

But was there an active slave market in these places? One Sam had had to dig a little harder to find? One Neville had ties to? One that traded in children? And if it existed, why had she never heard any rumors about it? She'd spent two years in Cairo, plus Middle Eastern cultures were supposed to be her field of expertise.

The questions ricocheted through her thoughts. But without Sam and his computer wizardry, she could only speculate. She couldn't retrace Sam's steps without a great deal of time—if at all. So she'd have to do it the old-fashioned way. Which meant a little breaking and entering was in order.

First, though, she'd check on Janie and Marta.

She wanted to talk to them, just to make sure they were okay. But a phone call in the middle of the night would do more harm than good. Marta, at least, would know something was wrong and would want to hurry home. Better to wait until morning, when everyone would be a little more clearheaded, before trying to explain why they both needed to stay in Miami longer than they'd planned.

Her other call to Miami, however, couldn't wait. She needed to have someone keep an eye on Marta and Janie, and within minutes she had made the arrangements. Her contact was more than willing to help out. After all, in their business, you never knew when you'd need a return favor.

Next, she dialed in to listen to her home messages. The first message was for Marta, from someone at Janie's school, and Erin pushed the skip button. The second was the one she'd been hoping for.

"Hello, Erin." It was Marta's voice. "I have someone here who wants to talk to you." Then in the background, "Go ahead, sweetie."

"Aunt Erin." Janie's voice was soft and tentative. "Where are you?"

Erin's heart clenched.

"Tell her what we did today." Another gentle instruction from Marta in the background.

"We went to the beach. It was really hot."

"What else?" Marta whispered.

"I found shells. And a starfish. Much better than the one we found last year. It's got no broken edges."

Erin smiled, remembering their hunt the year before for the perfect, intact starfish. They'd found one with only a single missing tip. She wished she'd been there when Janie found the one today.

"It was fun," Janie said. Then her voice turned whiny, in the way of tired children. "But I want to come home. I miss you."

Erin's heart melted, wishing she could call and reassure Janie.

"Say good-bye," came Marta's soft voice.

"Bye." It sounded more like tears than a word, and Erin fought back tears of her own.

Then Marta was back on the phone. "Janie's tired. We had a big day. So don't call back tonight. She's going to bed. But if you can, call in the morning. We'll be here until about ten. Talk to you then."

Marta hung up, and Erin fought the temptation to listen to the message again. She *would* call them in the morning, but she'd have to tell Marta to stay in Miami for a few more days. Until this was cleared up, it wasn't safe for them to come home. How could she explain that to a seven-year-old?

She went on to the last message on her answering machine, though she was tempted to skip it. In case Marta had called back, however, she let it run.

"Ms. Baker, this is Dr. Schaeffer at Gentle Oaks."

Erin felt a stab of guilt. When they'd left Gentle Oaks yesterday, Claire had been under a suicide watch. Erin had been so preoccupied with her investigation, she'd forgotten to call and check on her sister. "Your sister is very agitated and asking for you. Please give me a call at your earliest convenience."

"Damn." Erin looked at the time stamp on the message. Three this afternoon. If she'd listened to her messages when she'd gotten back from California, she could have run out to see Claire before going to the embassy.

Hanging up, she immediately dialed the home's number. Schaeffer would be long gone by now, but hopefully someone would be able tell her what was wrong. Within minutes, she was speaking to the resident on the graveyard shift.

"Your sister was very upset," he said. "She kept asking for you."

That couldn't be right. Claire never asked for her sister. "You mean, she was asking for Marta Lopez."

"No, she kept saying she needed to speak to Erin." His voice was tight, as if he was annoyed at having been questioned. "That's you, isn't it?"

"What else was she saying?"

"Look, Ms. Baker. Claire is asleep now. If you come out here in the morning, you can talk to her yourself. Also, Dr. Schaeffer will be in, and I'm sure he can give you much more information than I can."

"What else was she saying?" She heard the first niggling of fear in her own voice.

He must have heard it as well. "Don't worry about it. She wasn't making any sense."

"Tell me."

He sighed, obviously tired and irritated. Dealing with patients' relatives wasn't something he'd have to do very often on the late shift. "Something about ice cream and magic tricks. She kept saying, 'Tell Erin the Magic Man is here.' "

The dam of fear broke, wrapping ice around her heart. "I'll be right there."

"No, I told you—"

"Listen to me, Doctor, very carefully. Don't let anyone into her room until I get there."

"But—"

"No one. Do you understand?"

Another sigh. "Yes." He might not like taking her orders, but considering what she paid to keep Claire in his facility, he would at least pretend to go along.

"I'll be there within the hour," Erin said, searching for a way to make him take her seriously. "Oh, and Doctor—what's your name?"

"Temple."

"Dr. Temple, if anything happens to Claire before I get there, I'll hold you personally responsible. And believe me, I'll make a medical malpractice suit look like a walk in the park."

Erin set a record getting to Gentle Oaks, making the hour drive in a little over forty-five minutes. Fortunately no flashing blue lights appeared in her rearview mirror, because they would have just had to follow her to Fredericksburg. No one was getting between her and Claire. She was through the door and heading for her sister's room when the harried Dr. Temple stepped in her path.

"Ms. Baker, this is ridiculous. It's past visiting hours, and I told you your sister is sleeping."

"Get out of my way, Doctor. Or I'll move you."

Something in her face must have scared him because he stepped aside. Though he followed her the rest of the way, motioning to a nurse to come as well.

Inside Claire's room, Erin went to her sister's side, checking her pulse. She was restless but sleeping unharmed, and Erin took her first easy breath since getting off the phone with Dr. Temple.

"Who visited her yesterday after we left?" she asked, without taking her eyes off Claire.

"I don't know."

"Well, find out," she snapped.

Temple nodded to the nurse, who hurried out of the room with a frown. She obviously didn't approve of the way he was handling the irrational Ms. Baker and would have liked to take a crack at Erin herself.

"What is going on here?" he asked.

Erin ignored the question, brushing a wispy blond curl from Claire's cheek. Her sister sighed in her sleep, and Erin bent down to kiss her forehead. Erin had stirred things up, bringing the Magician out of whatever gutter he had occupied.

And she'd never forgive herself if anything happened to Claire as a consequence.

The nurse returned with the visitor registration book. "The last people who visited Claire were Erin Baker, Janie Baker, and Marta Lopez."

Erin turned to her. "Are you sure?"

"Do you want to look for yourself?" she asked.

"Could someone have visited without signing the book?"

The woman bristled. "We take our patients' safety very seriously here."

Erin sighed. "I'm sure you do." And she knew it was the truth. A facility of this caliber couldn't risk not taking security seriously. So the Magic Man had come in under the guise of a hospital employee—a male nurse, an orderly, or even a doctor. It's what she would have done in his shoes.

Turning back to Dr. Temple, she said, "I need you to wake her up."

"Whatever for? She needs to sleep."

"Claire needs to talk to me." Erin resisted the urge to shake this guy, who was probably considering the feasibility of sedating her as if she were a patient. "Wake her up."

"I can't be responsible—"

"I'll take full responsibility and sign whatever forms you need, but if you don't wake her up now, I'll call an ambulance and take her out of here unconscious. And you can explain to Dr. Schaeffer how you lost one of his prize patients in the middle of the night."

For a moment she thought he'd refuse. She could see the struggle racing across his face. He so wanted to score a point off her. But in the end, he complied, though clearly with disapproval, giving Claire a shot to wake her.

"Now leave us," Erin said, and that command he was more than willing to obey.

Claire came out of sleep slowly, stirring, then blinking her eyes into focus. "Erin?"

"It's me." Erin squeezed her hand. "I'm here."

Claire smiled, and for a moment, she was the gentle seven-year-old child whom Erin had lost all those years ago. "You came."

"All you had to do was ask." And it was true. All Claire had ever had to do was ask, and Erin would have done anything for her, for her baby sister. The realization sent a choke of emotion to her throat and a sting of tears to her eyes.

"He was here," Claire said, her voice hoarse from sleep.

"The Magic Man?"

Claire nodded. "He came into my room and told me he'd been watching me. And you. I told the doctors, but they didn't believe me."

"I believe you."

"What are we going to do?"

Erin's thoughts raced. Claire couldn't stay here, but Erin couldn't take her home, either. She couldn't go to the police or her own organization for help, but she had an idea where else she could find what she needed. "First, we're going to get you out of here. Then I'm going to take you somewhere safe."

Claire nodded. "I knew you'd know what to do."

"Come on." Erin helped her sister sit up, then handed her a glass of water.

As Erin started to move away, Claire grabbed her arm. "Don't leave me."

Erin again took her sister's hand. "I'm not going anywhere without you. I'm just going to get your clothes."

Claire released her reluctantly, following Erin with her eyes as she went to the closet and pulled out the dress Claire had worn on Sunday. Erin helped her change, and just as she slipped on a sweater over the dress, the doctor returned.

"What are you're doing?" he asked.

"I'm taking my sister out of here."

"But you said if I woke her . . ."

Erin felt a rush of sympathy for the man. He was so young, with no idea what he was up against. "Look, Dr. Temple. She'll be back. We're just . . ." If she explained that Claire was in danger, he'd insist on calling the police. Who wouldn't have a clue about how to protect Claire from the likes of the Magician. "We're just going for ride."

"In the middle of the night?"

"It calms her."

He watched in disbelief as Erin helped Claire off the bed and out into the hall. They walked slowly, arm in arm, while Erin looked at each person they passed, expecting the man with the magic hands. She didn't see him, but she had no doubt he was watching her, watching them, as they left the hospital.

He couldn't follow, though, not at night on the empty country roads, without her spotting him. And for that, at least, she was grateful. She'd get Claire somewhere safe. Then *she'd* find *him*.

She drove about fifteen minutes, then stopped outside Fredericksburg at an all-night 7-Eleven. Claire had drifted off to sleep again in the passenger seat, her trust so new and surprising that Erin didn't know quite what to make of it. Except that she would give her life to live up to it. For now, though, she didn't have time to dwell on those thoughts. She needed to find a place where Claire would be safe.

Getting out of the car, she went to a pay phone. She didn't want to take a chance on a cell, on either end, so she had to call directory assistance first to get the number she wanted. Then the voice that picked up was feminine.

"Cody Sanders tip line," she said. "Special Agent Cathy Hart speaking."

"This is Erin Baker, I need to speak with Agent Donovan."

There was a long pause at the other end of the line.

"I'm helping him with the Cody Sanders case," Erin explained.

"I know who you are, Officer Baker."

Erin sighed. So they'd figured it out. Not surprising really. She'd practically told Donovan herself. "Then you know why I need to speak with Donovan."

Another pause, a hesitation perhaps. "He's not here. As a matter of fact, I don't know where he is. I thought he might be with you."

"No. He's not."

"I'm sorry, then. I can't help you."

"Wait, don't hang up." Erin had the distinct feeling the woman on the other end was about to do just that. "If you know who I am, then you also know all about the Magician and my sister, Claire."

No reply.

"I'm calling from a phone booth about ten miles outside Fredericksburg, Virginia. I have my sister with me." She glanced back at the car, where Claire slept. "The Magician paid her a visit today, and I need your help to protect her."

XXIV

IT HAD BEEN YEARS since Alec had worked a stakeout, and he'd forgotten how much he disliked them. Sitting in an uncomfortable car, hot or cold, depending on the time of year, waiting for something to happen. For someone *else* to do something interesting.

After leaving Erin in the parking lot of Walter Reed Hospital, he'd started with the General's house in Georgetown, for no other reason than it was an easy place to blend in. Parked several houses down and across the street, he had a clear view of the front door. Later, he'd check out the estate in Middleburg and get a feel for the activity there as well. And at some point he'd have to decide which location would yield more information. For now, though, he planned to take a preliminary look at both.

In reality, it would take an entire team, at minimum four pairs of men working six-hour shifts, to properly cover both properties and watch the General's movements. But Alec had only himself, and that would have to do. Cathy was already risking her career by covering for him. He wouldn't make it worse by asking her for another set of eyes.

He rubbed at his right temple, at the headache forming behind it, and lifted his binoculars to get a better look at the structure. It was a large brick box, with white pillars framing the front door. A short wall fronted the property, topped by an iron fence. Alec wondered what the place cost. A mint—multiple mints—he was sure. Georgetown was so far beyond his bank account, he'd never even bothered to check out the price of homes.

The place was quiet but still alive. A stretch limo with diplomatic escort had pulled up earlier, and Neville had gone inside, surrounded by four burly bodyguards. Since then, lights had been blazing from a downstairs window, telling Alec that at least General Neville wasn't resting easy either.

Alec glanced at his watch. A little after midnight. Plenty of time before dawn for the man to stir up more trouble if he was so inclined.

Around one, a dark sedan pulled up and two men climbed out. Even from a distance, Alec could tell they were soldiers. They carried themselves in a straight, no-nonsense manner, watching the shadows as if expecting attack at any moment. After passing through the front gate, they circled the house to go in through some side or back entrances Alec couldn't see.

He suspected it was too much to hope that they didn't work for Neville, but were here to do the man some harm. Especially if theirs was the car that had put Erin's analyst, Sam, into the Potomac.

On the other hand, the nondescript sedan, the military types, a late-night visit to Georgetown, he hoped it all meant Erin had ditched her tail. And these two jokers were here to report the loss to their boss.

Man, would Alec love to be a fly on the wall for that conversation.

They weren't inside long, returning to their car in less than fifteen minutes. Alec waited until they were a block away before easing away from the curb to follow them. They worked their way west, crossing Francis Scott Key Bridge into Virginia, then turning onto 29 South.

Either they didn't know Alec was behind them or they didn't care, because they made no attempt to evade him. And well before they arrived in Erin's Arlington neighborhood, he knew where they were headed.

He let them turn onto her street without following, circled the block several times, then came back down past her house in the opposite direction. They'd parked at the end of the street, just close enough to take note of any cars pulling in or out of her driveway. Or a pedestrian approaching her front door. They were counting on her coming home, sooner or later.

Alec figured they'd have a long wait.

He considered his options. He could return to Georgetown and wait to see if Neville had any more late-night visitors. Or he could head out to the General's estate near Middleburg and take a look around.

Alec chose Middleburg.

Georgetown might be Neville's command post, but his secrets would be kept somewhere out of the way. A country estate, with lots of land, space, and no curious neighbors.

Even knowing that, Alec needed more time than he expected, nearly two hours, to find the place. It was north of Middleburg toward the Potomac, on an obscure country road that wasn't on any map. There was no marker, nothing to indicate Neville's ownership of the property. Nor had Alec expected that. People like the General didn't advertise their locations.

He actually drove by the main entrance twice before realizing he'd found it, and then only because there was nothing else around. On his third pass, he went slowly, noting the heavy iron gate, security cameras, and manned guardhouse. No house in sight, just a road disappearing over a woodsy rise.

Alec kept driving, watching for a break in the trees, finding what he wanted a quarter mile past the gate. A service road, overgrown now, but still visible within the thick undergrowth. He turned in, navigating the grassy road until his car was out of sight of the road. Anyone looking would spot the fresh tire tracks in the long grass, but he was betting no one would be looking. Not tonight anyway.

Maneuvering the car behind a tangled mass of greenery, he shut off the engine and got out. Around him, the woods went silent. Then came alive again with the night chatter of insects.

He checked his .38, for a full clip and a backup one, then returned it to his holster, leaving it unsnapped. From the trunk he retrieved a flashlight that he didn't turn on, and wouldn't, if he could help it. And night-vision binoculars, which were the only way he'd get close enough to see anything that would make this trip to the wilderness worthwhile.

Then he started down the overgrown road, picking his way carefully as he slipped deeper into the woods. He'd walked about ten minutes when he found the stone wall. At about six feet, it wouldn't keep even a determined teenager out, much less a serious trespasser. But he wasn't about to make any rash assumptions.

After climbing a nearby tree, he used his flashlight briefly to examine the top of the wall, looking for cameras, barbed wire, anything else that might surprise him. He saw nothing.

So the wall was a warning, a "Keep Out" sign.

He scaled it easily, dropping down on the other side, the sound muffled by a thick carpet of leaves. He expected he was officially trespassing on foreign soil now, stepping over the edge where his status as an FBI agent would no longer protect him.

Working his way through the woods, he kept his eyes open for security devices. Cameras in particular. Anything else out here would be too easily tripped by animals. He saw none, until the trees stopped, opening up to carefully manicured grounds, reaching at least an acre toward a stone mansion. It was like something you'd expect to find in Europe. Old. Massive. And ominous in the moonlight.

That's where he spotted the first cameras, on the trees edging the woods, their lenses aimed at the ground. Anyone moving past this point would be left to Neville's guards. Who, he realized, were out in force.

Alec dropped to the ground, belly to soft earth, and brought up his binoculars. He counted six men right off the bat. No. Make that eight. Six soldiers, uniformed and armed. Four patrolling the grounds close to the house, two posted near a second, stand-alone structure, much smaller and to the left.

About them all, tension charged the air. He sensed something about to happen. Or just over.

One possibility was the last two men. Not soldiers. But standing in pits already two or three feet deep, digging. Alec held his breath, afraid to speculate on the purpose of those holes. Eventually the diggers climbed out, leaving dark gaps in the earth, and went into the detached building—which looked like a combination garage and storage area for equipment.

Alec shifted back to the soldiers around the mansion. Still there, still on edge. Pacing the grounds. Checking doors and windows. Scanning the surrounding area.

Movement caught his eye, and he quickly refocused on the smaller building as the two men reemerged, each with a wrapped bundle that they carried to the open earth and dropped inside.

Alec's stomach clenched. Graves.

He thought immediately of Cody Sanders and dug the fingers of his free hand into the dirt. If one of those bundles contained a young boy's body, Alec was already too late. Racing down there, intent on seeking revenge would only get him killed. And the tragedy of Cody Sanders's fate would remain a mystery.

So he watched, his chest tight, while the men filled the holes with dirt, patted them with the flat of their shovels, then retreated. This time to the mansion.

Alec sighed and put down the binoculars.

Somehow he needed to get down there, past the security cameras, to see whose bodies were in those graves.

Again, motion brought his attention back to the scene below. One of the diggers had come back outside, hurrying across the opening between the two buildings, stopping only as a guard stepped into his path.

Alec was too far away to hear any of it, but the men's body language told him enough. They weren't exchanging pleasantries. The guard waved his gun toward the mansion, but Digger held his ground, even taking a step forward and poking a finger at the armed man's chest. The guard, smaller by a full head, took a backward step, intimidated despite his weapon. In the end, Digger threw up his hands, then stepped around the guard—who turned, as if trying to decide what to do—as Digger marched into the storage building and slammed the door.

For several long moments, Alec held his breath.

Until a large door slid up on the side of the garage, and he realized it was only one of six such doors. Then a flashy white import—a BMW—nearly leapt out through the opening and sped up the road toward the front gate.

Alex had just found his way in, a means to discover what had happened here and whose bodies were in those graves. And maybe what else was going on.

Pushing back away from the edge of the trees, he kept down until he was a good ten feet into the woods. Then he stood and raced toward the wall and over it, faster than was wise in the dark. He knew he wouldn't reach his car in time to follow the BMW, but he'd have to try to catch him.

As Alec expected, by the time he reached the road, the BMW was long gone. Hesitating, he considered which way to turn. Left was north, and there wasn't much that way for a hundred miles, except the Potomac and the Maryland border. So chances were Digger had gone right, heading south for Middleburg.

Alec turned right.

Though he questioned the decision a half-dozen times as he slid through the empty countryside with no sign of the other car. If Digger was running, he might be going for the state border. But he'd looked like a man anxious to get somewhere, not run from something. So Alec kept on toward town.

He was still on the outskirts of Middleburg when he spotted the BMW outside an all-night convenience store. Pulling in alongside it, he parked and went inside. Digger was filling a small handbasket from a shelf toward the back of the store.

"Evening." Alec nodded to the clerk and headed for the coffeepot, his eyes on Digger two aisles over.

"Sorry, man, the coffee's pretty stiff," the clerk called from across the store. "I can make a fresh pot, if you want."

"Sure." It would buy Alec some time and give him an excuse to linger. "That would be great."

The clerk, a kid in his midtwenties, shuffled out from behind the counter and started to put together the new batch of coffee.

Alec walked over and studied the display of ready-made sandwiches. "I should have stopped for dinner a long time ago. Now you're the only game in town."

The clerk threw him a quick, knowing grin. "Well, if you're desperate, those won't kill you. Otherwise . . ."

Alec laughed and grabbed a sandwich.

"Been on the road long?" the kid asked as he finished with the coffee and headed back to his stool and cigarettes.

Alec followed him. "Since early this morning." He nodded to Digger, who'd been waiting at the cash register. "I'm trying to get back to D.C. My wife went into labor this morning." He leaned against the counter, supposedly waiting for the fresh coffee.

"Hey, man, that's great."

"Yeah, thanks."

Digger had unloaded his basket. Rubbing alcohol. Iodine. Topical antibiotic. Aspirin. Ibuprofen. Gauze-pad rolls. A couple of Ace bandages.

"It's a boy," Alec said, eyeing the items, thinking they wouldn't do a dead body any good. Then he took his shot. "We're gonna name him Cody."

Digger flinched.

"Wow," Alec said, not giving the man time to recover. "Looks like you're stocking up for World War Three, fella."

Digger looked at him, his face hard and unmoving.

Alec lifted both hands, palms out. "Just kidding. It's good to be prepared."

Digger's lips turned up in a tight smile. Hesitated. Then he leaned down, grabbed a half-dozen candy bars, and dropped them on the pile with the rest of his items. He looked at Alec then. "These are for *my* son. Ryan. But he has a friend named Cody."

"Really." Alec didn't take his eyes off the other man's face. There was intelligence in those eyes, and something else. Fear maybe. But determination, too. "Well, I sure hope you've got good dental coverage, 'cause those things will rot your teeth." He paused, for half a heartbeat. "If you're not careful."

"I think there are more dangers than bad teeth."

"Maybe."

Digger shrugged, then paid for his purchases and headed for the door.

Alec grabbed a napkin and scribbled a number on it. "I'll be right back," he said to the clerk and hurried out the door after the other man. "Wait."

The big man stopped, turning slowly.

"My name's Alec," he said. "Alec Donovan." He shoved the napkin into Digger's shirt pocket. "This is for your son, for Ryan. And for his friend. I can help. In case all those candy bars rot his teeth. Call anytime."

XXV

Voices pulled at him. Distant. Hushed. Dragging him up toward . . . toward something he couldn't remember. Something important. He tried reaching them, but the darkness beckoned as well. A deep depth of silence that promised oblivion and peace. While the voices echoed with fear and memories best left forgotten. He wavered, caught between two worlds.

In the end, he chose the darkness.

Pain pulled him from the dark place a second time. Hours. Days. Years later. He didn't know or care. It drew him toward the surface with a slow recognition of a body. His? Damaged and hurting. No voices this time. Just the agony of awareness. Like a living, breathing entity, separate from himself, yet part of him as well. He couldn't remember what it was like not to feel pain, to live without it. Nor could he remember where it started. When? Or how?

It just existed.

He reached for the darkness, but it eluded him. Until the body moved. And the pain streaked through him, bringing momentary clarity. And memory.

Just before the darkness took him again.

When Ryan finally came back to himself, there was nothing gradual about it. Suddenly he was awake, conscious of the world around him and the way his body ached with each breath. He opened his eyes, but there was little difference between the darkness he'd just left and that which surrounded him.

His memories came intact as well. His decision to make a run for it. Going to Cody's room. Their race across the wet grass, the dark trees beckoning, promising freedom. The black shadow of a dog. His teeth viciously tearing at Ryan's arm. Cody facing the animal with nothing more lethal than a jagged stick. The crack of a rifle shot and spray of blood that had saved both boys' lives.

All relived like pieces of a film Ryan wished he hadn't seen.

He preferred the emptiness, but it was too late for that. As his eyes adjusted, the black eased to gray, revealing the boundaries of his world. Though not a cell, it was without question a prison. Four stone walls and a floor of cold concrete. A door he didn't need to try to know it was locked. No window. And a cot, where they'd put him to await whatever fate the General doled out.

They *would* kill him.

He had no doubt and could only wonder why he was still breathing. Unless the voiceless men who guarded this place waited on the General's order. Or his presence.

Funny, that the thought of dying no longer frightened Ryan. He was so tired. Tired of simply breathing. If he could make it happen with just a wish, he'd stop the air from filling his lungs.

But the body—his body, he reminded himself—refused to let go, leaving him trapped in its shell of agony.

He guessed he was in one of the mansion's deep cellars. He'd been down to the basement before, once while looking for a stray kitten the dogs had chased into hiding. But he'd never been this far down, never been tempted to explore beyond the cook's store of canned goods.

He thought of Cody.

Where would they have put him? Back in his own room? Why not? He was a valuable piece of merchandise, and without Ryan's help, the boy wasn't going anywhere.

Suddenly, there was a rattling at the door. Keys. And the turn of a lock.

Ryan closed his eyes. Better to let them think he was still asleep.

The door opened, squeaking on its ancient hinges.

"Still asleep." A woman's voice, familiar. Yet Ryan wouldn't risk opening his eyes to confirm the housekeeper's presence.

Except, the smell of food teased him.

"Wake him. There's not much time." A second voice, male, but not unkind. And Ryan remembered the hushed voices from his dream.

Still, fear kept his eyes closed. Though the food was closer now, set on something near the cot. And he remembered Cody's determination to keep up his strength by eating.

A weight settled beside him. A rough hand touched his face.

"Boy. You must wake." The woman again, the housekeeper who'd let him take her key without reporting him.

He opened his eyes, the light they'd brought with them hurting and making him squint.

She smiled. "See, he pretends only."

The man standing over them grunted and moved back to the door, which had been left partway open.

"You are well?" she asked, with more English than Ryan had known she could speak. Evidently he wasn't the only one with secrets in this place.

"I'm alive," he answered. "But no, not well."

Another grunt from the butler near the door. "He will live."

"Only if he goes," said the woman in response.

Ryan shifted his eyes back to her. "Is Cody all right?"

"Cody? The boy? Yes. Though angry."

Ryan almost smiled at the image, picturing the younger boy yelling and screaming, pounding at the hard wooden door until the General's guards were tempted to shoot him and be done with it.

"It was a brave thing you tried," she said. "Very brave."

"Stupid," came the rumble from the door, and Ryan had to agree with the man's assessment. Though he knew he'd do it again if given the chance. At some point he couldn't name, he'd crossed some invisible line and couldn't go back.

"The dogs," he said. "I used rat poison to put them to sleep. What happened?"

"Asleep? No. The . . ." She searched for the English word. "Female? Yes? She ate poison. Is dead."

That saddened him. He hadn't wanted to kill the animals, no matter how much he feared and hated them. "But I put the poison in both food dishes."

She shrugged. "A guard fed other meat. He not eat dog food."

"And is he . . . ?"

"*Ja.* The guard is good shot. Come." She reached behind his shoulders to lift him. It hurt to move, but her hands were both gentle and strong, so he ignored the discomfort and let her ease him into a sitting position. She set the tray on his lap. Rich stew. Thick bread. Cody could have his Whoppers.

"Eat now." She gathered a spoonful of stew for him, but he

took the utensil away from her. He had one good hand, his clumsy left, but he could still feed himself.

"Good." She nodded her approval. "Get strong. Tomorrow you go."

"Go?" He managed a mouthful without spilling any. "What do you mean 'go'? How?"

"We have way." She nodded toward the man standing watch at the door. "Herrick take you."

"But the General. He'll send you home. Or worse."

"Maybe." She shrugged. "Maybe not. I stupid country woman. I cook. I clean. I know nothing about bad boys."

Ryan grinned, almost laughed. Except he knew he'd pay for it if he did. "Were you the one who helped me the night Trader was here? After he . . ." *Beat the shit out of me.*

"Herrick found you. Carried you to your room. I . . ." She touched his freshly bandaged chest.

"And the food and aspirin. And this?" Ryan lifted his right arm, bound tightly where the dog had mauled him.

"No more talk." She nodded toward the tray, indicating he should eat. He did, gladly, quickly, imagining himself getting stronger with each mouthful. When he finished, she took the tray and started for the door.

"Wait," he said, not wanting them to leave. "What's your name?" He couldn't believe he'd lived here two years, in the same house with this kind woman, and didn't even know her name.

"Felda."

"Thank you, Felda."

She gave a smile, broad and warm. But as the door closed behind her and darkness settled back around him, fear crept in as well. And anger. He'd been better off before Felda and Herrick's visit because they'd given him hope, which was so much harder than surrender.

XXVI

CATHY HART MET THEM in McLean, the next town north of Arlington, in a strip-mall parking lot. From there, Erin followed her through predawn suburban streets to a small, unremarkable two-story house set among a neighborhood of similar houses. Agent Hart had claimed it had only recently been added to the FBI's ever-shifting number of safe houses.

They parked inside the garage, closing the doors behind them before climbing out of their cars.

"Where are we?" Claire asked, waking as Erin opened her door.

"Someplace safe. Come on." She helped Claire out of the car and into the house. It was a drab place, sparsely furnished and smelling of industrial cleanser.

Agent Hart had just finished making a sweep of the house. When she saw Erin and Claire, she holstered a 9mm automatic, her expression apologetic.

"Hi, Claire," she said. "I'm Special Agent Cathy Hart, with the FBI. And I'm here to help keep you and your sister safe."

Claire glanced at Erin, who nodded.

"Let's sit down for a minute." Cathy moved toward the kitchen. "And I'll explain what's going on."

The three women settled on chrome-and-vinyl chairs around an old Formica table, Claire's hand tight in Erin's.

"There'll be four agents here at all times," Cathy explained, still talking to Claire. Kindly. But like one adult to another instead of the way most people talked to Claire, as if she was a child. "Two on the inside, two out. We do this all the time. No one will get past them."

"What about you?" Claire asked.

"I'll be checking in regularly, but I'm going to spend most of my time trying to find the man you saw yesterday."

"And you'll catch him," Claire said.

Cathy hesitated. "I'll do my best."

Claire studied her for a moment, then nodded, accepting that she could expect no more.

"Meanwhile," Cathy said, "I'd like to ask you a few questions."

Claire tensed.

"I know you're tired, but anything you can tell me will help."

Claire visibly struggled, and Erin tightened her hold, willing her strength to pass to her sister. But Erin wouldn't push, wouldn't ask anything more from Claire than she could willingly give. It had to be her decision, one way or the other.

"I know it's hard on you, Claire," Cathy said, again kindly.

"Yes." Claire's voice was shaky but determined. "But you have to catch him, don't you? And you can't do that without me."

"You're right." Cathy's expression tightened. "He must be stopped. He's . . . a very evil man."

"Yes, that's a good way to describe him." For once, Claire sounded certain, mature, like the woman she would have become if things had been different.

"Tell me about him."

"I don't remember much." Claire closed her eyes, her hand trembling as she concentrated on some vision only she could see. "Except his hands. They were so . . . quick."

"Was he tall?"

"Yes. And very clean."

For the next fifteen minutes, Cathy asked questions, and Claire answered, doing her best, exhibiting a reserve of courage Erin hadn't known her sister possessed. But in the end, her answers wouldn't help find the Magician. She described two different men, contradicting one answer with the next, mixing a little girl's memories with those of the woman.

To her credit, Agent Hart showed none of the disappointment she must have felt. Instead, she rested a hand on Claire's and smiled. "Thank you, Claire. You've been a great help. And I promise I won't stop until I find him."

Claire beamed, her eyes filling with tears. She'd just triumphed over a fear that had held her captive for years.

"Get some sleep," Cathy said, removing her hand and looking suddenly very tired herself.

Alone upstairs, Claire let Erin help her out of the blue dress and into bed. "I'm so proud of you," Erin said. "I know that was hard."

Claire smiled tightly. "I want to go home. To the house you bought for Janie and Marta."

Erin settled on the bed next to her sister. "You will. Just as soon as we catch him."

"Promise me."

"If that's what you want, yes, I promise." Erin brushed the hair from her sister's face. "When this is over, I'll take you home."

Claire smiled, her eyes closing, the drugs they'd given her still in her system.

Erin stayed until Claire drifted off, thinking of the changes she'd seen in her sister. Were they new, or something Erin had just not noticed? Things between them had always been tense. Had she closed her eyes to the reality of Claire, seeing only the broken child instead of the woman she'd become?

It was an uncomfortable question, but one Erin couldn't ignore. It involved looking into the damaged parts of her own psyche. And she wasn't sure she'd like what she found.

Not tonight, though. Not until this was finished.

Erin went back downstairs, where Agent Hart was unloading groceries. She was a petite woman, blond, and might have been described as perky in her younger years, before the FBI had recast her features into a sterner mask. Now she was all business and obviously not pleased with Erin's role in all this. She'd been kind to Claire, however, and because of that, Erin could forgive a lot.

Noticing her standing in the doorway, Cathy said, "There's enough food here for several days."

"Thank you. For everything."

"I'm not doing this for you, Officer Baker. It's for your sister. No child should have to live through what she did. And I won't let him put his hands on her again."

Nor would she, Erin silently swore. But aloud she said, "Fair enough."

Cathy finished storing the groceries and brushed by Erin on the way to the living room. Glancing at her watch, she said, "The first two teams should be here any minute."

"Will you be leaving then?"

"I'm going out to Gentle Oaks. Not that I expect we'll find anything. The Magician is probably long gone."

"Even if he *is* there," Erin added, "you won't recognize him."

"No, but you and your sister will." She hesitated, then said, "I have to know what you're planning. Will you stay here with your sister and let us handle this?" Even though she'd phrased it as a question, Cathy sounded like she already knew the answer.

Erin turned to the windows, the outside world blocked by faded heavy curtains in avocado and gold, a relic of a long-gone decorating fashion.

She had no idea what to do next.

Her instincts urged her to steal into Neville's home and put a knife to his throat. He'd talk then. Or die. But in the end, who would that help? Not Claire. And not Cody Sanders.

She rubbed a hand back through her hair. "I need a few hours' sleep. Then I'll . . . think of something."

Cathy looked at her, surprise in her eyes.

"What?" Erin laughed shortly. "You thought I had all the answers."

"No, but I believed you thought you did."

Erin dropped into a nearby chair. "I have no answers, Agent Hart. None. I'm not an investigator. I don't know how to catch criminals or solve cases. It's not what I was trained for."

She leaned her head back and closed her eyes. She was so tired. "I know how to hunt and how to run. How to fight and kill. How to survive." She lifted her head, refocusing on the other woman. "I'm good at all those things. But someone else tells me where to go and what to do. This"—she made a sweeping gesture with her hand—"is so far out of my league."

"So why are you doing it?"

"Because I can't let it go. Because he took my sister and who knows how many others. I'm going to make him pay for that and make sure he can never hurt another child again."

Cathy studied her for a moment, then turned away.

"The last thing I knew," she said after a few moments of silence, "Donovan was planning to stake out both Neville's house in Georgetown and his estate in Middleburg. It's impossible for one man to watch two places at once. He could use an extra set of eyes."

Erin felt something unclench in her chest.

"Before that, though, you're probably going back out to Gentle Oaks. If the Magician's still there, which I doubt, you're our best chance of seeing him."

Erin realized this woman's kindness extended beyond broken children like Claire; it included damaged warriors like herself. "I'll do that."

Cathy turned back. Smiled at Erin. For the first time. "After you get some sleep, that is."

Erin slept like the dead, four hours, though she'd only allotted herself three. When she awoke it was midmorning, and the first thing she wanted was a phone. She needed to call Marta and Janie in Miami. They were supposed to come home today, and Erin had to stop them from getting on that plane. Calling from a safe house, however, was a sure way to reveal its location. So she'd have to wait until she could get to a pay phone.

Meanwhile, she checked on Claire, discovering her bed empty and made. Voices drew her downstairs, where she found her sister bustling around the kitchen, cooking breakfast for two strangers, a man and woman, sitting at the kitchen table.

"Morning, sleepyhead," Claire called when she spotted Erin. "Want some breakfast?"

"Your sister makes great blueberry pancakes," said the man.

A little stunned, Erin couldn't reply. She had no idea Claire even knew what a frying pan was, much less how to use one.

The female agent must have detected her confusion because she pulled out her identification. "Sorry, Ms. Baker. I'm Special Agent Randle, and this Neanderthal is Agent Nolan."

The man smiled sheepishly and started to reach into his pocket. Erin stopped him. "That's okay, I believe you. I'm just a little groggy."

"She makes great coffee, too," he said, lifting his cup from the table.

"That," Erin said, "sounds good." Though her thoughts were far from food or coffee, because she suddenly realized that in her hurry to get Claire beyond the Magician's reach, she'd put her sister in a different kind of danger. From herself.

Had these agents even been briefed on Claire, on the mood swings and depression that could surface at any time? Did they know she could appear perfectly fine, then lock herself in a bathroom and take a razor blade to her skin? Erin had been living with her sister's illness too long to trust the smiles and easy-going banter.

"I hate to interrupt your breakfast, Agent Randle," she said, "but could I speak with you for a minute?"

Randle put down her coffee cup and started to stand. "Of course."

"She's going to tell you to keep an eye on me," Claire said, her eyes locking on Erin. "Aren't you?"

Erin wished she could deny it. "I'm sorry, Claire. But this is the first time you've been out of the hospital for . . . a very long time."

Claire lifted her chin. "Nearly seven years."

"Yes." Erin felt the weight of those years, the torment of Claire's half-lived life.

"My sister is afraid I'll start cutting myself," Claire said to the agents, who'd watched the exchange in stunned silence. "And she's right." She looked back at Erin. "I fight the urge every day, every minute of every day."

Tears welled in Erin's eyes, her heart breaking for her sister and the nightmare she endured.

"So," Claire went on, turning back to the agents once again, "she wants you to keep a close eye on me." She paused, looking from one to the other before letting her gaze resettle on Erin. "And I want it, too." She smiled at Erin. "Is that about it?"

Erin nodded, unable to speak. Finally, she said, "That sums it up." She hesitated. "I love you, Claire." And had never meant it more in her life.

"Me, too, big sis." Claire grinned. "Now go get cleaned up."

Forty-five minutes later, after a quick shower and some food she ate only because of Claire's insistence, Erin left her sister in FBI hands. And as she was heading out, Claire was beating them soundly at poker. Which made Erin wonder just what the staff at Gentle Oaks had been teaching her sister.

First thing, she stopped at a pay phone. Of course, once Marta heard a modified version of what was happening, she wanted to come home immediately. Two of her chicks were in danger, and she wanted to gather them close. It was only by playing the Janie card that Erin got Marta even to consider staying in Miami.

"Just for a few days," Erin said. "The FBI will have this man in custody, and it will be safe for you and Janie to come home."

She could hear Marta's hesitation. "What about Claire? How is she holding up?"

Erin thought of Claire making pancakes and beating a couple of FBI agents at cards. "She's doing really well. In fact, she wants to move home when this is all over."

"Really?" And that was the promise that finally convinced Marta to stay put. If she waited a few days, until things settled down, she'd have all three of her chicks under one roof.

After hanging up, Erin headed for Gentle Oaks. To her surprise, it looked just as it always had. Quiet. Serene. With no signs of the FBI investigation Cathy Hart had promised.

In the lobby, however, the receptionist was expecting her. "Both Dr. Schaeffer and Agent Hart want to see you, Ms. Baker."

"Where is she?"

The woman frowned, obviously not pleased with having the FBI around. Or Erin. "In the conference room, interviewing employees."

"I'll start with Dr. Schaeffer, then. But will you tell Agent Hart I'm here?"

Another frown, but the woman escorted her back to the administration wing.

Dr. Schaeffer rose as she entered his office, crossing the room to take her hand. "Erin, what is going on here? The FBI is all over our records, talking to our employees."

Erin pulled her hand from his. "I'm sorry, Dr. Schaeffer, if the FBI has disrupted you or your staff."

"Yes, well, everyone is very upset. I've tried to tell Agent Hart that Claire is unstable, and nothing she says can be taken too seriously. Of all people, you should understand that. The very idea that she saw this man is ridiculous."

"I saw him as well."

He looked surprised. "You?"

"Yes, I was in the Glades Park with Claire the day he took her. And I saw the same man a couple of days ago in a park in Arlington."

"Erin, that was nineteen years ago. Your memory is playing tricks on you."

"It was the same man, Dr. Schaeffer. Now, I need to know who else had access to Claire yesterday."

He sighed and dropped into his desk chair. "That's the same question the FBI has been asking, and I'll tell you what I told them. Other than you and your family, no one but the staff has access to Claire." He lifted his hands, palms up, in exasperation. "And Agent Hart has the employee files and has been going through them all morning."

"There must be somebody." Erin folded her arms, looked at

the chair across from him, but knew she was too edgy to sit. She had all she could do to keep from pacing. "Someone new?"

He shook his head. "I can personally vouch for all my employees. We only hire—"

She cut him off. "Think, Dr. Schaeffer." She moved to his desk and rested her hands on the edge. "What about people visiting other patients? Could one of them have slipped into Claire's room? Maybe someone on the grounds crew? Or the kitchen staff?"

Pressing his lips together, he continued to shake his head. "We are very strict about that kind of thing, Erin. We never—" He suddenly stopped. "Wait, there was someone." He paused. "No, that can't be it."

She went still. "Who?"

"No, it's impossible."

"*Who,* Dr. Schaeffer?" It took all her willpower to keep from leaping across the desk and grabbing him by the collar.

"Well, Dr. Holmes was here yesterday. He spoke to Claire, but as I said, Dr. Holmes is . . ."

Coldness crept into her voice. "Is what?"

"He's a highly respected psychiatrist, who's just in town for a couple of days. He's attending a seminar in D.C. and wanted to see . . ." It hit him then. She could see it in his eyes.

"Claire?" Erin made an effort to remain calm.

"Yes, but—"

"Did he ask to *see* Claire?"

Fear had replaced the shock on Schaeffer's face. "I was with him the entire time. He didn't touch her."

No. He wouldn't. Not with witnesses around. "Is he still here?" Not daring to hope.

"He was this morning."

She pulled out the 9mm Beretta and checked the clip.

"What are you doing with that?"

"Whatever's necessary." Then, at his look of horror, she added, "Don't worry, I know how to use it."

She shoved the weapon back into the waistband of her jeans. "Let's go find this Dr. Holmes." She grabbed Schaeffer's arm and half pushed, half pulled him into the hall.

That's when Schaeffer seemed to get himself together, shaking free of her hold and straightening his jacket. "Shouldn't we let Agent Hart know about this?"

"She won't have a clue who to look for." *And she might get in my way.*

"And you will?"

"I told you, I've seen him."

Schaeffer pursed his lips, obviously doubting her, but no longer arguing. "I expect he's visiting with one of the patients. This way." He started down the hall toward the dayroom.

He wasn't there. Neither Schaeffer's Dr. Holmes, nor the man Erin knew as the Magician.

"He could be in one of the patients' rooms," Schaeffer said, and snagged a passing nurse. "Carol, have you seen Dr. Holmes?"

"Yes, Doctor. He's outside with Tara."

"Thank you," he said, hurrying to catch up to Erin, who was already moving toward the large doors leading to the patio.

Outside, Erin scanned the patients and staff scattered about the yard. At a distance, no one looked familiar. She needed to see the Magician up close or in motion in order to recognize him.

"There he is." Dr. Schaeffer nodded toward a tall man, garbed in the typical white jacket, across the expanse of manicured lawn. "With Tara."

"Are you sure?"

"Of course, I'd know Dr. Holmes anywhere."

That surprised her. She'd assumed Holmes was a fake. "You mean you know him?"

"Well, not personally. Or I didn't. But I've attended several of his lectures."

She took a deep breath. Was it too much to hope that they'd not only found the Magician but identified him as well?

"Okay, Doctor, I want you to go back inside and get Agent Hart. Tell her we've found the Magician."

He seemed ready to argue.

"Just do it," she emphasized.

He hesitated, not used to taking orders, then disappeared into the building.

Erin pulled out her weapon, holding it close to her leg, and started toward the couple. They were on the opposite side of the grounds, near the boundary between the grass and the trees. As she passed an orderly and an old woman in a wheelchair, the man's eyes widened at the sight of the gun.

"Get her inside," Erin said, without taking her eyes off Dr. Holmes and the woman with him.

The orderly obeyed.

Erin stopped a few hundred yards away from the distinguished doctor and Schaeffer's patient. "Dr. Holmes. Move away from her."

He looked up, surprised, then smiled. And she knew. Though they looked nothing alike, she'd seen him at least twice before. Once in Jamestown Park, three days ago. And before that in Miami, nineteen years ago.

"Is something the matter, Officer Baker?"

"Just step away from the woman. Slowly."

"And let you shoot me?"

The woman looked at Erin for the first time, her face registering shock. "She has a gun. Oh, my God. Dr. Holmes, that woman has a gun."

PATRICIA LEWIN

"You're frightening her, Officer Baker."

"She has nothing to do with this, Holmes. It's between you and me."

He raised his hands, mocking her. "Don't shoot."

"Oh, my God. Oh, my God." The woman folded in on herself, rocking in place.

"No one's going to get shot." Though Erin's finger itched on the gun at her side. "Just step away, Holmes."

"Whatever you say." He backed away, keeping the woman between them, easing around until he was just on the edge of the trees. His smile broadened. "I wasn't expecting to see you today, Erin. But since you're here . . ." Then he turned, darting into the woods.

Erin raised her gun, and the woman screamed.

"Damn." Erin couldn't fire and risk hitting the hysterical patient. Dropping the gun back to her side, she took off after him, leaving the woman's shrill voice behind.

Within a few feet, the woods closed in around her. Cool. Dark. And dense. She slowed. Leading with the gun, she kept moving. Ahead, a strip of white, and she picked up her pace. It was his coat, draped like a flag over a bush.

Silence. Not even the sound of insects.

He was close. She could feel him watching her, the sensation crawling over her skin. Then movement to her right, and she spun around as a blue blur disappeared into the trees.

She followed, breathing deeply to still the fear nudging at her insides. He was leading her deeper into the woods and farther away from the hospital grounds and help.

Behind her, a twig snapped.

Erin pivoted with the gun. Again. Nothing.

He was toying with her, making her jumpy. And it was working. She needed calm. Fear was a killer.

"Come on, Dr. Holmes," she said, using words to bolster her courage. "Let's not make this harder than it needs to be.

There's no way out. You can't hide anymore. We know who you are."

She sensed his amusement, like that day on the trail, floating toward her across the silence and sending a chill down her spine. Stirring fear. It was his specialty. His special gift. Knowing that, however, did little to ease hers.

To her right again, a rustling of bushes. She swung around, barely keeping herself from firing. Panic. She had to fight it. It would kill her, like fear, only faster.

In the distance, she heard shouts from the hospital grounds and clung to the sound.

"Hear that," she said. "Pretty soon these woods will be crawling with FBI agents." *Only two,* whispered the fear. *And too far away.* "Make it easy on yourself and surrender. That way, no one will get hurt."

Too late she sensed it. The swoosh of air. As something hard came down on her hands, breaking her gun grip. Sending it skittering into the underbrush. Pain rippling up her arms. So fast. She'd only begun to react, to turn toward the assault, when a heavy stick slammed into her head, buckling her knees, dazing her.

She saw the next strike coming. The black boot. And tried to roll. Her body responding in slow motion. And the kick caught her in the shoulder, sending her sprawling.

Then he was on her, one hand in her hair, the other wrenching her arm behind her back, pressing her face into the moldy forest floor.

"And here I thought you were going to be a challenge." His breath was hot and sickly on her cheek.

"Let me up, you son of a bitch."

"I don't think so. You see, you ruined everything, all my plans. Claire was supposed to die first."

Erin shoved against him with all her strength, but his hold was too tight, too secure. "Haven't you hurt her enough?"

"I wasn't going to touch her. She was going to do it herself. Fitting, don't you think?"

"I'll kill you, you—"

"Such brave words. Or is it just anger I hear in your voice, knowing you won't be there to protect your sister next time I go for her? Or little Janie?"

A blinding rage ripped through her. And frustration.

Suddenly, from the direction of the hospital, she heard shouts. And found a thread of hope. "They're coming for you," she said, the words coming out in a broken gasp, the pain in her arm, her shoulder, making it difficult to speak. But she forced the words out. "And you're going to pay for every child you hurt."

"Maybe." He wrenched her arm a little higher, a little more painfully, and she bit her tongue to keep from keening in pain. "But they won't be in time to save you."

Again, the sounds of approaching voices gave her strength, and she opened her mouth to scream. Again, she was too slow. And saw the big silver ring seconds before it slammed into her temple.

Everything went black.

XXVII

THEY BROUGHT HER out on a stretcher.

Alec met them at the edge of the woods, taking in her pale features, her bandaged wrists, the angry red lump and ragged cut across her temple.

"Jesus," he whispered.

"Yeah," said one of the paramedics. "She's lucky to be alive. That blow to the temple could have killed her. If he'd had better aim, it would have."

"What about her wrists?" Alec asked.

"Can't be sure without an X ray, but they look to be severely bruised, not broken."

Erin's eyes opened, disoriented and unfocused. Then they found Alec's, and she blinked into awareness. "Holmes?" Her voice was weak and hoarse.

"We're combing the woods and surrounding area," Alec answered. "And we've set up roadblocks. We'll get him."

She stirred, as if trying to rise, and Alec pressed her back down. "Don't try to move. You're in pretty bad shape."

"Just need some aspirin." She lifted a trembling hand to her temple. "Feels like he stomped on my head."

They'd reached the parking lot, and the paramedics set the stretcher atop a collapsible gurney behind the ambulance.

"Can we have a few minutes?" Alec asked.

"Sure." The paramedics disappeared, and Erin again tried to sit up.

"Will you stop?" Alec again refused to let her rise. "We've already established that you're Superwoman, you don't need to keep proving it."

She frowned at him, a sure sign she was going to live. "What are you doing here, anyway? I thought you were off watching Neville."

"I was. But Agent Hart contacted me about Claire, and I thought I could help out here."

"Well, you're too late. The bad guy's already fled the scene."

He had to smile, though he'd already kicked himself for not getting there sooner. Before Erin. Or at least before she'd gone chasing after Holmes in the woods. If Alec hadn't stopped at his motel for a shower and a few hours' sleep, he would have arrived first.

"Did you find out anything about Neville?" she asked.

He hesitated. She needed rest, not more to worry about.

"Donovan, tell me."

She still sounded tired and weak, but determined, and he knew she wouldn't let up. So he told her about the graves on Neville's property and his encounter with Digger.

He glanced at his watch. "I thought he'd call by now. He's unhappy about whatever's going on out there, and I think he's on the verge of asking for help."

"Give him time. Meanwhile, we need to find out whose bodies are in those graves."

"*We* don't need to do anything. You're going to the hospi-

tal for X rays and observation. I'll find out about the graves."
Though he hadn't yet figured out how.

Cathy joined them, having obviously overheard the last
part of their conversation, and said, "Why not go to Neville
and ask his permission to dig up the graves? He's not going to
refuse. If he does, he'll look guilty."

"She's right," Erin agreed, again attempting to sit up, and
this time succeeding only because Cathy gave her a hand.

Alec shot the other agent a look meant to maim.

"All he can do is refuse," Erin was saying as she gripped the
side of the gurney. "And I don't think he will. He's just arrogant
enough to let us. He'll either claim no knowledge or diplomatic
immunity."

"You okay?" Cathy asked.

"Just a little dizzy."

Cathy held up a plastic evidence bag, containing a 9mm
Beretta. "Is this yours?"

"A lot of good it did me."

"Don't be too hard on yourself. It looks like he did a number on your wrists."

Erin lifted her bandaged arms, her disgust obvious. "Yeah."

"The gun's evidence," Cathy said, "so I can't return it to
you right now, but you'll get it back later. Anything else out
there we should be looking for?"

"Just whatever club he used to hit me with."

Cathy smiled tightly and nodded, then to Alec said, "What
about Neville?"

"I'll pay him a visit," Alec agreed.

"I'm going," Erin said.

"No, you're not." Then, directly to Cathy, he said, "Officer
Baker needs to go to the hospital."

"Help me down," Erin said to Cathy, ignoring him. "I'm
going with Donovan."

Alec tried again. "You're in no condition to go anywhere."

Ignoring him, she slid off the gurney, Cathy taking one hand, Alec grabbing the other when he saw she was going to try to stand, with or without his help.

"This is not a good idea," he said.

"Just give me a minute," she replied. "If I can't walk, then I'll do what you say and go to the hospital." She tried a tentative step, then another. Although she looked like she'd had a few too many, she kept her feet under her.

"Okay," she admitted. "I may not be ready to drive, but I can walk."

In the end, he agreed to let her come along. He knew if he didn't, she'd find some other way to get to Washington and into Neville's face.

The paramedic had protested, as had Dr. Schaeffer after a quick examination. Neither man had any better luck than Alec at changing her mind. So, with warnings about possible sleepiness or nausea, Erin climbed into the front seat of Alec's FBI-issued Taurus.

Cathy remained behind to oversee the manhunt for Jacob Holmes and start the investigation into his past. With luck she'd be able to either confirm or eliminate him as the Magician.

They drove for about fifteen minutes without speaking, then Alec glanced at her to see how she was holding up. She sat with her head against the headrest, her eyes closed.

"Are you okay?" he asked.

"I'm not sleeping, Donovan. Just waiting for the aspirin to kick in."

"Are you sure you don't want to go to a hospital?"

"Positive. Except for the mother of all headaches, I'm fine."

Another hesitation, then he asked, "What happened out there?"

At first, he thought she wouldn't answer. Then she said,

"Did you know I give martial-arts demonstrations to ex-military types?"

He didn't, but it didn't surprise him either.

"I show them how someone my size can take down some-one a lot bigger." She paused. "And in every class some form of the same question always comes up. Usually from one of the women, because the men, well, they never consider the possi-bility. But the women—they live every day with the realities of their sex.

"Anyway, the question is always something like, what hap-pens, Officer Baker, when you run into someone just as good but bigger? How do you come away in one piece?"

"What's your answer?"

"I tell them it comes down to one simple factor. Who gets meaner quicker." She looked at Alec then, and he saw true fear in her eyes. "That's what happened. I never even saw him coming, and by the time I knew I was in a fight for my life, it was already over." She closed her eyes again. "He got meaner quicker."

For long moments, the silence settled around them as the car sped east toward Washington. Overhead, clouds moved in to ob-scure the sunlight, promising a dreary afternoon. Along the road, the first flash of fall had touched the trees. Almost overnight.

He thought of the woman sitting in the passenger seat be-side him. The more time he spent with her, the more she in-trigued him. She was complex, made up of layers upon layers, overlapping and entwined.

He'd seen the warrior first. It was the person she showed the world, her strength a shell that protected her and kept everyone else at a distance. But he'd seen flashes of the nurturer as well, the woman who took care of her broken sister and young niece, vulnerable and compassionate, the guilt tearing at her from the inside, carefully hidden.

Now he'd just gotten his first glimpse of the woman facing her own mortality, and he found himself wanting to step between her and whatever threatened her.

"You're lucky to be alive," he said, careful not to look at her in case she could read his thoughts.

"Yes."

"Why was he still there?"

She turned her head to look at him, without lifting it from the seat.

"I mean . . ." Alec hesitated. "If he'd gone to Gentle Oaks to kill Claire, and you got to her first, then why stick around? Why wait for you to come looking for him?"

"Maybe he thought I'd bring Claire back, or he could find out where I'd taken her." She turned her head and closed her eyes again.

He thought about it, and threw out another possibility. "Maybe he was waiting for you."

She shook her head. "I don't think so. He looked surprised to see me, and he told me Claire was supposed to die first."

"First?"

For a moment she didn't answer. "Yeah," she said finally. "It seems I messed up his plans."

General Neville's butler allowed them into the front hall of the Georgetown mansion, though he wasn't happy about it. Alec's badge had no effect. The man obviously knew the FBI had no jurisdiction over his employer and wasn't even moderately intimidated. Finally, it was their simple refusal to leave the premises before seeing Neville that got them through the door.

They waited. Ten minutes. Fifteen.

Erin lowered herself onto the front steps because there was nowhere else to sit. Alec fumed at her because she belonged in a hospital, and at Neville for leaving them waiting, no doubt just because he could. Alec considered barging through the house looking for the man but thought better of it. That action, of course, would be stupid enough to land his ass behind bars.

Finally, after forty-five minutes, the butler reappeared, shooting Erin a disapproving look where she rested on the front steps. "General Neville will see you now."

Alec could tell the words pained the man, but he led them down a narrow hallway and through a set of double doors into William Neville's study.

Everything about the room screamed money. Dark, heavy furniture. Rugs worth more than Alec earned in a year. Artwork that looked familiar enough to be authentic and original. Even the man himself, sitting behind an ornately carved wooden desk, impeccably groomed and polished.

He kept them waiting again as he perused some papers on his desk and signed a couple of others. Alec had about run out of patience when Erin lost hers.

"Excuse us, General," she said, "but we really don't have all day."

He looked up then. Smiled. "Why, Ms. Baker, how good it is to see you again. And you're looking particularly lovely this afternoon."

"You like it?" There was an edge to her voice that hadn't been there the night of the embassy party. "It's the barroom-brawl look. I thought maybe you had arranged it for me."

"Me? No. Although I have to tell you, I'm not surprised someone else did. It was only a matter of time."

She opened her mouth to respond, but Alec touched her arm to remind her why they were here. Then he pulled out his identification and flipped it open. "General, I'm Special Agent Alec Donovan—"

"Yes, yes," Neville interrupted. "I know who you are,

Agent Donovan. You've been entertaining Ms. Baker here ever since that unfortunate incident with the missing girl. So what does the United States FBI want with me?"

"Just information." Alec returned the leather ID to his jacket pocket, not bothering to question Neville about how he knew him. Or Chelsea Madden. Asking would only exaggerate the farce.

"We have a report that several of your household staff were burying bodies on your property in Middleburg last night."

"A report?" Neville leaned back in his chair, tenting his fingers beneath his chin.

"Yes, sir."

"And where did you get such a report?" Neville spread his hands before leaning forward and folding them on his desk. "I would hate to think that the U.S. government was spying on its foreign diplomats." Of course, surveillance of that kind was standard operating procedure, though everyone pretended otherwise.

"The information came from hikers who wandered onto your property by mistake."

"At night?"

"They were lost." He could feel Erin's impatience beside him, but she held her tongue. Fortunately. And her temper. Alec understood. It took all his resolve to remain polite—when he would have preferred stringing up this guy by his silk necktie.

"Of course. And now you want to know about the bodies."

"I'm certain we want the same thing, General."

"I doubt it." Neville arched an eyebrow. "Besides, I already know what bodies are in those graves, Agent Donovan."

Of course you do. "Would you care to enlighten us?"

"If you like." Again he leaned back in his chair, relaxed and confident. "I lost two of my dogs yesterday. Loyal, good animals. The first was poisoned. By your hikers perhaps?" He shifted his attention to Erin, briefly, then refocused on Alec.

"And the second was shot before he could maul a trespasser. Again, maybe your hikers know something of that."

"I'm sorry to hear about your pets, General—"

"Not pets, Agent Donovan. Guard dogs."

"We'd still like your permission to dig up the graves, General."

Neville studied them, then dismissed them with a flick of his wrist. "A waste of time. But it is your time." Nodding to one of his men, he added, "Accompany Agent Donovan and Ms. Baker out to the estate and make sure everyone cooperates with them."

"Will you be joining us, General?" Alec asked.

"I am afraid not," he said. "I'm leaving your country to-morrow, and I have work to do."

Alec would have preferred watching Neville's reaction to the graves, but he couldn't insist. So he expressed his gratitude, and he and Erin followed two men in a dark sedan, the same two Alec had seen the night before while watching the George-town address.

About thirty miles outside the city, it started to rain. A slow, steady drizzle that was somehow harder to take than a down-pour. They rode in silence for some time, the wipers clicking against the windshield, the tires streaming across wet asphalt.

"That was too easy," Erin said finally.

"Yep. Makes me think we're going to find dogs in those graves." A good thing, though it got them no further with the hunt for Cody Sanders.

"Maybe he's already moved the bodies you saw buried last night."

"And killed his dogs to cover it up?" He shook his head. "I don't think so. No, I think Neville's telling the truth." Alec paused, running the previous night's events through his mind. "But those dogs hurt someone before they died. Digger bought enough medical supplies to stock a small emergency room."

"Cody?"

Alec considered. "Possibly. But Digger talked about his son, and called him Ryan. Though I'm willing to bet he knows something about Cody. He reacted when I used the name and said his son had a friend named Cody."

They'd arrived, following the other car through the gates. As they passed the mansion, Erin said, "Looks like something out of a horror movie."

"Yeah."

"I think we need to get a look at more than just those graves."

He glanced at her. "It's a good way to get yourself killed." Though he'd thought the same thing himself.

She wasn't fooled. "Tell me you wouldn't go in if you knew that boy was inside."

He couldn't, and they both knew it.

"I counted eight armed guards," she said. "Including the two at the gate. It's not an army."

"And the cameras?"

"Near the gatehouse. Along the perimeter of the trees. Ringing the house. No doubt they'd see us coming."

"As I said, it's a death trap."

"Maybe." She shrugged. "And maybe we don't have a choice. Not if we want to see who or what is buried in those graves."

They stopped behind the dark sedan, near the building where Alec had watched the men bury the bodies. Besides the guards, two other men waited for them, standing under the eaves of the garage, shovels in hand.

"The big guy on the right is Digger," Alec said.

"Our weak link."

"The question is how to get to him."

"There's always a way. Our problem is we're running out of

time. Neville's leaving the country tomorrow. If we don't find Cody before then, my guess is we won't find him at all."

Which had occurred to Alec as well, and they climbed out of the car, careful to avoid eye contact with the man with the shovel.

They stood in the drizzle as the men attacked the freshly turned earth, turned muddy now. And when the small bundles were finally pulled from the earth, Alec stepped forward to see them uncovered. As he expected, they were dogs.

Back in the car, as they drove toward the house, Erin spoke his thoughts aloud. "As I said. Maybe we don't have a choice."

The room was dark, cheap vinyl-backed curtains blocking the watery afternoon sun. Only the television provided light, though Isaac watched without sound. The picture telling him all he needed to know.

A reporter stood outside Golden Oaks, police and FBI vehicles in the background. An ambulance. For Erin Baker, no doubt. He wondered if she was alive. He hoped so. He'd so enjoyed nearly killing her once, he wanted the pleasure of doing it thoroughly.

His name and picture were all over the news.

Dr. Jacob Holmes, internationally known psychiatrist, wanted for questioning in the assault of a young woman. No name. Or picture of the woman. And, of course, nothing to indicate she was an armed CIA officer.

In the end, she'd been a disappointment. Her eye keen and mind interesting, but her warrior spirit weak. He'd thought she'd put up more of a fight, but he'd put her down almost too easily. It was a shame. He'd such a grand finale planned.

He'd always been a master of improvisation, taking the

unexpected and turning it to his advantage. And what he'd come up with this time was no exception. Better to end it all this way, with a surprise or two still waiting for Erin Baker and her sister.

He glanced around the room. Everything was ready. Smiling, he lifted the gun in his lap, the steel cold, even through his latex gloves.

It was time. Jacob Holmes was a dead man.

XXVIII

Ryan fell in and out of sleep.

Each time he woke, he felt both stronger and more anxious. He couldn't tell how much time had passed. Was it already too late for Cody? And for him? Was the other boy already in some foreign place, learning lessons Ryan couldn't teach him? And would the General's staff forget Ryan, leaving him here to die in the dark, alone?

The questions teased a panic he barely suppressed, and he'd retreat to the darkness of sleep.

Once, he awoke and found a tray of food by his cot along with a flashlight, and he cried to think he'd missed Felda's visit. He'd even be happy to see Herrick's grim face. Or the General's. Instead, he ate the food, the memory of Cody's determination daring him to give up, to let the General kill him with fear.

Still, by the time he heard the rattle of keys and the groan of ancient hinges, he would have welcomed anyone. Even Trader. At least then, it would be over.

Herrick stepped through the door, running a light over Ryan on the cot. "You awake, boy?"

Ryan made an effort to sit up, and managed to lift himself from the stale mattress to lean against the wall. "Yeah."

"It is time."

Fear gripped Ryan's stomach. "Time?"

"To go." Herrick crossed the dark space and dropped a soft bundle on the cot. "Come, I get you away from here."

Ryan touched the bundle. Clothes. Clean and fresh, smelling of detergent. A welcome scent after the dankness of this cellar and his own blood. "What about the General?"

Herrick frowned, his expression more stern than normal, and moved to stand watch at the door. "We go before he comes."

"What about Cody?" Ryan asked as he awkwardly slipped on the clothes. He ached, everywhere, though the pain in his ribs had eased a bit. His arm, however, where the dog had sunk his teeth, felt heavy and unnatural beneath Felda's dressing.

"I can do nothing for the other boy," Herrick said. "They watch him too closely."

"Then he's still here." Excited, Ryan crossed to Herrick.

"The Trader will come for him tonight."

Ryan grabbed the man's arm. "Then we can't just leave him here."

"If you stay, they will kill you."

Ryan struggled with his fear. He didn't want to die. Yet leaving without Cody felt wrong, like betrayal. "I can't go without him."

"You can do nothing," Herrick said. "They will kill us *both* before we get close to the boy's room."

Ryan couldn't let that happen. Herrick had been good to him, and Ryan couldn't ask the man to risk his life more than he already had. Still, leaving Cody . . .

Herrick made the decision for him, taking Ryan's arm and

gently leading him out the door, locking and closing it behind them. "Stay close, and stay quiet."

Ryan followed the big man down a narrow, dark corridor, the flashlight playing over cold concrete walls. They emerged into a big circular room, with more gaping holes than the one they'd just left. The thought scampered through Ryan's mind that this was a real, live dungeon, deep beneath the gilded prison.

He shivered.

Herrick crossed to a set of stone steps and started up. At the top, he motioned for Ryan to stay back as he opened a door and went through. After a couple of minutes, he returned, gesturing for Ryan to come up.

They were in the laundry room.

Herrick closed the door behind them, then slid a storage shelf in place to hide the entrance. Unless you knew where to look, you'd never know the door, or the warren of damp rooms below, existed.

Suddenly, voices reached them from above, coming closer.

"Hurry," Herrick said, and led Ryan over to a large canvas-lined bin used for gathering and moving laundry. "Inside."

Ryan climbed in atop a layer of sheets, and Herrick covered him with several more. Then they started to move, the wheels creaking as Herrick pushed the cart up a ramp into the main part of the house.

Normal household sounds and bustle closed in around him. A couple of young maids hurried by, chattering. The clang of pots and dishes. Laughter. The cook lecturing one of her girls in harsh German. Ryan felt an unexpected pang of longing. He'd belonged here, fit here in a way. Until Cody showed up and ruined everything. If he could take it all back . . .

Then Herrick's deep voice, telling Felda this was the last of the linens for cleaning and storage, cut through Ryan's regret. Her reply was curt and quick. He was to hurry back because they had more work to close up the house. But Ryan heard more than their words. He heard their defiance of the General, and their willingness to risk their lives to save Ryan's life. So he refused to regret his own decision. No matter what happened. He'd done the right thing by trying to help Cody escape.

A brush of cool, damp air eased over him as they moved outside. The wobbly wheels hit metal, and he pictured Herrick easing his last load into the back of the white panel truck he used for household errands. The motion stopped, and his footsteps retreated, followed by the clang of the doors closing and the snap of a lock.

A few minutes later, the truck started.

Ryan began to breathe easier. They might just get away with this. He might actually be free of the General and men like him. And as the motion of the truck settled into an easy rumble, he drifted toward sleep, finally daring to hope that he might actually live to see the morning.

XXIX

ERIN WANTED TO GET into that house.

Her instincts told her Neville was involved. He had the connections and resources, and the history. Yet they had no hard evidence, nothing to positively tie him to either Cody's disappearance or Jacob Holmes. But she suspected that if she could get inside and take a look around, she'd find all the proof they needed.

As they left Neville's estate behind and night settled damply around them, she considered one scenario after another, throwing out each in turn. Sam had given her the mansion's floor plan, but it wouldn't help much. It was a large place, which she didn't doubt had dozens of nooks and crannies big enough to hide a small boy. But even if she knew right where to find Cody, there was the security system to consider.

She'd seen the cameras and guards herself, but besides that, she didn't know what to expect. With Neville's resources, there could be anything. Alarms, silent or otherwise, motion and light sensors, infrared. Granted, with the mansion fully staffed, there would be limits to the elaborateness of the security system, but counting on that could get her killed. And Cody left to his fate.

Reaching up, she touched her bandaged forehead. The aspirin had eased the sharp pain to a dull ache. One she could ignore. Her wrists, too, were sore, but functional. She could hold a gun steady and fight. If she had to.

A shiver of fear went through her at the thought.

She'd told Donovan the truth; she hadn't seen Holmes coming and that's why he'd so easily overwhelmed her. What she hadn't said, nor ever shared with a class of CTs, was that she usually had one advantage when fighting a man. It was a small one, for sure, but one that had never failed her. Men never expected women to challenge them physically. They didn't expect aggression, or for a woman to come at them first. It was that split second of hesitation, before realizing she wasn't going to fall back and cower, when Erin would press her advantage.

Holmes had not suffered from that misconception. He'd come at her hard and fast. And she couldn't lie—not even to herself—and pretend that it hadn't frightened her.

Still, she had no reason to believe he'd be anywhere near Cody. She'd seen a half-dozen armed men at the estate, hired men, with no stake in the fight except money. A weak motivator when it came to putting your life on the line. Holmes, on the other hand, was on the run, with the FBI and half the state of Virginia on his tail.

Alec's cell phone rang.

"Donovan," he answered, went silent, listening, and finally said, "Where?" Then, "We're twenty minutes away," and pushed the disconnect button.

"It's Holmes," he said as he swung the car around, heading back the way they'd come. "They've found him. Dead."

"Dead? How?"

"Looks like a suicide."

No. She didn't believe it. "That doesn't make sense." The man who'd attacked her wasn't suicidal. Far from it.

"They found him in a motel room outside Warrenton. One of the other guests heard the shot."

It had to be a trick, a setup. Then she caught Donovan's eye. He was keeping something from her.

"What else?" she asked.

"He left a suicide note." He hesitated, obviously not thrilled with this latest development. "Addressed to you."

Sunshine Manor was a dive.

On the outskirts of Warrenton, it clung to the side of a two-lane highway that had been deserted with the completion of the interstate. Consisting of a series of small cabins in a horseshoe configuration, on the surface the place was in bad need of a paint job. Beyond that, one didn't want to look too closely.

Several police cars blocked off the parking lot, their blue lights strobing the rain-streaked night. Alec pulled up, showed his badge, and was waved through. They parked, and Cathy Hart met them at the door to room number three.

"It's not a pretty sight," she said to Erin. "Are you sure you want to go in?"

Erin shook her head. "Not sure at all, but I need to see for myself." Until she saw his face, his hands, she wouldn't believe he was dead.

"That's what I thought you'd say." Cathy stepped aside. "Just don't touch anything."

Inside, the motel room was in worse shape than out. Paint faded to gray, carpet worn to threadbare strips, an ancient television bolted to a cheap dresser. And, on the bed, lay Jacob Holmes. Pressed khaki slacks, a navy polo shirt. His long fingers and quick hands limp at his sides. A Colt .38 revolver on the floor. A heavy silver ring on his right hand that she could still feel ripping her skin. And a neat little hole in his temple.

"It's him," she said, and turned to leave the room.

Alec followed her outside. "Are you okay?"

She moved farther away from the grisly room without answering. She desperately wanted to believe Holmes was dead, that the man lying on that bed was the Magician, the monster who'd stolen Claire's life and attacked Erin in the woods. But even seeing him, she couldn't quite make herself accept it.

"Erin?"

She looked up, seeing the concern on Donovan's face. "I'm fine," she said, realizing he'd misinterpreted her silence. "I just need more to believe it's him."

"Maybe I can help with that," Cathy said, joining them. She held up a clear plastic evidence bag with a single sheet of paper inside.

Without taking the note from her, Erin read:

To MY FRIEND, OFFICER ERIN BAKER:
YOU WIN. OR DO YOU? ENJOY THE REST OF YOUR LIFE AS YOU LOOK OVER YOUR SHOULDER. OH, AND KEEP A CLOSE EYE ON YOUR DERANGED SISTER AND HER LOVELY DAUGHTER.

JACOB HOLMES

Erin shuddered.

"Sick," Donovan muttered.

"And smart," Cathy said. "Alive or dead, he's messing with your mind, Erin. I wouldn't even have showed this to you, except news of these things has a way of getting out, and I didn't want you to hear about it from some other source."

"He's right, you know," Erin said, fighting down the panic that would send her back to town, to her sister. Even knowing he was playing with her mind didn't ease her worries. "I need to see Claire. And Janie."

"That's not a good idea," Donovan said. "If this is a setup, he'll be waiting for you. It's you he wants."

"And I'm already ahead of you," Cathy said. "I just checked in with the agents at the safe house, and everything is quiet. But we're going to move Claire just in case. And we've assigned a team to keep an eye on your niece and Marta Lopez in Miami. Just until we're sure the body inside is Jacob Holmes, and that he's the same man who attacked you in the woods."

"And how are you going to know that?" Erin asked, unconvinced. "This man has been eluding you for twenty years."

"First," Cathy said, "we'll analyze the note for fingerprints and compare handwriting samples. Also, the man who attacked you spent a lot of time at Gentle Oaks over the last two days. We're dusting for prints now, and if they match the man on that bed, we can be fairly certain of his identity.

"Meanwhile, I have a team of agents looking into Holmes's background and activities. Including cross-checking his movements to unsolved kidnappings over the last twenty years. It will take time, but we should be able to determine if it's even possible that Holmes is responsible."

"What about Claire?"

Cathy threw Donovan a glance, obviously uncomfortable with the question and the answer. "It's inconclusive, and we still have a lot of digging to do. But so far we've learned he did a lot of traveling, speaking at medical conventions, consulting at various medical schools. And he was in the same town as several of the unsolved child abduction cases. Which means he had access and could have taken those children."

She stopped, folding her arms. "There are also cases where we can verify he was nowhere near the right area. Again, that doesn't mean anything, because even if he is the Magician, he couldn't possibly have been responsible for all the open missing child cases. But he's been in the D.C./Virginia area for the past couple of weeks, and—"

"And he was in Miami in 1985," Erin supplied.

Cathy hesitated. "Yes. He was consulting at UM." She took Erin's arm and drew her away from the building and Donovan. "You have to let us do our job, Erin. You said yourself you're not an investigator. Well, I am, and Donovan's one of the best. We'll find out what's going on here."

The EMTs wheeled out the body, loading it into a waiting ambulance. Erin watched, knowing she wasn't certain she'd ever believe Jacob Holmes had committed suicide. Cathy, however, was right. Erin couldn't let that fear stop her either.

"Okay," she said. "Let's see what you come up with." Then she'd decide whether she believed, or whether she'd spend the rest of her life looking over her shoulder as the note indicated.

Cathy smiled tightly and motioned for Donovan to join them. "Now, what happened with Neville?"

Donovan explained what they'd found—and not found—at Neville's estate.

"Which leaves us no closer to finding Cody Sanders." She sighed, her frustration showing.

"There's Digger," Donovan said. "And there's Neville's morbid mansion."

"And we can't touch it," Cathy said, eyeing him closely.

Erin met Donovan's gaze, realizing that for once they agreed on a course of action. One way or another, Middleburg held the answers. All they needed was one small push, just one shred of hope that the key to finding Cody Sanders was inside.

Again, Donovan's phone rang, and Erin held her breath, hoping it was the call they'd been waiting for.

Donovan answered, listened, then nodded to Erin that they'd finally gotten a break. "Wait," he said as the caller disconnected. A couple of seconds later, Donovan did the same. "That was Digger," he said. "He told us where to find the boy."

Erin expected it was too much to hope that the boy who was waiting for them was Cody Sanders. Just as it was too much to believe that the Magician was really dead. It was more likely they'd find the second boy Digger had mentioned, the one he'd referred to as his son.

Or an ambush, courtesy of the General.

"The boy needs help," Digger had said, without identifying himself or which boy he meant. Then he'd instructed Donovan to follow a small, rural route off one of the smaller back highways, giving the distances in kilometers.

"Look to the left," he'd said, just before ending the abbreviated, one-sided conversation. "Behind the trees."

It wasn't until they'd reached the location that they'd seen the dilapidated barn, sitting well back from the road, almost hidden from sight. Donovan turned onto an overgrown road and parked behind the shabby building.

For a moment neither he nor Erin spoke.

The place looked like it had been deserted for years. Broken glass etched the dark windows. Long grasses grew up to the foundation, and kudzu marched up the walls. Yet it was impossible to tell whether the actual structure was sound or not.

Erin pulled out the Glock Cathy had lent her and checked the clip.

Alec reached across her to the glove compartment and grabbed a flashlight. "Here," he said, handing it to her. "I have another in the trunk."

Quickly, he'd retrieved a second flashlight and they moved quietly toward the barn. At the rear wall, they split up, each taking a different side, working toward the front, ducking beneath the glassless windows, listening for some sound from inside, and finally meeting up again at the entrance.

Stopping. Erin braced herself, watching Donovan do the same.

Going through the door was the dangerous part. If this was an ambush, here was where it would hit them.

"Wait here," Alec mouthed, and went in first, slipping into the dark interior, leading with his gun.

Erin waited. Ten seconds. Twenty.

She was just about to follow him, despite his instructions, when he cracked the door and motioned her inside.

Silence. And a heavy darkness, ripe with the smell of rotting hay.

Alec pointed toward the first stall, and they split up again. She took the right side, he the left, cautiously working their way down toward the back, flashlights level with their weapons, sweeping each stall in turn.

Erin found him.

The boy. Cowering in the last stall, wrapped in a heavy plaid blanket. Her flashlight played over his face, and she saw his fear. And the bruises. Not Cody.

Lowering the Beretta, she held up a hand. "It's okay. I won't hurt you."

He didn't look convinced.

"Donovan, over here," she said.

She slipped the gun into the waistband of her jeans and edged into the stall. The boy, though obviously frightened, didn't back away. She approached slowly, and as she got closer, she realized he was older than she'd first thought. Probably in his early teens.

"My name's Erin," she said.

The boy looked behind her, and she glanced back to see Donovan standing just outside the stall door.

"That's Agent Donovan," she said. "He's not coming in here, but he's with the FBI, and he's here to help you."

"What about you? Are you with the FBI, too?"

Reaching his side, Erin dropped to her knees. "No, I'm just helping out. What's your name?"

A brief hesitation, then, "Ryan."

Digger's son. She reached up to brush the hair from his forehead and got a better look at his injuries. "How did you get here, Ryan?"

"Did he send you?"

Erin again glanced back at Donovan, who nodded. "We don't know his name. We just got a call that you needed help."

"Big man, heavy accent," Donovan said, keeping his distance so as not to startle the boy.

"Yes, Herrick, that's him," the boy supplied, a ghost of a smile teasing his mouth. Or maybe just relief. "He got me out and brought me here."

"Is he your father?" Erin asked.

Ryan brow furrowed. "No, he works for the General."

"The General?" Though she knew whom Ryan meant, she didn't want to put a name in his mouth.

"General Neville."

Erin sighed. Maybe not Cody, but another boy caught beneath Neville's thumb. "Okay, Ryan, let's get you out of here." She reached out to touch him. He winced, and she noticed the dressing on his arm. "What happened?"

"I was trying to run, and one of the dogs caught me."

"And your face?"

He shuddered. "No, that was Trader."

Erin understood his fear and held the flashlight beneath her face so he could see. "I think I met him as well. Come on, we'll get you to a hospital."

Behind her, she could hear Donovan talking into his cell phone, calling for backup and an ambulance.

"Wait," Ryan said. "Cody needs your help more than me."

Erin went very still.

"Cody?" Donovan stepped into the stall.

Ryan focused on Donovan. "Trader is coming for him tonight, and they're going to send him away. Out of the country. You've got to help him."

"Where is he?" Donovan asked, crouching down beside Erin.

"In the mansion."

"Do you know where?"

Ryan hesitated. "I think so. But after we tried to run—" He shook his head. "I'm not sure."

"Cody tried to run, too?" Erin said.

"Yes, but the dogs caught us. Then the guards locked me in the cellar, but they probably just put Cody back in his room."

"Was he hurt?"

"I don't think so. But you've got to get him out." He looked from one to the other of them. "Herrick said he couldn't do anything, but you could. He said to tell you he'd take care of the cameras."

Erin looked to Donovan and saw the resignation and determination in his eyes. They were going in, and to hell with the consequences. This was all the push, all the incentive, they needed.

XXX

ALEC WOULDN'T TRADE one child's life for another.

So he and Erin waited for the ambulance, despite Ryan's insistence that they didn't have time. Once the paramedics had arrived, along with a couple of local police cars, he knew the boy was in good hands, and it was time.

Alec and Erin headed toward Neville's estate.

As they drove, they went over their plan, what there was of it. Basically, they were counting on Herrick shutting down the cameras long enough for them to get in, grab the boy, and get out before anyone noticed.

Of course, Alec knew it wouldn't go that smoothly and expected Erin understood this as well. But they had no other choice. They were mounting a raid on a foreign diplomat's property, breaking enough laws to put them both away for a very long time. They couldn't call for backup or ask for help. Nor could they afford the time to go through the proper channels. Even if that worked, which Alec doubted, Cody Sanders would be long gone by then.

So they were going to do this. Legal or not. Good idea or not. Alone.

As they'd agreed, he pulled off to the side of the road, just out of sight of the guardhouse. Quickly, they checked their cache of weapons, stashing extra clips in their pockets. He had a SIG and a backup Glock 19 on his ankle. Erin had Cathy's Glock and her own Ruger.

"Ready?" she asked.

He took a deep breath. "As I'll ever be."

She smiled tightly and opened the door.

"Erin," he said, and she looked back at him. "Be careful."

She grinned. "Always." Then closed the door and faded into the trees.

He counted to a hundred, slowly, then started up again, driving toward the estate entrance and turning in. Neville's guard flagged him down, walking to the side of his car as he rolled down his window, his FBI identification ready.

"Special Agent Donovan, FBI, here to see General Neville."

The guard shook his head. "No. Not here."

"What do you mean, he's not here? I have an appointment."

"Not here."

Alec spotted movement behind the man. "You better check with your supervisor, Buddy, because—"

With a grunt, the man slid to the ground, the butt of Erin's Ruger rendering him unconscious.

Alec jumped out of the car. "I'll take care of him. You get the gate."

He grabbed the man's arms, dragging him toward the woods, as Erin scaled the iron railing. Quiet. Nimble. Perfectly at home stealing onto foreign territory in the dead of night. Alec found it a bit unsettling.

By the time he'd tied up the man and gotten back to the car, the heavy gate was open and Erin was behind the wheel. Alec didn't argue with her.

Climbing into the passenger seat, he said, "Let's hope Herrick wasn't lying about those cameras. Otherwise, this is going to get rough real fast."

"Hey, I like it rough," Erin countered, and drove through the gates.

"Oh, yeah? Well, we'll have to talk about that if we make it through the next hour alive."

She laughed, in her element in a way that unnerved and surprised him. He'd seen the fighter in her, the warrior, and had thought it was merely a way to disguise her vulnerability. Now he saw that it was more than that. She thrived on the danger, the challenge of it, and that made him nervous.

She navigated the winding road without lights, until just before leaving the shelter of the trees. Then she turned off the engine and let the car glide soundlessly down the hill to the mansion.

When they came to a stop, Alec slipped out, keeping low and leaving the door ajar. Erin shimmied across the front seat to join him, crouching beside the passenger side of the vehicle.

So far, so good. No signs that anyone knew they were here.

"Cover me," he whispered, and darted for the front door, where he pressed his back against the wood within the shadows.

Erin, a two-fisted grip on her gun, took up a position by the car's fender.

Alec picked the lock, then signaled to her.

After another quick glance around, she darted to his side. Together, they slipped into the mansion's main foyer, closing the door soundlessly behind them.

Empty. Quiet.

It should have been a relief. Instead, it felt suddenly all wrong.

"I don't like this," Erin said, voicing his thoughts as she scanned the room. "It just doesn't feel right."

"Yeah. Let's find the boy and get out."

She nodded, nervous, and followed him as he took the wide front steps two at a time. Three quarters of the way up, the staircase forked. He veered left, as Ryan had instructed, and met a locked door sealing off the entrance to the east wing.

Again, Alec pulled out his pick to attack the locks.

Suddenly, from below them, came approaching voices, harsh and urgent.

Erin dove to the floor, taking aim through the balustrade. "Get the boy, I'll cover you."

Alec worked the lock, and just as it clicked open, a shout went out, the voices below rising to shouts as the men spotted the intruders.

Erin dropped the first man, while the second fell back, returning fire.

"Hurry," she said. "Neville's entire army's going to be breathing down our necks any minute."

Alec slipped into the corridor, his SIG pointed toward the ceiling as he counted doors. "The seventh room on the left," Ryan had said. "If they haven't moved him." Alec was on five when a big man bolted from a room two doors away.

Herrick.

"Go back," he called. "It's a trap."

Behind him, a second man burst into the hallway, shooting, his expression shocked when he spotted Alec.

Herrick stumbled, then staggered forward, as a bullet caught him in the back.

Alec fired, dropping the attacker in the doorway, then went to Herrick and pulled him to the side.

"The boy? Cody?" Alec asked. "Where is he?"

"Gone. Out the back. A few minutes ago. I tried to stop them."

"Where are they taking him?"

Herrick shook his head, licked his lips. "Airport, I think."

"Which airport?"

"Ryan?" Herrick gripped Alec's hand, his eyes losing focus. "Is he—"

"He's safe. Which airport, Herrick?"

But the man had uttered his last words.

Another burst of gunfire came from the foyer, snapping Alec back to awareness of his own precarious position.

"What's the holdup?" Erin called.

Alec raced out to take a position beside her. "I think we're in trouble."

"Herrick?" she asked.

"Dead."

"What about Cody?"

"Gone. They took him out a back way."

"Come on, then," she said. "We need to get out of here."

She was truly crazy, he decided, though he followed her as she inched along the railing toward the steps.

"Do you have a death wish or something?" he asked.

"There's only a few of them left, about three or four." She shot him a grin. "We can take them. Besides, how long before they come at us from one of these upper hallways, and we're pinned down from both sides?"

"You have a point."

"On the count of three." She had the Glock in one hand and the Ruger in the other. "You take the left. I'll take the right."

Alec grabbed his backup weapon from his ankle. "Okay, let's go."

They stood together, firing, scrambling toward the steps and down.

He spotted two men in the left, first-floor corridor, one behind the other, using a massive pillar for coverage. He was just past the fork in the stairway when one swung out while the other covered him with a spray of bullets. Alec dropped to his side, sliding, and put a bullet in the exposed man. The other fell back along the wall and out of sight.

"Shit." Alec was going to pay for that maneuver. If they lived that long. He rolled, at the bottom now, as Erin's Ruger chased her men into hiding as well.

Silence again. And empty, save the half-dozen bodies littering the foyer and side corridors.

"Man," he said. "You've been a busy girl."

"There wasn't much else to do," she said as they sprinted across the foyer. "You were off playing with the boys."

They flanked the double front doors, the car and relative safety on the other side, only yards away. Yet it might as well have been a mile.

"How many do you think are out there?" she asked.

Alec shook his head. "Haven't a clue."

"Me, neither, but we can't stay here."

For once he agreed with her. The retreating guards would return, with reinforcements. And soon. "We'll have to make a dash for it. Can you cover me?"

"I'm going first this time." Before he could protest, she was out the door, zigzagging.

Gunfire came from around the corner of the mansion, chasing her across the wide porch. Alec swung out, firing both weapons at the hidden shooter. Erin leapt from the porch, tucking and rolling as she hit the ground. She came up unhurt against the rear fender and ducked behind it as she assumed a shooter's stance.

Alec took a deep breath, then raced across the slick concrete. A bullet grazed his sleeve, sending a sliver of sweat down his spine, and he slid in beside her. "Damn, that was close."

"You okay?"

"Yeah, but I think we've overstayed our welcome. Let's get the hell out of here."

"Easier said than done."

From the garage, farther down the hill, came the roar of an engine. Alec squinted into the approaching lights, then flattened against the sedan's fender as a black Lincoln Town Car raced past, splattering muddy water as it headed for the gate.

"Cody's in the car," he said. "We have to—"

A fresh burst of gunfire erupted. Two men, dark shadows in the moonless night, automatics blazing, started up the hill toward him and Erin. They brought out the other two guards as well, the ones who'd been using the side of the mansion for cover.

Alec dropped, returning fire. "It's now or never. If we don't get out of here before the others reach the front door, we'll be sitting ducks."

"Who's driving?"

"Me." He scrambled, crablike, toward the driver's door and pulled it open.

Erin clambered into the passenger seat, leaning half in, half out, as she fired through the crack in the open door. "Let's go."

"Hold on," he said, and threw the car in gear.

Erin slammed her door, and Alec switched on the brights.

A guard, close, reflexively tossed up his hands to shield his eyes. Alec floored the accelerator and yanked the steering wheel hard to the left, forcing the vehicle into a sharp U-turn. The guard dove sideways, but not before the sedan clipped his leg, sending him flying.

Heading back in the right direction, Alec gunned it, and the car leapt forward.

The back window exploded, spraying glass.

Alec ducked, looking to Erin, who'd crouched down as well across the seat. "You okay?"

"Just pissed off." She turned, taking aim through the shattered back window, the Ruger searching out one final target as the men rapidly faded behind them.

"Where's the closest airport?" he asked as he headed toward the front gate.

"Leesburg, I think."

"Works for me."

The gate was closing, but Alec sped up, scraping metal as the sedan shot through. They hit the wet asphalt, skidded, fishtailed, then straightened.

"We can't help Cody if we're roadkill," Erin said, grabbing the armrest.

He threw her a quick glance. "Hey, I thought you liked it rough."

"Yeah," she said. "But only when I'm in the driver's seat."

Alec laughed, realizing he really needed to get to know this woman better.

XXXI

ERIN ACHED.

Oh, she'd forgotten about it for a while. Adrenaline had carried her through, but as her heart rate and the rest of her returned to normal, she felt Holmes's attack all over again. Her wrists and shoulder complained bitterly, and her head, well, she wasn't sure her stomach would tolerate the amount of aspirin it would take to stop the pounding.

The worst part?

She knew she wasn't done pushing her tired body to the limit. And she'd be damned before admitting any of it to Donovan.

They caught up to the Town Car within a few miles of Neville's estate, the diplomatic plates a dead giveaway.

"Got you," Erin said.

"Oh, yeah?" Donovan closed the distance between the two vehicles, but the other driver made no attempt to speed up or lose them. "Now what?"

Good question. Anything they did to force the other car off

the road would endanger Cody. And neither of them wanted that. "Just stay with them. They've got to stop eventually."

"I've got an idea." Alec pulled out his cell phone and tossed it to Erin. "Let's see if we can get some local help."

"The police won't interfere with a car sporting diplomatic plates."

Alec shot her a grin. "So don't tell them. By the time they figure it out, it'll be all over."

Erin made the call, giving the local police Alec's FBI information and requesting assistance with the apprehension of a kidnapping suspect. Meanwhile, the Town Car kept a steady pace, well within the posted speed limit.

"They know we can't touch them," Erin said.

"Let them keep thinking that."

Erin smiled, liking this side of Donovan. A little reckless, a little dangerous. It made her think the straitlaced, overprotective FBI-agent act was all a sham.

They were closing in on Leesburg and its small executive airport when the sounds of sirens came from behind and blue lights flashed in his rearview mirror.

"Here comes the cavalry," Alec said.

Erin still wasn't sure the locals were a good idea, but it was worth a shot. "Let's just hope they don't decide we're the bad guys."

"As long as we get Cody out of that car first," he said, "that's all that matters."

This side of Donovan, too, was nice, she thought. He had his priorities straight, with no chance of his confusing the right moral choice for the most useful career choice.

Two police cars sped past them, screeching to a halt in front of the airport entrance, blocking it. The Town Car slammed on its breaks, skidded on the wet asphalt, and came to rest sideways in the road.

Alec stopped a few yards back, flanked by two more patrol cars. Erin jumped from the car, the FBI Glock already in hand. Donovan joined her, and shortly after, four officers from the two patrol cars were at their sides. Across the way, on the other side of the Town Car, four more officers took up position.

"Special Agent Donovan." Donovan flashed his ID without taking his eyes off the silent Town Car. "She's Erin Baker," he added, letting them make their own assumptions about her role in all this.

"What's the story here, Agents?" asked the cop, whose name tag read *Sergeant Reynolds*, nearest Donovan.

"We have reason to believe that the Lincoln is transporting a kidnap victim. A nine-year-old boy. Cody Sanders. Heard of him?"

"Yeah," said one of the other officers. "He's been missing for nearly a week now. From up around the Baltimore area."

"That's him," Alec confirmed.

"Well, let's see if we can flush them out." Sergeant Reynolds raised a bullhorn. "This is the police. You're surrounded. Throw out your weapons and come out with your hands up."

No response from the Town Car.

"Agent," said one of the officers to Erin, "that car's got diplomatic plates."

She'd known that sooner or later one of the cops would notice. "It's stolen," she said.

He looked doubtful. Or maybe just worried.

"I'll take full responsibility, Officer," Alec said, then reached for the bullhorn. "Let me try."

The officer handed it over.

"This is Agent Donovan with the FBI." Donovan's voice boomed across the empty space. "We know you're holding Cody Sanders. Let him go, and we can all go home in one piece."

Still no response.

"They know we can't approach," Erin said, "or fire on them without hurting Cody." They knew something else as well. Something that gave them an incentive to just sit tight.

From behind them on the road, a stream of headlights cut through the dark. Erin turned to look, thinking this was what—or whom—the Town Car was waiting on. Getting closer, the lights took on dark shapes. A stretch limousine, flags flying on its bumper, and four sedans, two in front, two in back. A diplomatic escort.

Neville.

The reason the Town Car's occupants felt safe just waiting it out. She was willing to bet her life on it.

The caravan stopped.

After a moment's hesitation, a suited muscle got out of the front car. As he approached the police officers, Erin recognized him as one of Neville's men, one of those who'd escorted her and Donovan out to the estate to dig up the graves.

Had that been only this afternoon? It felt like days ago.

"Excuse me, Officer," he said. "Why are you blocking that car?"

"Sorry, buddy," the cop answered. "You'll have to move along. We have a situation here."

"I don't think you understand. That car belongs to my employer and is protected by his diplomatic rights."

Donovan stepped up beside the sergeant. "And just who is your employer?" Though Erin knew he recognized the man as well.

"I think you know the answer to that, Agent Donovan."

"Yeah, well, you tell Neville that if he wants his car, he'll have to come get it personally. And I want Cody Sanders."

The man looked ready to argue. Instead, he turned and walked back to the limousine, disappearing into its interior.

"What's going on here?" asked Reynolds. "This looks like much more than just a kidnapping."

Erin stepped up beside Donovan. "We just want the boy returned home, Sergeant. We won't ask you to step over any lines."
She only hoped she was telling the truth.

A moment later, the muscle reemerged from the limo. Then
Neville followed, with two other bodyguards behind him. The
four men covered the distance between the cars, stopping in
front of Erin and Donovan.

Neville sighed. "Agent Donovan and Officer Baker, you've
gone too far this time." Then, turning to Sergeant Reynolds by
their side, he said, "I'm General William Neville, attached to
the German Embassy, and that is one of my cars you're holding
hostage. If you don't want to create an international incident,
and consequently lose your job and face criminal charges from
your own government, I suggest you move aside and let me and
my entire entourage pass."

Reynolds squirmed but held his ground. "Agent Donovan
says the car was stolen and used in a kidnapping."

Neville bristled. "That's ridiculous."

"Who's in the car, then, sir?"

"I don't need to answer your questions."

"No, sir, you don't." The cop was holding his own. "But it
might help to expedite this situation."

Neville looked from one to the other of them, calculating,
weighing his next move. Then he motioned to his man, the
muscle in a suit. "Go see who's in the car."

The man looked surprised, but did as instructed. As he approached the Town Car, the front passenger door opened, and
a man stepped out. They talked for a minute, then Neville's
man returned.

"They thought you were trying to rob them," he said.
"That's why they stayed in the car."

"And Cody?" Erin said, feigning patience.

"There's a boy with them. They picked him up by the side
of the road. He was lost."

"Bring the boy," Neville said.

Erin felt the anger roll over her. He was going to get away with this.

The man returned to the car, and a few minutes later, Cody Sanders climbed out. Blinking. Sleepy. Or just awakening from a different type of nightmare.

One of the police officers hurried to the boy's side and led him to one of the cruisers.

Neville pasted on a smile. "This has been a terrible misunderstanding."

"You son of a bitch." Erin started forward, but Alec grabbed her arm before she could launch herself at the man.

Neville's smile turned chilly. "You shouldn't play games you can't win, Officer Baker."

She pulled at Donovan's grip, but he held tight.

From the road, another stream of headlights flashed toward them, traveling fast. A half-dozen cars pulled in behind Neville's caravan and four times that many men spilled out. Most held back, though, standing by their vehicles, except for the four walking directly toward them, stunning Erin.

Associate Deputy Director for Intelligence Thomas Ward led the group.

He approached the police sergeant and flashed his identification. "This is an international incident, Sergeant. We'll take it from here."

The man hesitated—he had guts—and glanced back at Erin and Donovan, then nodded his acceptance of Ward's authority. "Let's go," he said to his colleagues.

As they started for their patrol cars, Ward turned to Neville. "General, I apologize on behalf of my government for this. You and your people are free to go."

Neville looked from Ward to Erin, still caught in Donovan's grip. Then he gave the CIA director a curt nod and motioned for his men to follow as he headed for his limousine.

"You can't let him go," Erin said.

Ward ignored her. "Agent Donovan, I think young Mr. Sanders is your responsibility."

She saw the stubborn set of Donovan's jaw but knew he could do nothing more for her here. She was at the mercy of the Agency, and to be honest, she didn't give a damn if they threw the book at her.

"Go ahead, Donovan," she said. "Take the boy home."

Donovan hesitated a bit longer, then went to retrieve Cody from the waiting patrol car.

Meanwhile, Erin watched Neville's limousine slide past to the airport. "I can't believe you're just going to let him go. He's a monster."

"That he is."

She crossed her arms, holding in the anger that was still bubbling inside her. "If you know, then why?"

Ward moved away from the other men, nodding for Erin to follow. "We've been watching General Neville for some time."

"And you let him continue selling children?"

"It's not children he's selling." Pushing back his jacket, Ward slid his hands into his pockets and rocked a bit on his heels. "They're more of a sideline for his more lucrative business dealings."

"Which are?"

"He sells information. Biological formulas mostly, to the Middle East. Viruses. Antidotes. Anything desperate people are willing to sell, and disreputable governments are eager to buy."

She still didn't understand, and to be honest, she wasn't sure she wanted to. If the CIA knew about Neville's business dealings and were turning a blind eye, she wanted no part of it. "If you know what he's doing, why don't you stop him?"

"The enemy you see is far less dangerous than the enemy you don't." He pressed his lips together. "Tonight he's on his way home with a formula for a new strain of anthrax. A particularly virulent strain. A disgruntled employee at the CAC sold it to him. Only"—he shrugged—"his buyers will never be able to reproduce the results."

"You're feeding him disinformation."

"Yes."

"The enemy you control . . ."

"Is valuable indeed." She backed away, understanding, but not liking it. She'd never had any illusions about the Company, yet this infuriated her. Because of the children. "You knew all along that Neville had Cody, and you let me go after him. Why?"

"I actually thought you had a good chance of rescuing the boy." He smiled. "Which you did. But the real reason was that Neville found out you were CIA, and thought you were officially coming after him." He shrugged. "We didn't want to disabuse him of that notion. You kept him busy, preoccupied."

"While someone else . . ."

"Was able to take the place of his seller and slip him a phony formula."

"You used me."

"Yes, but then, that's your job. You do what we want, when we want. Without question."

The truth, but it stung. "You should have told me."

"You were more effective not knowing."

"And what about the children who are Neville's sideline?"

"There are casualties in every war, Officer Baker."

XXXII

The following ten days were particularly intense.

Erin had spent hours at Langley, days it seemed, in endless meetings. Debriefings. Inquiries. She'd broken more rules and protocols than she could count, and not a few laws. In the end, she wasn't certain if she still had a career with the Agency, or whether she even still wanted one. They didn't dismiss her immediately, so she guessed that was something.

The days had proffered good things as well. Marta and Janie had returned from Miami, sun-kissed and relaxed. Claire had moved home, despite her doctor's protest. Erin had kept her promise. The situation was far from perfect. Claire would still have her moments of depression and withdrawal, and Erin and Marta would have to watch her closely. But Claire was family, their family, and they all wanted it to work.

Also, Donovan stopped by with information about Cody and Ryan.

They'd found Ryan's family in Colorado: parents and three

siblings, all younger, two sisters and a brother. Evidently he'd been taken when he was four, little more than a toddler, and sold. He claimed to have had four owners over the years, and the authorities were hunting them down. He, too, was going to have a difficult adjustment, but he'd shown remarkable courage in trying to help Cody, and everyone expected he'd do well with his family.

As for Cody, he was back home. Where evidently nothing had changed, except maybe Cody himself.

The two boys, though half a continent apart, were determined to keep in touch. And Erin suspected they could do anything they set their minds to.

There was also news about Jacob Holmes. Donovan also told her what the FBI had found out about Jacob Holmes. Although no one could prove conclusively that he was the legendary Magician, everything pointed in that direction. On ten different occasions Holmes had been attending meetings or seminars in a city at the time that an unsolved kidnapping case occurred. But more damning than that were the charges filed against him, then dropped, when he was barely out of his teens. Charges of child molestation.

So, after hearing the FBI evidence herself, Erin admitted that the man who'd attacked her was most likely Jacob Holmes, and he was indeed dead.

After that, the silence between her and Donovan grew awkward and uncomfortable. He stood, and she walked him to the front hallway, a part of her searching for a way to keep him from leaving, while another part held back, telling her to let him go. They'd made a tentative personal connection while searching for Cody, but the circumstances had been unreal, exaggerated, and maybe it was best if they just put it behind them. He was a reminder of everything that had happened, and a lot she'd rather forget.

At the door, he turned, and she held her breath, afraid he would force the issue. And that he wouldn't.

"I'll check back with you," he said, "just to see how things are going with Claire."

"That's not necessary."

He searched her face, and she kept her expression carefully neutral. Just two colleagues saying good-bye.

"Maybe not," he said. "But I'd like to anyway."

Again, she didn't know how to answer, didn't know what she wanted from this man. If anything. Then she heard herself saying, "If things were different, if we'd met under different circumstances—"

He cut her off. "That's just an excuse, Erin. Another time, another place, you'd find another excuse."

She knew he was right, it *was* an excuse. There was more to her reluctance than wanting to forget. Getting involved with him would be dangerous in a way she couldn't, wouldn't risk. She had all she could handle with Claire and Janie. "Let it go, Alec."

"I'll give you some time . . ." He glanced toward the stairs, then back at her. "But I won't just walk away. This is not finished between us." He leaned over and kissed her gently, quickly, before she could think to step away. Then he said, "It hasn't even begun yet."

Then he was gone, and she felt his absence like a chill. Or maybe it was his promise to come back that had her wrapping her arms around her middle. Either way, she knew he'd keep his word. The only question was what she was going to do about it.

Finally, the intense days came to an end. And a Friday came when Langley seemed finished with her for a time. It was late, and she was looking forward to a long, uninterrupted weekend with Janie and Claire.

And there was comfort in coming home, in stepping into the dim kitchen with the faint scent of a dinner cooked hours earlier. Everything was clean now, put away, but the warmth lingered, like the echoes of a child's laughter. Marta and Janie, and now Claire, had brought this into Erin's life, this warmth, this sense of belonging and comfort she'd never known before. Not even in her mother's house.

Erin closed and locked the door.

The house was quiet, though she could hear the faint sounds of the television in the living room. Marta had waited up, or had more likely fallen asleep in front of the television. Claire and Janie would be sound asleep upstairs, lost in their dreams.

As she'd guessed, Erin found Marta asleep in her favorite chair—an overstuffed recliner—while some late-night host chattered to some overendowed celebrity. Erin switched it off, then made her way to the other woman's side.

"Marta?"

She stirred, sleepily opening her eyes and smiling at Erin. "You're home."

"And you were sleeping in your chair again."

"I was just resting my eyes."

"Uh-huh. Well, how about if I help you upstairs so you can rest them in bed. Otherwise you'll be stiff in the morning."

"That's a good idea, but I can make it." Marta pulled the lever that dropped the footrest, but let Erin help her to her feet. "This getting old thing is no fun."

Erin smiled and kissed her on the cheek. "See you in the morning."

"Good night, dear."

Erin watched her slow walk toward the steps, then Marta stopped and said, "I made lasagna tonight and left you a plate in the oven."

"Thank you."

Marta never forgot to take care of her chicks. "Oh, and Janie left you a picture. It's on the table. It's very good."

"Really?"

"Yes, they had a special treat in school today. A magician."

Erin froze. "A magician?"

"Yes, and Janie drew his picture. Good night."

For several long minutes, as Marta made her way up the stairs, Erin couldn't make her feet move. Her heart pounded, the only sound in the silent house. Then it was if a dam burst. She couldn't get to the kitchen fast enough.

As Marta said, Janie's pad lay open on the kitchen table. And the top picture, the one she'd prayed Marta had been wrong about, was of a middle-aged man, holding a rabbit he'd pulled from a hat.

Erin's hands shook. The face was unfamiliar, but even in the child's drawing she knew the man. Those hands.

They needed to get out of the house. Fast.

Dropping the drawing, she started for the stairs. And stopped short, just inside the dining room. He stood not ten feet away, on the other side of their living room couch.

"Hello, Erin." She'd have recognized that voice anywhere. "Are you surprised to see me?" He held a knife, a long knife, its tip stained with still-wet blood.

She fought down the fear racing through her.

He lifted the knife, just a fraction, and smiled. "Oh, my, whose blood is it? The old woman's? Maybe your sister's? Or that sweet, sweet child?"

Again, Erin fought for control, when what she wanted was to throw herself at him. "If you hurt them . . ."

"What will you do?"

Fear. It would kill her. And those she loved. "You won't get away with this."

"Why not? I always have. Even that little ruse with Jacob Holmes. I wasn't sure it would even work, but you fell for it so easily." He tossed the knife from one hand to the other. Graceful. His hands so quick. So nimble. "You see, I've known about Jacob for years and suspected there would come a time when I could use his past indiscretions."

"So you posed as him at Gentle Oaks."

"I'm always someone else, someone the police know about and can go after while I get away. This time, things were just a tad different. I had Jacob safely tucked away, and his death was a perfect cover."

"So why are you here? What do you want from me?"

"You are a loose end. As long as you're alive, I can never be certain we won't run into each other again. And *you* would recognize me. Wouldn't you, Erin."

She wouldn't panic, couldn't let him rattle her. He'd caught her off guard once before and nearly killed her. Not this time. This time she'd see him coming. This time Janie and Claire were upstairs . . .

The blood on the knife caught her eye, jarred her, and suddenly she had control. Her years of training came back to her, and she shut down. A cold determination settled over her, blocking out all other feelings.

He grinned. "You want this?" He waggled the knife, then tossed it on the couch between them. "I'll even make it a fair fight. We're both about the same distance from it. Let's see who gets there first."

He wanted her to go for it, was daring her. And she was tempted. But she couldn't survive playing by his rules. She had to make her own.

Inching toward the couch, she put a tremble in her voice she no longer felt. "This is between you and me. You don't have to involve the others." She saw her target without ever taking her eyes from him.

"That's where you're wrong. They've all seen me, now, even your Marta. I can't risk it. You understand, don't you?"

With that, she dove for the fireplace. He went for the knife. Grabbing the poker, she came up swinging. He ducked. But not fast enough. She caught his arm and he let out a grunt of surprise.

"That's for my shoulder, you son of a bitch."

He spun around with the knife, taking a fighter's stance. "Why, you—"

She didn't give him time to finish or regroup, charging forward, swinging the poker. He backed. Once. Twice. Got his feet under him and sprang forward with the knife.

He was a tall man, not bulky, but with a long reach.

Still, she sidestepped him easily, pivoting. And brought the poker down across his back.

He went down on his knees. The knife skating across the hard wood floor to catch on the rug. She swung again, but he caught her leg. Too close. And she toppled on her back, the poker flying from her grasp. Slamming against the wall. As he scrambled for the knife.

She sprang back to her feet. And he, too, found his footing. Back around. Charging her.

She blocked him, her body falling into the fluid rhythm it had followed since childhood. It was no different because of the knife. Her foot outside his. Ankle to ankle. The heel of her right hand slamming against the underside of his chin. Her left struck his biceps, delivering a stunning blow to the side of his neck, and forcing his head sideways into his shoulder.

The look in his eyes was pure shock.

She seized his elbow, twisted, and the knife rattled to the floor. He landed on his back, grabbed the knife, slashed upward, missed. And she kept him rolling onto his stomach, the knife caught beneath him as she wrenched his arm behind him, wrist bent, her knee jammed against his kidney.

His body stiffened. Then went limp.

Erin held on, afraid to let go, until the blood seeped out to soak the aged wood floors. Then she leapt back, long suppressed tears streaming down her face. She looked up. Two horrified women watched from the steps, Claire and Marta, with Janie's face tucked unseeing against Claire's side.

Erin shook her head, unable to speak.

In the distance, a siren shattered the stillness, and she noticed the portable phone in Marta's hand. Help. She'd called for help.

Claire passed her daughter to Marta and came down to her sister. Folding Erin into her thin arms.

"That's okay, sweetie," Claire said, as sounds of help drew closer. "It's over now. Really over."

Erin let Claire hold her, giving in to the need for someone else to take control, to comfort. If just for a minute. While the adrenaline drained from her body with the tears that streaked her face. Until the sirens shrieked to a halt outside. Then Erin straightened, pulled back, and wiped the tears from her eyes.

"Yes, it's over." She tested a tentative smile on her sister and felt a swell of warmth for this woman who'd been through so much. "And we," she touched Claire's cheek, "we can move on."

Claire nodded, her own eyes bright with unshed tears. "Yes."

Suddenly everything seemed lighter, as if the dark shroud that had encased their lives had been lifted. Maybe now they could begin to heal. Claire's trauma. Erin's guilt. They could put it behind them, and if not forget, they could forgive each other and begin anew.

Erin thought fleetingly of Alec Donovan and it, too, warmed her. Now she could even risk letting him into their lives. Into hers.

Someone pounded on the door, and a male voice called, "Open up, police."

Claire smiled and motioned toward the sound. "I think you better open the door before they break it down."

Erin answered her sister's smile with one of her own. Yes, things would be better now. She and Claire would face the future together. And they would make it better.

Then Erin moved off to open the door for the police.